Miss Lulu Bett

(A Novel)

and

Miss Lulu Bett

An American
Comedy of Errors

Miss Lulu Bett
(A Novel)

and

Miss Lulu Bett
An American
Comedy of Errors

Zona Gale

Introduction by Marc Seals

Hastings College Press | Hastings, Nebraska

Production Staff

Emilie Barnes

Megan Beirow

Jordan Brown

Natalee Hanway

Nicole Havlik

Alexandria Kreikemeier

Gabrielle Rodgers

Makenzie Shofner

Carly Spotts-Falzone

Jeri Thompson

Anna Weber

ISBN-10: 1942885393
ISBN-13: 978-1-942885-39-9

Note on the text: This edition has been reset from the first editions. Original spelling and grammatical conventions have been maintained, except in the case of publishing errors in the first edition. The original punctuation has been maintained but updated using modern conventions (e.g., eliminating spaces around dashes).

Manufactured in the United States of America.

Text is printed on acid-free, chlorine-free paper with 30% postconsumer recycled content. Cover is printed on 100% recycled paper.

Contents

Introduction

Marc Seals

Zona Gale's *Miss Lulu Bett* was the best-selling novel of 1920, and you've probably never heard of it. Let that sink in for a moment—*Miss Lulu Bett* sold as many copies as Sinclair Lewis's 1920 novel *Main Street*, but, while Lewis's novel holds a secure position in the American literary canon, Gale's novel seems all but forgotten. Even more remarkable is the fact that Gale won the 1921 Pulitzer Prize for Drama for the theatrical adaptation of the novel, making her the first woman to be awarded that prize. The play ran for nearly 200 performances between December 27, 1920, and June 18, 1921, at the Belmont Theatre on Broadway. There was even a 1921 Paramount silent film version, adapted by Clara Beranger and directed by William C. de Mille. Consider all of these factors— *Miss Lulu Bett* was a best-selling novel, a Pulitzer Prize-winning Broadway play, and a successful film released by Paramount Pictures—and one must confess that it is remarkable that most well-read Americans have never heard of the novel.[1] Let's examine the history, critical reception, and significance of *Miss Lulu Bett*.

Between 1906 and 1917, Zona Gale had established a reputation as a sentimental writer, penning novels and short stories of idyllic small-town life. She cast this aside with her fifth novel, 1918's *Birth*, a realistic and even tragic tale that Gale considered her best novel (Simonson 77). Though *Birth* was not a commercial success, the book was well-received by critics

---

[1] Special thanks are due to my very capable research assistant, Dori Kornacker; her insights into the four endings of the various versions of *Miss Lulu Bett* were invaluable.

(Williams 110). Gale took a discarded portion of *Birth* and developed it into *Miss Lulu Bett*. The result is a novel of feminist awakening; critic Deborah Lindsay Williams calls Lulu "a kind of self-actualized Cinderella" (109).

As the title indicates, *Miss Lulu Bett* is the story of Lulu Bett—a classic spinster who lives with her sister Ina's family and serves as domestic drudge. Lulu's brother-in-law, Dwight Deacon, is an officious oaf who cruelly mistreats Lulu. When Dwight's brother Ninian visits after an absence of nearly twenty years, he quickly charms Lulu and they marry (through a humorous series of events). (Spoilers ahead!) Lulu leaves with her new husband for a honeymoon in Savannah, Georgia, but returns a month later after Ninian confesses that he was previously married (and, having never divorced, does not know if his first wife is alive). Lulu returns to her life of servitude with the Deacon family but quickly realizes that she cannot remain in such an oppressive situation. When she decides to leave to seek a life elsewhere, Neil Cornish (a friend, confidant, and music-shop owner) proposes marriage. Having received word that Ninian's lost wife is indeed still alive (thus annulling her marriage), Lulu is free to accept. The novel ends with the newlyweds rushing to the train station.

Miss Lulu Bett was an immediate best seller (Williams 111, Simonson 79). Reviewers were also positive in their reception of the novel. The unsigned *New York Times* review (28 March 1920) was effusive in its praise:

> Miss Gale has so absolutely realized the story she tells, and knows so intimately the folks she draws, that "Miss Lulu Bett" speaks forcibly to those who care for actual human life and its problems in fictions. The book is simple in its elements, but it is wrought with careful detail.... Lulu Bett herself is an exquisite piece of portrayal.... The story is charming, but the interesting thing is the effect on Lulu of her encounter with life, her experience of being a personage rather than an appendage.... To

us it seems the best thing Miss Gale has yet done.…
"Miss Lulu Bett" is one of the books that ought
not to be missed by any one [*sic*] who cares for a
distinctively American story that is also a genuine
human relation, well told and lighted throughout
by a comprehending humor. (1)

Like most reviewers of the day, the *New York Times* lauded *Miss Lulu Bett* as an important work of American realism. The review went on to say that the novel was "a promise of a new type of work from her" (1).

In 1922, the *Milwaukee Journal* serialized *Miss Lulu Bett*, saying in an April 30th advertisement for the upcoming serialization that Lulu Bett "has taken her place among the greater characters of fiction." The *Journal's* advertisement quotes several contemporary reviews of the novel, including the *New York Times* review cited above, the *New York Tribune* (in which Heywood Broun proclaimed the novel as being "at the top of the list" of recently received novels), *The Chicago Evening Post* (which praised the novel's characters as "typically Midwestern"), *The St. Louis Globe-Democrat* (which declared that the novel placed Gale "in the highest class of American writers"), *The New York Evening Post* (which called the novel's main characters "vignettes done with exquisite deftness, no stroke misspent"), *The Duluth Herald* (which declared that the novel's "stark realism" placed Gale "in a class by herself"), and novelist Meredith Nicholson (who declared that the novel was "a work of genius" that would "last a long time"). A similar advertisement in Colorado's *Craig Courier* (28 December 1922) contained several of the same reviews, but added a blurb from Hildegarde Hawthorne's *Chicago Daily News* review (which argued that the novel presented "real human beings" and "a shining line of humor" which ran throughout).

This praise is typical of the overall critical reception of *Miss Lulu Bett*. One of the earliest reviews (27 March 1920) appeared in Philadelphia's *Evening Public Ledger*, calling *Miss Lulu Bett* "an important novel" that does for "the Middle West" what Edith Wharton had done for New England[2]. The *New York Tribune* teased the novel by quoting (among others) Yale literature professor William Lyon Phelps, who thought that *Miss Lulu Bett* was an "admirable novel" and "a notable example of realistic art" ("Book Gossip"); in their full review a week later (2 May 1920), the *Tribune* declares that *Miss Lulu Bett* is Gale's "first significant contribution to American literature" and praises the novel's "unerring insight" and "utter lack of sentimentality" ("Small-Town Folks"). Calling Lulu Bett a "latter day Cinderella," the review published by the *Evening Star* (Washington, D.C.) on 2 May 1920 notes the "delicacy and understanding" of the novel's treatment of the theme of "the unloved and unsought woman." Constance Mayfield Rourke (in *The New Republic*, 11 August 1920) hails the book as "a signal accomplishment in American letters" (316). The Atlantic Monthly pronounced *Miss Lulu Bett* "without flaw," concluding, "The book does not just contain felicities; it is stamped with felicity. We can show it to Europe without the sign of a blush in deprecation of our provincial rawness" (722–23). Frederic Taber Cooper wrote in *The Publishers' Weekly* that "to say that here also the author rises to the occasion is simply to credit her once again with that fine and finished art that make all her writing an abiding joy to the discriminating" (992). Lastly, widely syndicated columnist O.O. McIntyre wrote in late 1920, after he had just begun reading Sinclair Lewis's *Main Street*, that while many have praised *Main Street* as "the best novel of a small town yet written," he doubts it can compare with *Miss Lulu Bett* (4).

I was able to find only one negative review of the novel; this appeared in the April 1921 issue of *The Double Dealer* (an important but short-lived "little magazine"). The dissenting reviewer, identified only as "J.M.," acknowledges that "the

---

[2]   Edith Wharton, in fact, was impressed with *Miss Lulu Bett*, calling it (in a September 1922 letter to Gale) one of "the two significant books in recent American fiction" (qtd. in Williams 15). Sinclair Lewis's *Main Street* was the other book.

chorus of praise has not been marred by a single dubious discord." J.M.[3] then provides the previously absent "dubious discord," writing,

> The facts are these: Considered as literature, permanent or ephemeral, "Miss Lulu Bett" is a bubble blown up with air. The book is almost unbelievably slight: there is next to *nothing* in it. The plot is bizarre and tenuous. None of the characters (not excepting Lulu herself) has any vitality: they are manikins.... The style of the book is as strained and as painful in its way of speech as this gently humorous Dwight, Lulu's brother-in-law, whom in part it ridicules. The novel is distressingly empty. (165)

Though perhaps unreasonably harsh, J.M.'s opinion seems to be the only one that predicted the demise of the novel's place in American literary history.

The place of *Miss Lulu Bett* seemed to have been secured in October 1921 when influential literary critic Carl Van Doren singled out Zona Gale (along with Edgar Lee Masters, Sherwood Anderson, Floyd Dell, E.W. Howe, Sinclair Lewis, Mary Borden, and F. Scott Fitzgerald) as a leader in what he termed "the revolt from the village." In a landmark essay in *The Nation*, Van Doren argued that, while earlier fiction had presented small towns as idyllic, a new generation of authors was presenting readers with a darker take on village life. The idea of "the revolt from the village," though perhaps out of fashion today, was considered an important literary movement for several decades. Van Doren found Zona Gale particularly useful in this model because she had made her initial reputation writing the Friendship Village stories, which

---

[3] "J.M." is almost certainly John McClure, poet and one of the founding editors of *The Double Dealer*. McClure was one of the primary book reviewers for *The Double Dealer*.

fit neatly in the mold of the idyllic village myth. Van Doren suggests that Warbleton (the setting of *Miss Lulu Bett*) might well be Friendship "seen during a mood when its creator had grown weary of the eternal saccharine" (411). Van Doren continues, "Her story is as spare as the virgin frame of Lulu Bett; her style is staccato in its lucid brevity, like Lulu's infrequent speeches; her eloquence is not that of a torrent of words and images but that of comic or ironic or tragic meaning packed in a syllable, a gesture, a dumb silence" (411). Though the literary style of *Miss Lulu Bett* may seem quaint and dated today, Gale's simple, terse prose might usefully be seen as a forerunner of Ernest Hemingway's style of American modernism[4].

Such was the commercial and critical success of *Miss Lulu Bett* that it must have been no surprise when, in October 1920, Gale was asked by Broadway producer Brock Pemberton to adapt the novel for the stage. Gale finished the play in a mere ten days (Simonson 84). Gale stayed close to the novel—until the play's conclusion, which is drastically different. After discovering that Ninian's first wife is alive (thus nullifying Lulu's marriage), Lulu declines Cornish's proposal and leaves to become an independent woman. As she leaves, Lulu declares, "Goodby. Goodby, all of you. I'm going I don't know where—to work at I don't know what. But I'm going from choice!" (287). Biographer Harold Simonson suggests that the play's original "unromantic ending creates a more artful ambiguity" than the more traditional happy ending of the novel (84), and critic Marilyn Atlas argues in a 2003 essay that "Zona Gale dares to show [in this version] that even more important than marriage is the freedom and right of women to choose" (38).

---

[4]   The idea of connecting Gale to the modernist movement is not new. Catherine Kalish argues in her 2003 essay on Gale's Friendship Village (1908) that Friendship Village is not merely a collection of short stories, but rather a progressive novel with "a structure similar to that of James Joyce's *Dubliners*" (25), and Marilyn Judith Atlas suggests that the first ending of the play version of Miss Lulu Bett "embrace[s] a modern attitude toward closure" (35).

The play was previewed to over 1000 prisoners at the Sing
Sing Correctional Facility on 26 December 1920 and had its
official debut the next day at the Belmont Theatre in New York.
The initial reviews were mixed. The *New York Times* review,
written by Alexander Woollcott, begins mildly, noting that
the play was "warmly welcomed" (17). He posits that while a
viewer familiar with the "admirable" novel might find "genuine
pleasure," he is less confident that "a stray visitor" would
find the same; rather, such an audience member "would find
there a rather dull and flabby play, one somewhat sleazily put
together by a playwright who has but a slight sense of dramatic
values and no instinct at all for the idiom of the theatre" (17).
Woollcott praises the actors at the expense of the play, saying
that they are "all adroitly cast and played by a company that
does handsomely by a play that is not, by a good deal, as worth
their while as it might have been" (17). Heywood Broun's
review (in the *New York Tribune*) was similar, noting that the
play is well acted and "admirably" staged, but is marred by a
playwright who is "still too much of the novelist in her method"
("'Miss Lulu Bett'" 6). Pemberton, Woollcott, and Broun
were all charter members of the Algonquin Round Table (the
celebrated group of wits who met for lunch each day at New
York City's Algonquin Hotel); their next luncheon together
must have been a particularly interesting affair. *The New York
Herald*'s reviewer echoed an opinion similar to that of Woollcott
and Broun, writing that the play remained too much a book:
"The actors indeed all read their lines of the book intelligently.
But it was still a book they were working on, not a play, so their
efforts were only partly successful" ("'Miss Lulu Bett' Remains"
9). Burns Mantle's *Chicago Tribune* review notes the "small
but distinguished" audience at the Broadway premiere (which
included Zona Gale herself) and says that he would like to say
that the play is as successful as the novel, but "it can't be done"
(part 7, p. 3); again, the acting is fine, but the play is too much
like the novel.

The *Evening World*'s Charles Darnton offers a dissenting
and positive review; Darnton acknowledges that the play might

be even better had it been adapted by "an expert dramatist," but he still praises the ever-present "human touch," concluding that it is "a scandalous thing to say, but the whole town is likely to fall in love with and want to marry 'Miss Lulu Bett'" (19). *The Bookman*'s review was also positive, calling the play "an arresting dramatic picture" that might be called "one of the finest" productions of the year ("Seven Plays" 567–68). The review that ran in *The New Republic* actually takes the negative reviewers to task for criticizing Gale's skills as a playwright, declaring that Gale has "shown, in perfect American terms, the serious comedy of an emancipation" ("After the Play" 204).

Gale was flooded with letters from disappointed playgoers who expected "Lulu to get her man" (Craig 40). She took the complaints (and perhaps the negative reviews and weak ticket sales) to heart and rewrote the third act after just ten performances. In this new ending, Ninian discovers that his wife has been dead for years and asks for Lulu's forgiveness and pleads with her to come back to him; Lulu replies, "I forgave you in Savannah, Georgia" (271). The change seemed to have had the desired effect on audience approval—the play ran for about 200 performances before going on tour for another 600 (Williams 116). Critics, however, were less kind with regards to the revision. The *New York Tribune*'s Heywood Broun dismisses the new conclusion, writing, "But the 'happy ending' tradition for the whole of the theater, whether in terms of marriage or wealth or anything else, seems about as wise as demanding feathers on the tail of everything, from a tomtit to a mountain lion" ("As We Were Saying" part II, p. 1). Ludwig Lewisohn, in *The Nation*, defends the original "weightier and severer ending" and argues that audiences were perhaps swayed by the negative reviews (like Broun's) to "find the play dull" (198). Lewisohn argues that the happier ending sacrifices "the significance and strength of the dramatic action" (198). Even so, he finds the play saved by the characters and "moral atmosphere" created by Gale, calling the play "an enormous advance in the American drama" (189). Gale herself defended the new ending in a letter to newspaper editors: "Why in Miss Lulu Bert is Lulu less artistic in marriage at the final curtain than in going off to work for herself?… Why is marriage inartistic?" She agrees that the "open ending is the artistic ending," but argues that life has no "'ending' happy or unhappy" and questions the validity of any such labeling (qtd. in Williams 117).

It was the happier, crowd-pleasing version of the play that toured the country for 600 performances. When the touring company reached Madison and Baraboo (only a few miles from Gale's home in Portage, Wisconsin), Gale was in attendance. A *New York Times* theatre column (22 January 1922) quoted a letter that Gale wrote to producer Brock Pemberton:

> Baraboo and Madison were lovely—the real
> openings. I wish you had been there. I never had
> six dozen American Beauties at once before—not
> counting chrysanthemums…. I wish that you
> would hear us here at home. We are all so surprised
> in town that we liked it so much. The postman
> said: "You know, the boys thought it would be
> something highbrow, but they came back raving."
> And the druggist said: "I liked it four times as
> much as I expected to. It was great." And the coal
> man said: "Seventy-five percent of those who went
> over went because it was your play—but a hundred
> percent came back crazy about it." ("Gossip")

The touring production of the play was a hit, and reviewers across the country praised the play's realistic portrayal of domestic life (Chansky 60).

In addition to its modest success on Broadway and its broader success on tour, the play *Miss Lulu Bett* was awarded the 1921 Pulitzer Prize for Drama for being the American play performed in New York that best represented "educational value and power of the stage in raising the standard of good morals, good taste and good manners." (This was the stated criteria for the award until 1930.) Gale received $1000 and was the first woman to win the award. Again, the *New York Tribune*'s

Heywood Broun weighed in, condemning the selection: "Few, we think, will agree with the committee in giving the play prize to Zona Gale's 'Miss Lulu Bett.' Miss Gale might well have taken the prize for the best novel of the year with her book of this name, but it seems to me that she has not been as successful with the theme in its dramatic form" ("Books" 10).

In December of 1921, the film version of *Miss Lulu Bett* was released by Paramount Pictures. Directed by William C. de Mille (who specialized in adapting Broadway shows for the silver screen) and adapted by Clara Beranger (who eventually married de Mille), the film, which combines some elements of both the novel and the play, provides a conclusion similar to that of the novel. As in the novel, Lulu decides to leave the Deacon household, but in the film she does so with a dish-breaking tantrum. Lulu gets a job at the local bakery, and—after receiving a letter from Ninian telling her that his wife is alive and Lulu is free—she stops to show the letter to Cornish (who has been transformed from a hapless music store proprietor into a more respectable schoolteacher); they confess their love for one another with a charming bit on the classroom chalkboard (as Cornish's precocious students watch in delight).

Prior to the film's general release, *The Logan Republican* (Utah) reported that Paramount had received a letter from Gale expressing her approval of the screen adaptation: "At more than one point the picture of 'Miss Lulu Bett' improves upon both book and play. By such work as this, Paramount is doing a service not only to the screen but to fiction and drama" ("At the Movies" 8). Critics of the day seemed to agree that the film was superior to the play. The reviewer for *The New York Herald* writes, "'Miss Lulu Bett' of the stage seems to be 'Miss Lulu Better' on the screen" ("'Miss Lulu Bett' Is Produced" 11). This reviewer thought that the skillful performance of Lois Wilson (who played Lulu) prevented the kitchen violence of the film's ending from descending into slapstick. Harriette Underhill, of the *New York Tribune*, calls the china smashing a "glorious scene" and thinks Cornish a "rather more romantic figure" than in the previous incarnations (which is perhaps because he is played by matinee idol Milton Sills) (6). Underhill also gives a thumbs-up to the performance of Lois Wilson, saying, "Miss Wilson is a clever enough actress to make you believe almost anything save that she is a beauty" (6). Underhill's opinion of Wilson's appearance is perhaps a testament to Wilson's performance, considering that Wilson was the first Miss Alabama and went on to play Daisy Buchanan in the film adaptation of *The Great Gatsby* (1926).

Further, film scholars seem to feel that the film adaptation of *Miss Lulu Bett* has aged well. In 2001, the film was selected by the National Film Registry as one of the "culturally, historically, or aesthetically significant films" deemed worthy of preservation in the Library of Congress (making it one of the first 325 films chosen for preservation). Daniel Eagan, author of *America's Film Legacy: The Authoritative Guide to the Landmark Movies in the National Film Registry*, argues that, in *Miss Lulu Bett*, de Mille "captures a nostalgic but clear-eyed view of small-town culture with… grace and dignity" (74).

While the four versions of *Miss Lulu Bett* each provide the audience with a slightly different moral statement, the underlying theme is the same—Lulu consciously chooses her future. This theme was certainly timely, as the novel was published the same year that the 19th Amendment (giving women the right to vote) went into effect. When Ninian first meets Lulu, he asks, "Is it Miss Lulu Bett? Or Mrs.?"—Lulu replies, "Miss. From choice" (24, 166). This exchange is virtually unchanged in all four incarnations of the tale. In the original version of the play, Lulu declares at the end that she is leaving "from choice!" (287). This ending may be the strongest statement of female agency, but a strong statement in a play that no one sees is of limited value. By catering to her audience's desire for what they considered a happy ending, Gale allowed her basic (and still intact) message of choice and the inherent worth of all people to be heard—a culturally safe feminism for the era, perhaps, and a message that resonates even today. This edition—the first to contain all three print editions of *Miss Lulu Bett*—allows us to revisit a neglected American classic.

Works Cited

Advertisement for serialization of *Miss Lulu Bett. Craig Courier.* vol. 32, no. 21, 28 Dec. 1922, p. 5. *Colorado Historic Newspapers Collection.*

Advertisement for serialization of *Miss Lulu Bett. Milwaukee Journal.* 30 Apr. 1922, sec. 2 p. 5. *JSOnline.*

"After the Play." *The New Republic.* vol. XXV, no. 319, 12 Jan. 1921, pp. 204–5.

"At the Movies." *The Logan Republican* (Utah). 8 Dec. 1921, p. 11. *Chronicling America: Historic American Newspapers.* Lib. of Congress.

Atlas, Marilyn Judith. "From Novel to Plays: Zona Gale and the Marriage Plot in Three Versions of *Miss Lulu Bett*." *Midwestern Miscellany*, vol. 30, Spring 2002, pp. 35–43.

"Book Gossip." *New York Tribune.* 25 April 1920, section VII, p. 11. *Chronicling America: Historic American Newspapers.* Lib. of Congress.

Broun, Heywood. "As We Were Saying." *New York Tribune*, 6 Feb. 1921, part III, p. 1. *Chronicling America: Historic American Newspapers.* Lib. of Congress.

———. "Books." *New York Tribune*, 1 Jun. 1921, p. 6. *Chronicling America: Historic American Newspapers.* Lib. of Congress.

———. "'Miss Lulu Bett' Is of Fine Fabric Though Often Crude." *New York Tribune*, 28 Dec. 1920, p. 6. *Chronicling America: Historic American Newspapers.* Lib. of Congress.

Chansky, Dorothy. *Kitchen Sink Realisms: Domestic Labor, Dining, and Drama in American Theatre.* U of Iowa P, 2015.

Cooper, Frederic Taber. "A Family Beast of Burden." Rev of *Miss Lulu Bett*, by Zona Gale. *The Publishers' Weekly*, 20 March 1920. 991–2.

Craig, Carolyn Casey. *Women Pulitzer Playwrights: Biographical Profiles and Analyses of the Plays.* McFarland, 2004.

Darnton, Charles. "'Miss Lulu Bett' Homely, Human and Amusing." *The Evening World* (New York). 28 Dec. 1920, p. 19. *Chronicling America: Historic American Newspapers.* Lib. of Congress.

Eagan, Daniel. *America's Film Legacy: The Authoritative Guide to the Landmark Movies in the National Film Registry.* Continuum, 2010.

Gale, Zona. *Miss Lulu Bett (A Novel) and Miss Lulu Bett: An American Comedy of Errors.* Hastings College Press, 2016.

"Gossip of the Rialto." *New York Times.* 22 Jan. 1922, p. 85. *New York Times Archive.*

Kalish, Catherine. "Nobody Sick, Nobody Poor: Zona Gale's Construction of a Feminist Utopia." *Midwestern Miscellany*, vol. 31, Spring 2003, pp. 25–33.

Lewisohn, Ludwig. "Drama: Native Plays." *The Nation.* vol. CXII, no. 2900, 2 Feb. 1921, p. 198.

Mantle, Burns. "'Miss Lulu Bett' Lacks Essential Outlines of Drama." *Chicago Tribune.* 9 Jan. 1921, part 7, p. 3. *Chicago Tribune Archives.*

McIntyre, O.O. "Gotham Easy, Says Essayist." *The Washington Herald* (Washington, D.C.). 01 Nov. 1920, p. 4. *Chronicling America: Historic American Newspapers.* Lib. of Congress.

Miss Lulu Bett. Dir. William C. de Mille. Perf. Lois Wilson, Mabel Van Buren, and Theodore Roberts. Paramount Pictures, 1921. *Internet Archive*, https://archive.org/details/ Miss_Lulu_Bett.

"'Miss Lulu Bett' Is Produced as Movie." *The New York Herald.* 19 Dec. 1921, p. 11. *Chronicling America: Historic American Newspapers.* Lib. of Congress.

"'Miss Lulu Bett' Remains but a Book Even Upon the Stage." *The New York Herald.* 28 Dec. 1920, p. 9. *Chronicling America: Historic American Newspapers.* Lib. of Congress.

Rev. of *Miss Lulu Bett*, by Zona Gale. *The Atlantic Monthly*, May 1920, pp. 722–3.

Rev. of *Miss Lulu Bett*, by Zona Gale. *The Double Dealer*, April 1921, pp. 165–6.

Rev. of *Miss Lulu Bett*, by Zona Gale. *Evening Public Ledger* (Philadelphia), 27 March 1920, p. 6. *Chronicling America: Historic American Newspapers*. Lib. of Congress.

Rev. of *Miss Lulu Bett*, by Zona Gale. *Evening Star* (Washington, D.C.), 02 May 1920, p. 22. *Chronicling America: Historic American Newspapers*. Lib. of Congress.

Rev. of *Miss Lulu Bett*, by Zona Gale. *New York Times Book Review*. 28 Mar. 1920, p. 1+. *New York Times Archive*.

Rourke, Constance Mayfield. "Transitions." *The New Republic*, vol. XXIII, 11 Aug. 1920, 315–16.

"Seven Plays" (rev. of *Miss Lulu Bett*). *The Bookman*, vol. LII, no. 6, pp. 567–68.

Simonson, Harold Peter. *Zona Gale*. Twayne, 1962.

"Small-Town Folks." *New York Tribune*, 02 May 1920, section VII, p. 9. *Chronicling America: Historic American Newspapers*. Lib. of Congress.

Underhill, Harriette. "On the Screen: 'Miss Lulu Bett' Transferred to Screen with Surprisingly Few Changes." *New York Tribune*, 20 Dec. 1921, p. 6. *Chronicling America: Historic American Newspapers*. Lib. of Congress.

Van Doren, Carl. "Contemporary American Novelists, Part X. The Revolt from the Village: 1920." *The Nation*, vol. CXIII, no. 2936, 12 Oct. 1921, pp. 407–12.

Williams, Deborah Lindsay. *Not in Sisterhood: Edith Wharton, Willa Cather, Zona Gale, and the Politics of Female Authorship*. Palgrave, 2001.

Woollcott, Alexander. "The Play: Zona Gale's Play." *New York Times*. 28 Dec. 1920, section Amusements, p. 17. *New York Times Archive*.

Additional Reading

Bilderback, Riann. "Male Fraud: Zona Gale Travesties Patriarchy." *Midwestern Miscellany*, vol. 31, Spring 2003, pp. 17–23.

Burkardt, Barbara. "A Feminist Influence: Zona Gale and
     William Maxwell." *Midwestern Miscellany*, vol. 31, Spring
     2003, pp. 42–52.
Noe, Marcia, and Nancy Neff. "Reading *Miss Lulu Bett*: The
     Reception History of a Midwestern Classic." *Midwestern
     Miscellany*, vol. 31, Spring 2003, pp. 9–16.

....

Marc Seals is an Associate Professor of English at the
University of Wisconsin campus in Baraboo. Though he is an
American modernist by training, teaching at a small liberal arts
college has gradually made him into a flexible generalist. He
teaches courses in American literature, composition, and film.
His primary research interests include Raymond Chandler,
Ernest Hemingway, Gwendolyn Brooks, Dashiell Hammett,
F. Scott Fitzgerald, and Zona Gale. He is the President of the
University of Wisconsin Colleges chapter of the American
Association of University Professors.

Miss Lulu Bett

(A Novel)

I

April

The Deacons were at supper. In the middle of the table was a small, appealing tulip plant, looking as anything would look whose sun was a gas jet. This gas jet was high above the table and flared, with a sound.

"Better turn down the gas jest a little," Mr. Deacon said, and stretched up to do so. He made this joke almost every night. He seldom spoke as a man speaks who has something to say, but as a man who makes something to say.

"Well, what have we on the festive board to-night?" he questioned, eyeing it. "Festive" was his favourite adjective. "Beautiful," too. In October he might be heard asking: "Where's my beautiful fall coat?"

"We have creamed salmon," replied Mrs. Deacon gently. "On toast," she added, with a scrupulous regard for the whole truth. Why she should say this so gently no one can tell. She says everything gently. Her "Could you leave me another bottle of milk this morning?" would wring a milkman's heart.

"Well, now, let us see," said Mr. Deacon, and attacked the principal dish benignly. "*Let* us see," he added, as he served.

"I don't want any," said Monona.

The child Monona was seated upon a book and a cushion, so that her little triangle of nose rose adultly above her plate. Her remark produced precisely the effect for which she had passionately hoped.

"*What's* this?" cried Mr. Deacon. "*No* salmon?"

"No," said Monona, inflected up, chin pertly pointed. She felt her power, discarded her "sir."

"Oh now, Pet!" from Mrs. Deacon, on three notes. "You liked it before."

"I don't want any," said Monona, in precisely her original tone.

"Just a little? A very little?" Mr. Deacon persuaded, spoon dripping.

The child Monona made her lips thin and straight and shook her head until her straight hair flapped in her eyes on either side. Mr. Deacon's eyes anxiously consulted his wife's eyes. What is this? Their progeny will not eat? What can be supplied?

"Some bread and milk!" cried Mrs. Deacon brightly, exploding on "bread." One wondered how she thought of it.

"No," said Monona, inflection up, chin the same. She was affecting indifference to this scene, in which her soul delighted. She twisted her head, bit her lips unconcernedly, and turned her eyes to the remote.

There emerged from the fringe of things, where she perpetually hovered, Mrs. Deacon's older sister, Lulu Bett, who was "making her home with us." And that was precisely the case. *They* were not making her a home, goodness knows. Lulu was the family beast of burden.

"Can't I make her a little milk toast?" she asked Mrs. Deacon.

Mrs. Deacon hesitated, not with compunction at accepting Lulu's offer, not diplomatically to lure Monona. But she hesitated habitually, by nature, as another is by nature vivacious or brunette.

"Yes!" shouted the child Monona.

The tension relaxed. Mrs. Deacon assented. Lulu went to the kitchen. Mr. Deacon served on. Something of this scene was enacted every day. For Monona the drama never lost its zest. It never occurred to the others to let her sit without eating, once, as a cure-all. The Deacons were devoted parents and the child Monona was delicate. She had a white, grave face, white hair, white eyebrows, white lashes. She was sullen, anaemic. They let her wear rings. She "toed in." The poor child was the late birth of a late marriage and the principal joy which she had provided them thus far was the pleased reflection that they had produced her at all.

"Where's your mother, Ina?" Mr. Deacon inquired. "Isn't she coming to her supper?"

"Tantrim," said Mrs. Deacon, softly.

"Oh, ho," said he, and said no more.

The temper of Mrs. Bett, who also lived with them, had days of high vibration when she absented herself from the table as a kind of self-indulgence, and no one could persuade her to food. "Tantrims," they called these occasions.

"Baked potatoes," said Mr. Deacon. "That's good—that's good. The baked potato contains more nourishment than potatoes prepared in any other way. The nourishment is next to the skin. Roasting retains it."

"That's what I always think," said his wife pleasantly.

For fifteen years they had agreed about this.

They ate, in the indecent silence of first savouring food. A delicate crunching of crust, an odour of baked-potato shells, the slip and touch of the silver.

"Num, num, nummy-num!" sang the child Monona loudly, and was hushed by both parents in simultaneous exclamation which rivalled this lyric outburst. They were alone at table. Di, daughter of a wife early lost to Mr. Deacon, was not there. Di was hardly ever there. She was at that age. That age, in Warbleton.

A clock struck the half hour.

"It's curious," Mr. Deacon observed, "how that clock loses. It must be fully quarter to." He consulted his watch. "It is quarter to!" he exclaimed with satisfaction. "I'm pretty good at guessing time."

"I've noticed that!" cried his Ina.

"Last night, it was only twenty-three to, when the half hour struck," he reminded her.

"Twenty-one, I thought." She was tentative, regarded him with arched eyebrows, mastication suspended.

This point was never to be settled. The colloquy was interrupted by the child Monona, whining for her toast. And the doorbell rang.

"Dear me!" said Mr. Deacon. "What can anybody be thinking of to call just at meal-time?"

He trod the hall, flung open the street door. Mrs. Deacon listened. Lulu, coming in with the toast, was warned to silence by an uplifted finger. She deposited the toast, tiptoed to her chair. A withered baked potato and cold creamed salmon were on her plate. The child Monona ate with shocking appreciation. Nothing could be made of the voices in the hall. But Mrs. Bett's door was heard softly to unlatch. She, too, was listening.

A ripple of excitement was caused in the dining-room when Mr. Deacon was divined to usher some one to the parlour. Mr. Deacon would speak with this visitor in a few moments, and now returned to his table. It was notable how slight a thing would give him a sense of self-importance. Now he felt himself a man of affairs, could not even have a quiet supper with his family without the outside world demanding him. He waved his hand to indicate it was nothing which they would know anything about, resumed his seat, served himself to a second spoon of salmon and remarked, "More roast duck, anybody?" in a loud voice and with a slow wink at his wife. That lady at first looked blank, as she always did in the presence of any humour couched with the least indirection, and then drew back her chin and caught her lower lip in her gold-filled teeth. This was her conjugal rebuking.

Swedenborg always uses "conjugial." And really this sounds more married. It should be used with reference to the Deacons. No one was ever more married than they—at least than Mr. Deacon. He made little conjugal jokes in the presence of Lulu who, now completely unnerved by the habit, suspected them where they did not exist, feared lurking *entendre* in the most innocent comments, and became more tense every hour of her life.

And now the eye of the master of the house fell for the first time upon the yellow tulip in the centre of his table.

"Well, *well!*" he said. "What's this?"

Ina Deacon produced, fleetly, an unlooked-for dimple.

"Have you been buying flowers?" the master inquired.

"Ask Lulu," said Mrs. Deacon.

He turned his attention full upon Lulu.

"Suitors?" he inquired, and his lips left their places to form a sort of ruff about the word.

Lulu flushed, and her eyes and their very brows appealed.

"It was a quarter," she said. "There'll be five flowers."

"You *bought* it?"

"Yes. There'll be five—that's a nickel apiece."

His tone was as methodical as if he had been talking about the bread.

"Yet we give you a home on the supposition that you have no money to spend, even for the necessities."

His voice, without resonance, cleft air, thought, spirit, and even flesh.

Mrs. Deacon, indeterminately feeling her guilt in having let loose the dogs of her husband upon Lulu, interposed: "Well, but, Herbert—Lulu isn't strong enough to work. What's the use...."

She dwindled. For years the fiction had been sustained that Lulu, the family beast of burden, was not strong enough to work anywhere else.

"The justice business—" said Dwight Herbert Deacon—he was a justice of the peace—"and the dental profession—" he was also a dentist—"do not warrant the purchase of spring flowers in my home."

"Well, but, Herbert—" It was his wife again.

"No more," he cried briefly, with a slight bend of his head. "Lulu meant no harm," he added, and smiled at Lulu.

There was a moment's silence into which Monona injected a loud "Num, num, nummy-num," as if she were the burden of an Elizabethan lyric. She seemed to close the incident. But the burden was cut off untimely. There was, her father reminded her portentously, company in the parlour.

"When the bell rang, I was so afraid something had happened to Di," said Ina sighing.

"Let's see," said Di's father. "Where is little daughter to-night?"

He must have known that she was at Jenny Plow's at a tea party, for at noon they had talked of nothing else; but this was his way. And Ina played his game, always. She informed him, dutifully.

"Oh, *ho*," said he, absently. How could he be expected to keep his mind on these domestic trifles.

"We told you that this noon," said Lulu. He frowned, disregarded her. Lulu had no delicacy.

"How much is salmon the can now?" he inquired abruptly—this was one of his forms of speech, the can, the pound, the cord.

His partner supplied this information with admirable promptness. Large size, small size, present price, former price— she had them all.

"Dear me," said Mr. Deacon. "That is very nearly salmoney, isn't it?"

"Herbert!" his Ina admonished, in gentle, gentle reproach. Mr. Deacon punned, organically. In talk he often fell silent and then asked some question, schemed to permit his vice to flourish. Mrs. Deacon's return was always automatic: "*Her*bert!"

"Whose Bert?" he said to this. "I thought I was your Bert."

She shook her little head. "You are a case," she told him. He beamed upon her. It was his intention to be a case.

Lulu ventured in upon this pleasantry, and cleared her throat. She was not hoarse, but she was always clearing her throat.

"The butter is about all gone," she observed. "Shall I wait for the butter-woman or get some creamery?"

Mr. Deacon now felt his little jocularities lost before a wall of the matter of fact. He was not pleased. He saw himself as the light of his home, bringer of brightness, lightener of dull hours. It was a pretty rôle. He insisted upon it. To maintain it intact, it was necessary to turn upon their sister with concentrated irritation.

"Kindly settle these matters without bringing them to my attention at meal-time," he said icily.

Lulu flushed and was silent. She was an olive woman, once handsome, now with flat, bluish shadows under her wistful eyes. And if only she would look at her brother Herbert and say something. But she looked in her plate.

"I want some honey," shouted the child, Monona.

"There isn't any, Pet," said Lulu.

"I want some," said Monona, eyeing her stonily. But she found that her hair-ribbon could be pulled forward to meet her lips, and she embarked on the biting of an end. Lulu departed for some sauce and cake. It was apple sauce. Mr. Deacon remarked that the apples were almost as good as if he had stolen them. He was giving the impression that he was an irrepressible fellow. He was eating very slowly. It added pleasantly to his sense of importance to feel that some one, there in the parlour, was waiting his motion.

At length they rose. Monona flung herself upon her father. He put her aside firmly, every inch the father. No, no. Father was occupied now. Mrs. Deacon coaxed her away. Monona encircled her mother's waist, lifted her own feet from the floor and hung upon her. "She's such an active child," Lulu ventured brightly.

"Not unduly active, I think," her brother-in-law observed.

He turned upon Lulu his bright smile, lifted his eyebrows, dropped his lids, stood for a moment contemplating the yellow tulip, and so left the room.

Lulu cleared the table. Mrs. Deacon essayed to wind the clock. Well now. Did Herbert say it was twenty-three to-night when it struck the half hour and twenty-one last night, or twenty-one to-night and last night twenty-three? She talked of it as they cleared the table, but Lulu did not talk.

"Can't you remember?" Mrs. Deacon said at last. "I should think you might be useful."

Lulu was lifting the yellow tulip to set it on the sill. She changed her mind. She took the plant to the wood-shed and tumbled it with force upon the chip-pile.

The dining-room table was laid for breakfast. The two women brought their work and sat there. The child Monona hung miserably about, watching the clock. Right or wrong, she was put to bed by it. She had eight minutes more—seven—six—five—

Lulu laid down her sewing and left the room. She went to the wood-shed, groped about in the dark, found the stalk of the one tulip flower in its heap on the chip-pile. The tulip she fastened in her gown on her flat chest.

Outside were to be seen the early stars. It is said that if our sun were as near to Arcturus as we are near to our sun, the great Arcturus would burn our sun to nothingness.

In the Deacons' parlour sat Bobby Larkin, eighteen. He was in pain all over. He was come on an errand which civilisation has contrived to make an ordeal.

Before him on the table stood a photograph of Diana Deacon, also eighteen. He hated her with passion. At school she mocked him, aped him, whispered about him, tortured him. For two years he had hated her. Nights he fell asleep planning to build a great house and engage her as its servant.

Yet, as he waited, he could not keep his eyes from this photograph. It was Di at her curliest, at her fluffiest, Di conscious of her bracelet, Di smiling. Bobby gazed, his basic aversion to her hard-pressed by a most reluctant pleasure. He hoped that he would not see her, and he listened for her voice.

Mr. Deacon descended upon him with an air carried from his supper hour, bland, dispensing. Well! Let us have it. "What did you wish to see me about?"—with a use of the past tense as connoting something of indirection and hence of delicacy—a nicety customary, yet unconscious. Bobby had arrived in his best clothes and with an air of such formality that Mr. Deacon had instinctively suspected him of wanting to join the church, and, to treat the time with due solemnity, had put him in the parlour until he could attend at leisure.

Confronted thus by Di's father, the speech which Bobby had planned deserted him.

"I thought if you would give me a job," he said defencelessly.

"So that's it!" Mr. Deacon, who always awaited but a touch to be either irritable or facetious, inclined now to be facetious. "Filling teeth?" he would know. "Marrying folks, then?" Assistant justice or assistant dentist—which?

Bobby blushed. No, no, but in that big building of Mr. Deacon's where his office was, wasn't there something… It faded from him, sounded ridiculous. Of course there was nothing. He saw it now.

There was nothing. Mr. Deacon confirmed him. But Mr. Deacon had an idea. Hold on, he said—hold on. The grass. Would Bobby consider taking charge of the grass? Though Mr. Deacon was of the type which cuts its own grass and glories in its vigour and its energy, yet in the time after that which he called "dental hours" Mr. Deacon wished to work in his garden. His grass, growing in late April rains, would need attention early next month… he owned two lots—"of course property *is* a burden." If Bobby would care to keep the grass down and raked… Bobby would care, accepted this business opportunity, figures and all, thanked Mr. Deacon with earnestness. Bobby's aversion to Di, it seemed, should not stand in the way of his advancement.

"Then that is checked off," said Mr. Deacon heartily.

Bobby wavered toward the door, emerged on the porch, and ran almost upon Di returning from her tea-party at Jenny Plow's.

"Oh, Bobby! You came to see me?"

She was as fluffy, as curly, as smiling as her picture. She was carrying pink, gauzy favours and a spear of flowers. Undeniably in her voice there was pleasure. Her glance was startled but already complacent. She paused on the steps, a lovely figure.

But one would say that nothing but the truth dwelt in Bobby.

"Oh, hullo," said he. "No. I came to see your father."

He marched by her. His hair stuck up at the back. His coat was hunched about his shoulders. His insufficient nose, abundant, loose-lipped mouth and brown eyes were completely expressionless. He marched by her without a glance.

She flushed with vexation. Mr. Deacon, as one would expect, laughed loudly, took the situation in his elephantine grasp and pawed at it.

"Mamma! Mamma! What do you s'pose? Di thought she had a beau—"

"Oh, papa!" said Di. "Why, I just hate Bobby Larkin and the whole *school* knows it."

Mr. Deacon returned to the dining-room, humming in his throat. He entered upon a pretty scene.

His Ina was darning. Four minutes of grace remaining to the child Monona, she was spinning on one toe with some Bacchanalian idea of making the most of the present. Di dominated, her ruffles, her blue hose, her bracelet, her ring.

"Oh, and mamma," she said, "the sweetest party and the dearest supper and the darlingest decorations and the gorgeousest—"

"Grammar, grammar," spoke Dwight Herbert Deacon. He was not sure what he meant, but the good fellow felt some violence done somewhere or other.

"Well," said Di positively, "they *were*. Papa, see my favour."

She showed him a sugar dove, and he clucked at it.

Ina glanced at them fondly, her face assuming its loveliest light. She was often ridiculous, but always she was the happy wife and mother, and her rôle reduced her individual absurdities at least to its own.

The door to the bedroom now opened and Mrs. Bett appeared.

"Well, mother!" cried Herbert, the "well" curving like an arm, the "mother" descending like a brisk slap. "Hungry *now?*"

Mrs. Bett was hungry now. She had emerged intending to pass through the room without speaking and find food in the pantry. By obscure processes her son-in-law's tone inhibited all this.

"No," she said. "I'm not hungry."

Now that she was there, she seemed uncertain what to do. She looked from one to another a bit hopelessly, somehow foiled in her dignity. She brushed at her skirt, the veins of her long, wrinkled hands catching an intenser blue from the dark cloth. She put her hair behind her ears.

"We put a potato in the oven for you," said Ina. She had never learned quite how to treat these periodic refusals of her mother to eat, but she never had ceased to resent them.

"No, thank you," said Mrs. Bett. Evidently she rather enjoyed the situation, creating for herself a spot-light much in the manner of Monona.

"Mother," said Lulu, "let me make you some toast and tea."

Mrs. Bett turned her gentle, bloodless face toward her daughter, and her eyes warmed.

"After a little, maybe," she said. "I think I'll run over to see Grandma Gates now," she added, and went toward the door.

"Tell her," cried Dwight, "tell her she's my best girl."

Grandma Gates was a rheumatic cripple who lived next door, and whenever the Deacons or Mrs. Bett were angry or hurt or wished to escape the house for some reason, they stalked over to Grandma Gates—in lieu of, say, slamming a door. These visits radiated an almost daily friendliness which lifted and tempered the old invalid's lot and life.

Di flashed out at the door again, on some trivial permission.

"A good many of mamma's stitches in that dress to keep clean," Ina called after.

"Early, darling, early!" her father reminded her. A faint regurgitation of his was somehow invested with the paternal.

"What's this?" cried Dwight Herbert Deacon abruptly.

On the clock shelf lay a letter.

"Oh, Dwight!" Ina was all compunction. "It came this morning. I forgot."

"I forgot it too! And I laid it up there." Lulu was eager for her share of the blame.

"Isn't it understood that my mail can't wait like this?"

Dwight's sense of importance was now being fed in gulps.

"I know. I'm awfully sorry," Lulu said, "but you hardly ever get a letter—"

This might have made things worse, but it provided Dwight with a greater importance.

"Of course, pressing matter goes to my office," he admitted it. "Still, my mail should have more careful—"

He read, frowning. He replaced the letter, and they hung upon his motions as he tapped the envelope and regarded them.

"Now!" said he. "What do you think I have to tell you?"

"Something nice," Ina was sure.

"Something surprising," Dwight said portentously.

"But, Dwight—is it *nice?*" from his Ina.

"That depends. I like it. So'll Lulu." He leered at her. "It's company."

"Oh, Dwight," said Ina. "Who?"

"From Oregon," he said, toying with his suspense.

"Your brother!" cried Ina. "Is he coming?"

"Yes. Ninian's coming, so he says."

"Ninian!" cried Ina again. She was excited, round-eyed, her moist lips parted. Dwight's brother Ninian. How long was it? Nineteen years. South America, Central America, Mexico, Panama "and all." When was he coming and what was he coming for?

"To see me," said Dwight. "To meet you. Some day next week. He don't know what a charmer Lulu is, or he'd come quicker."

Lulu flushed terribly. Not from the implication. But from the knowledge that she was not a charmer.

The clock struck. The child Monona uttered a cutting shriek. Herbert's eyes flew not only to the child but to his wife. What was this, was their progeny hurt?

"Bedtime," his wife elucidated, and added: "Lulu, will you take her to bed? I'm pretty tired."

Lulu rose and took Monona by the hand, the child hanging back and shaking her straight hair in an unconvincing negative.

As they crossed the room, Dwight Herbert Deacon, strolling about and snapping his fingers, halted and cried out sharply:

"Lulu. One moment!"

He approached her. A finger was extended, his lips were parted, on his forehead was a frown.

"You *picked* the flower on the plant?" he asked incredulously.

Lulu made no reply. But the child Monona felt herself lifted and borne to the stairway and the door was shut with violence. On the dark stairway Lulu's arms closed about her in an embrace which left her breathless and squeaking. And yet Lulu was not really fond of the child Monona, either. This was a discharge of emotion akin, say, to slamming the door.

II

May

Lulu was dusting the parlour. The parlour was rarely used, but every morning it was dusted. By Lulu.

She dusted the black walnut centre table which was of Ina's choosing, and looked like Ina, shining, complacent, abundantly curved. The leather rocker, too, looked like Ina, brown, plumply upholstered, tipping back a bit. Really, the davenport looked like Ina, for its chintz pattern seemed to bear a design of lifted eyebrows and arch, reproachful eyes.

Lulu dusted the upright piano, and that was like Dwight— in a perpetual attitude of rearing back, with paws out, playful, but capable, too, of roaring a ready bass.

And the black fireplace—there was Mrs. Bett to the life. Colourless, fireless, and with a dust of ashes.

In the midst of all was Lulu herself reflected in the narrow pier glass, bodiless-looking in her blue gingham gown, but somehow alive. Natural.

This pier glass Lulu approached with expectation, not because of herself but because of the photograph on its low marble shelf. A large photograph on a little shelf-easel. A photograph of a man with evident eyes, evident lips, evident cheeks—and each of the six were rounded and convex. You could construct the rest of him. Down there under the glass you could imagine him extending, rounded and convex, with plump hands and curly thumbs and snug clothes. It was Ninian Deacon, Dwight's brother.

Every day since his coming had been announced Lulu, dusting the parlour, had seen the photograph looking at her with its eyes somehow new. Or were her own eyes new? She dusted this photograph with a difference, lifted, dusted, set it back, less as a process than as an experience. As she dusted the mirror and saw his trim semblance over against her own bodiless reflection, she hurried away. But the eyes of the picture followed her, and she liked it.

She dusted the south window-sill and saw Bobby Larkin come round the house and go to the wood-shed for the lawn mower. She heard the smooth blur of the cutter. Not six times had Bobby traversed the lawn when Lulu saw Di emerge from the house. Di had been caring for her canary and she carried her bird-bath and went to the well, and Lulu divined that Di had deliberately disregarded the handy kitchen taps. Lulu dusted the south window and watched, and in her watching was no quality of spying or of criticism. Nor did she watch wistfully. Rather, she looked out on something in which she had never shared, could not by any chance imagine herself sharing.

The south windows were open. Airs of May bore the soft talking.

"Oh, Bobby, will you pump while I hold this?" And again: "Now wait till I rinse." And again: "You needn't be so glum"— the village salutation signifying kindly attention.

Bobby now first spoke: "Who's glum?" he countered gloomily.

The iron of those days when she had laughed at him was deep within him, and this she now divined, and said absently:

"I used to think you were pretty nice. But I don't like you any more."

"Yes, you used to!" Bobby repeated derisively. "Is that why you made fun of me all the time?"

At this Di coloured and tapped her foot on the well-curb. He seemed to have her now, and enjoyed his triumph. But Di looked up at him shyly and looked down. "I had to," she admitted. "They were all teasing me about you."

"They were?" This was a new thought to him. Teasing her about him, were they? He straightened. "Huh!" he said, in magnificent evasion.

"I had to make them stop, so I teased you. I—I never wanted to." Again the upward look.

"Well!" Bobby stared at her. "I never thought it was anything like that."

"Of course you didn't." She tossed back her bright hair, met his eyes full. "And you never came where I could tell you. I wanted to tell you."

She ran into the house.

Lulu lowered her eyes. It was as if she had witnessed the exercise of some secret gift, had seen a cocoon open or an egg hatch. She was thinking:

"How easy she done it. Got him right over. But *how* did she do that?"

Dusting the Dwight-like piano, Lulu looked over-shoulder, with a manner of speculation, at the photograph of Ninian.

Bobby mowed and pondered. The magnificent conceit of the male in his understanding of the female character was sufficiently developed to cause him to welcome the improvisation which he had just heard. Perhaps that was the way it had been. Of course that was the way it had been. What a fool he had been not to understand. He cast his eyes repeatedly toward the house. He managed to make the job last over so that he could return in the afternoon. He was not conscious of planning this, but it was in some manner contrived for him by forces of his own with which he seemed to be coöperating without his conscious will. Continually he glanced toward the house.

These glances Lulu saw. She was a woman of thirty-four and Di and Bobby were eighteen, but Lulu felt for them no adult indulgence. She felt that sweetness of attention which we bestow upon May robins. She felt more.

She cut a fresh cake, filled a plate, called to Di, saying: "Take some out to that Bobby Larkin, why don't you?"

It was Lulu's way of participating. It was her vicarious thrill.

After supper Dwight and Ina took their books and departed to the Chautauqua Circle. To these meetings Lulu never went. The reason seemed to be that she never went anywhere.

When they were gone Lulu felt an instant liberation. She turned aimlessly to the garden and dug round things with her finger. And she thought about the brightness of that Chautauqua scene to which Ina and Dwight had gone. Lulu thought about such gatherings in somewhat the way that a futurist receives the subjects of his art—forms not vague, but heightened to intolerable definiteness, acute colour, and always motion— motion as an integral part of the desirable. But a factor of all was that Lulu herself was the participant, not the onlooker. The perfection of her dream was not impaired by any longing. She had her dream as a saint her sense of heaven.

"Lulie!" her mother called. "You come out of that damp."

She obeyed, as she had obeyed that voice all her life. But she took one last look down the dim street. She had not known it, but superimposed on her Chautauqua thoughts had been her faint hope that it would be to-night, while she was in the garden alone, that Ninian Deacon would arrive. And she had on her wool chally, her coral beads, her cameo pin....

She went into the lighted dining-room. Monona was in bed. Di was not there. Mrs. Bett was in Dwight Herbert's leather chair and she lolled at her ease. It was strange to see this woman, usually so erect and tense, now actually lolling, as if lolling were the positive, the vital, and her ordinary rigidity a negation of her. In some corresponding orgy of leisure and liberation, Lulu sat down with no needle.

"Inie ought to make over her delaine," Mrs. Bett comfortably began. They talked of this, devised a mode, recalled other delaines. "Dear, dear," said Mrs. Bett, "I had on a delaine when I met your father." She described it. Both women talked freely, with animation. They were individuals and alive. To the two pallid beings accessory to the Deacons' presence, Mrs. Bett and her daughter Lulu now bore no relationship. They emerged, had opinions, contradicted, their eyes were bright.

Toward nine o'clock Mrs. Bett announced that she thought she should have a lunch. This was debauchery. She brought in bread-and-butter, and a dish of cold canned peas. She was committing all the excesses that she knew—offering opinions, laughing, eating. It was to be seen that this woman had an immense store of vitality, perpetually submerged.

When she had eaten she grew sleepy—rather cross at the last and inclined to hold up her sister's excellencies to Lulu; and, at Lulu's defence, lifted an ancient weapon.

"What's the use of finding fault with Inie? Where'd you been if she hadn't married?"

Lulu said nothing.

"What say?" Mrs. Bett demanded shrilly. She was enjoying it.

Lulu said no more. After a long time:

"You always was jealous of Inie," said Mrs. Bett, and went to her bed.

As soon as her mother's door had closed, Lulu took the lamp from its bracket, stretching up her long body and her long arms until her skirt lifted to show her really slim and pretty feet. Lulu's feet gave news of some other Lulu, but slightly incarnate. Perhaps, so far, incarnate only in her feet and her long hair.

She took the lamp to the parlour and stood before the photograph of Ninian Deacon, and looked her fill. She did not admire the photograph, but she wanted to look at it. The house was still, there was no possibility of interruption. The occasion became sensation, which she made no effort to quench. She held a rendezvous with she knew not what.

In the early hours of the next afternoon with the sun shining across the threshold, Lulu was paring something at the kitchen table. Mrs. Bett was asleep. ("I don't blame you a bit, mother," Lulu had said, as her mother named the intention.) Ina was asleep. (But Ina always took off the curse by calling it her "si-esta," long *i*.) Monona was playing with a neighbour's child—you heard their shrill yet lovely laughter as they obeyed the adult law that motion is pleasure. Di was not there.

A man came round the house and stood tying a puppy to the porch post. A long shadow fell through the west doorway, the puppy whined.

"Oh," said this man. "I didn't mean to arrive at the back door, but since I'm here—"

He lifted a suitcase to the porch, entered, and filled the kitchen.

"It's Ina, isn't it?" he said.

"I'm her sister," said Lulu, and understood that he was here at last.

"Well, I'm Bert's brother," said Ninian. "So I can come in, can't I?"

He did so, turned round like a dog before his chair and sat down heavily, forcing his fingers through heavy, upspringing brown hair.

"Oh, yes," said Lulu. "I'll call Ina. She's asleep."

"Don't call her, then," said Ninian. "Let's you and I get acquainted."

He said it absently, hardly looking at her.

"I'll get the pup a drink if you can spare me a basin," he added.

Lulu brought the basin, and while he went to the dog she ran tiptoeing to the dining-room china closet and brought a cut-glass tumbler, as heavy, as ungainly as a stone crock. This she filled with milk.

"I thought maybe..." said she, and offered it.

"Thank *you!*" said Ninian, and drained it. "Making pies, as I live," he observed, and brought his chair nearer to the table.

"I didn't know Ina had a sister," he went on. "I remember now Bert said he had two of her relatives—"

Lulu flushed and glanced at him pitifully.

"He has," she said. "It's my mother and me. But we do quite a good deal of the work."

"I'll bet you do," said Ninian, and did not perceive that anything had been violated. "What's your name?" he bethought.

She was in an immense and obscure excitement. Her manner was serene, her hands as they went on with the peeling did not tremble; her replies were given with sufficient quiet. But she told him her name as one tells something of another and more remote creature. She felt as one may feel in catastrophe— no sharp understanding but merely the sense that the thing cannot possibly be happening.

"You folks expect me?" he went on.

"Oh, yes," she cried, almost with vehemence. "Why, we've looked for you every day."

"'See," he said, "how long have they been married?"

Lulu flushed as she answered: "Fifteen years."

"And a year before that the first one died—and two years they were married," he computed. "I never met that one. Then it's close to twenty years since Bert and I have seen each other."

"How awful," Lulu said, and flushed again.

"Why?"

"To be that long away from your folks."

Suddenly she found herself facing this honestly, as if the immensity of her present experience were clarifying her understanding: Would it be so awful to be away from Bert and Monona and Di—yes, and Ina, for twenty years?

"You think that?" he laughed. "A man don't know what he's like till he's roamed around on his own." He liked the sound of it. "Roamed around on his own," he repeated, and laughed again. "Course a woman don't know that."

"Why don't she?" asked Lulu. She balanced a pie on her hand and carved the crust. She was stupefied to hear her own question. "Why don't she?"

"Maybe she does. Do you?"

"Yes," said Lulu.

"Good enough!" He applauded noiselessly, with fat hands. His diamond ring sparkled, his even white teeth flashed. "I've had twenty years of galloping about," he informed her, unable, after all, to transfer his interests from himself to her.

"Where?" she asked, although she knew.

"South America. Central America. Mexico. Panama." He searched his memory. "Colombo," he superadded.

"My!" said Lulu. She had probably never in her life had the least desire to see any of these places. She did not want to see them now. But she wanted passionately to meet her companion's mind.

"It's the life," he informed her.

"Must be," Lulu breathed. "I—" she tried, and gave it up.

"Where you been mostly?" he asked at last.

By this unprecedented interest in her doings she was thrown into a passion of excitement.

"Here," she said. "I've always been here. Fifteen years with Ina. Before that we lived in the country."

He listened sympathetically now, his head well on one side. He watched her veined hands pinch at the pies. "Poor old girl," he was thinking.

"Is it Miss Lulu Bett?" he abruptly inquired. "Or Mrs.?"

Lulu flushed in anguish.

"Miss," she said low, as one who confesses the extremity of failure. Then from unplumbed depths another Lulu abruptly spoke up. "From choice," she said.

He shouted with laughter.

"You bet! Oh, you bet!" he cried. "Never doubted it." He made his palms taut and drummed on the table. "Say!" he said.

Lulu glowed, quickened, smiled. Her face was another face.

"Which kind of a Mr. are you?" she heard herself ask, and his shoutings redoubled. Well! Who would have thought it of her?

"Never give myself away," he assured her. "Say, by George, I never thought of that before! There's no telling whether a man's married or not, by his name!"

"It don't matter," said Lulu.

"Why not?"

"Not so many people want to know."

Again he laughed. This laughter was intoxicating to Lulu. No one ever laughed at what she said save Herbert, who laughed at *her*. "Go it, old girl!" Ninian was thinking, but this did not appear.

The child Monona now arrived, banging the front gate and hurling herself round the house on the board walk, catching the toe of one foot in the heel of the other and blundering forward, head down, her short, straight hair flapping over her face. She landed flat-footed on the porch. She began to speak, using a ridiculous perversion of words, scarcely articulate, then in vogue in her group. And,

"Whose dog?" she shrieked.

Ninian looked over his shoulder, held out his hand, finished something that he was saying to Lulu. Monona came to him readily enough, staring, loose-lipped.

"I'll bet I'm your uncle," said Ninian.

Relationship being her highest known form of romance, Monona was thrilled by this intelligence.

"Give us a kiss," said Ninian, finding in the plural some vague mitigation for some vague offence.

Monona, looking silly, complied. And her uncle said my stars, such a great big tall girl—they would have to put a board on her head.

"What's that?" inquired Monona. She had spied his great diamond ring.

"This," said her uncle, "was brought to me by Santa Claus, who keeps a jewellery shop in heaven."

The precision and speed of his improvisation revealed him. He had twenty other diamonds like this one. He kept them for those Sundays when the sun comes up in the west. Of course—often! Some day he was going to melt a diamond and eat it. Then you sparkled all over in the dark, ever after. Another diamond he was going to plant. They say—He did it all gravely, absorbedly. About it he was as conscienceless as a savage. This was no fancy spun to pleasure a child. This was like lying, for its own sake.

He went on talking with Lulu, and now again he was the tease, the braggart, the unbridled, unmodified male.

Monona stood in the circle of his arm. The little being was attentive, softened, subdued. Some pretty, faint light visited her. In her listening look, she showed herself a charming child.

"It strikes me," said Ninian to Lulu, "that you're going to do something mighty interesting before you die."

It was the clear conversational impulse, born of the need to keep something going, but Lulu was all faith.

She closed the oven door on her pies and stood brushing flour from her fingers. He was looking away from her, and she looked at him. He was completely like his picture. She felt as if she were looking at his picture and she was abashed and turned away.

"Well, I hope so," she said, which had certainly never been true, for her old formless dreams were no intention—nothing but a mush of discontent. "I hope I can do something that's nice before I quit," she said. Nor was this hope now independently true, but only this surprising longing to appear interesting in his eyes. To dance before him. "What would the folks think of me, going on so?" she suddenly said. Her mild sense of disloyalty was delicious. So was his understanding glance.

"You're the stuff," he remarked absently.

She laughed happily.

The door opened. Ina appeared.

"Well!" said Ina. It was her remotest tone. She took this man to be a pedlar, beheld her child in his clasp, made a quick, forward step, chin lifted. She had time for a very javelin of a look at Lulu.

"Hello!" said Ninian. He had the one formula. "I believe I'm your husband's brother. Ain't this Ina?"

It had not crossed the mind of Lulu to present him.

Beautiful it was to see Ina relax, soften, warm, transform, humanise. It gave one hope for the whole species.

"Ninian!" she cried. She lent a faint impression of the double *e* to the initial vowel. She slurred the rest, until the *y* sound squinted in. Not Neenyun, but nearly Neenyun.

He kissed her.

"Since Dwight isn't here!" she cried, and shook her finger at him. Ina's conception of hostess-ship was definite: A volley of questions—was his train on time? He had found the house all right? Of course! Any one could direct him, she should hope. And he hadn't seen Dwight? She must telephone him. But then she arrested herself with a sharp, curved fling of her starched skirts. No! They would surprise him at tea—she stood taut, lips compressed. Oh, the Plows were coming to tea. How unfortunate, she thought. How fortunate, she said.

The child Monona made her knees and elbows stiff and danced up and down. She must, she must participate.

"Aunt Lulu made three pies!" she screamed, and shook her straight hair.

"Gracious sakes," said Ninian. "I brought her a pup, and if I didn't forget to give it to her."

They adjourned to the porch—Ninian, Ina, Monona. The puppy was presented, and yawned. The party kept on about "the place." Ina delightedly exhibited the tomatoes, the two apple trees, the new shed, the bird bath. Ninian said the unspellable "m—m," rising inflection, and the "I see," prolonging the verb as was expected of him. Ina said that they meant to build a summer-house, only, dear me, when you have a family—but there, he didn't know anything about that. Ina was using her eyes, she was arch, she was coquettish, she was flirtatious, and she believed herself to be merely matronly, sisterly, womanly…

She screamed. Dwight was at the gate. Now the meeting, exclamation, banality, guffaw… good will.

And Lulu, peeping through the blind.

When "tea" had been experienced that evening, it was found that a light rain was falling and the Deacons and their guests, the Plows, were constrained to remain in the parlour. The Plows were gentle, faintly lustrous folk, sketched into life rather lightly, as if they were, say, looking in from some other level.

"The only thing," said Dwight Herbert, "that reconciles me to rain is that I'm let off croquet." He rolled his r's, a favourite device of his to induce humour. He called it "croquette." He had never been more irrepressible. The advent of his brother was partly accountable, the need to show himself a fine family man and host in a prosperous little home—simple and pathetic desire.

"Tell you what we'll do!" said Dwight. "Nin and I'll reminisce a little."

"Do!" cried Mr. Plow. This gentle fellow was always excited by life, so faintly excited by him, and enjoyed its presentation in any real form.

Ninian had unerringly selected a dwarf rocker, and he was overflowing it and rocking.

"Take this chair, do!" Ina begged. "A big chair for a big man." She spoke as if he were about the age of Monona.

Ninian refused, insisted on his refusal. A few years more, and human relationships would have spread sanity even to Ina's estate and she would have told him why he should exchange chairs. As it was she forbore, and kept glancing anxiously at the over-burdened little beast beneath him.

The child Monona entered the room. She had been driven down by Di and Jenny Plow, who had vanished upstairs and, through the ventilator, might be heard in a lift and fall of giggling. Monona had also been driven from the kitchen where Lulu was, for some reason, hurrying through the dishes. Monona now ran to Mrs. Bett, stood beside her and stared about resentfully. Mrs. Bett was in best black and ruches, and she seized upon Monona and patted her, as her own form of social expression; and Monona wriggled like a puppy, as hers.

"Quiet, pettie," said Ina, eyebrows up. She caught her lower lip in her teeth.

"Well, sir," said Dwight, "you wouldn't think it to look at us, but mother had her hands pretty full, bringing us up."

Into Dwight's face came another look. It was always so, when he spoke of this foster-mother who had taken these two boys and seen them through the graded schools. This woman Dwight adored, and when he spoke of her he became his inner self.

"We must run up-state and see her while you're here, Nin," he said.

To this Ninian gave a casual assent, lacking his brother's really tender ardour.

"Little," Dwight pursued, "little did she think I'd settle down into a nice, quiet, married dentist and magistrate in my town. And Nin into—say, Nin, what are you, anyway?"

They laughed.

"That's the question," said Ninian.

They laughed.

"Maybe," Ina ventured, "maybe Ninian will tell us something about his travels. He is quite a traveller, you know," she said to the Plows. "A regular Gulliver."

They laughed respectfully.

"How we should love it, Mr. Deacon," Mrs. Plow said. "You know we've never seen *very* much."

Goaded on, Ninian launched upon his foreign countries as he had seen them: Population, exports, imports, soil, irrigation, business. For the populations Ninian had no respect. Crops could not touch ours. Soil mighty poor pickings. And the business—say! Those fellows don't know—and, say, the hotels! Don't say foreign hotel to Ninian.

He regarded all the alien earth as barbarian, and he stoned it. He was equipped for absolutely no intensive observation. His contacts were negligible. Mrs. Plow was more excited by the Deacons' party than Ninian had been wrought upon by all his voyaging.

"Tell you," said Dwight. "When we ran away that time and went to the state fair, little did we think—" He told about running away to the state fair. "I thought," he wound up, irrelevantly, "Ina and I might get over to the other side this year, but I guess not. I guess not."

The words give no conception of their effect, spoken thus. For there in Warbleton these words are not commonplace. In

Warbleton, Europe is never so casually spoken. "Take a trip abroad" is the phrase, or "Go to Europe" at the very least, and both with empressement. Dwight had somewhere noted and deliberately picked up that "other side" effect, and his Ina knew this, and was proud. Her covert glance about pensively covered her soft triumph.

Mrs. Bett, her arm still circling the child Monona, now made her first observation.

"Pity not to have went while the going was good," she said, and said no more.

Nobody knew quite what she meant, and everybody hoped for the best. But Ina frowned. Mamma did these things occasionally when there was company, and she dared. She never sauced Dwight in private. And it wasn't fair, it wasn't *fair*—

Abruptly Ninian rose and left the room.

The dishes were washed. Lulu had washed them at break-neck speed—she could not, or would not, have told why. But no sooner were they finished and set away than Lulu had been attacked by an unconquerable inhibition. And instead of going to the parlour, she sat down by the kitchen window. She was in her chally gown, with her cameo pin and her string of coral.

Laughter from the parlour mingled with the laughter of Di and Jenny upstairs. Lulu was now rather shy of Di. A night or two before, coming home with "extra" cream, she had gone round to the side-door and had come full upon Di and Bobby, seated on the steps. And Di was saying:

"Well, if I marry you, you've simply got to be a great man. I could never marry just anybody. I'd *smother*."

Lulu had heard, stricken. She passed them by, responding only faintly to their greeting. Di was far less taken aback than Lulu.

Later Di had said to Lulu: "I s'pose you heard what we were saying."

Lulu, much shaken, had withdrawn from the whole matter by a flat "no." "Because," she said to herself, "I couldn't have heard right."

But since then she had looked at Di as if Di were some one else. Had not Lulu taught her to make buttonholes and to hem—oh, no! Lulu could not have heard properly.

"Everybody's got somebody to be nice to them," she thought now, sitting by the kitchen window, adult yet Cinderella.

She thought that some one would come for her. Her mother or even Ina. Perhaps they would send Monona. She waited at first hopefully, then resentfully. The grey rain wrapped the air.

"Nobody cares what becomes of me after they're fed," she thought, and derived an obscure satisfaction from her phrasing, and thought it again.

Ninian Deacon came into the kitchen.

Her first impression was that he had come to see whether the dog had been fed.

"I fed him," she said, and wished that she had been busy when Ninian entered.

"Who, me?" he asked. "You did that all right. Say, why in time don't you come in the other room?"

"Oh, I don't know."

"Well, neither do I. I've kept thinking, 'Why don't she come along.' Then I remembered the dishes." He glanced about. "I come to help wipe dishes."

"Oh!" she laughed so delicately, so delightfully, one wondered where she got it. "They're washed—" she caught herself at "long ago."

"Well then, what are you doing here?"

"Resting."

"Rest in there." He bowed, crooked his arm. "Señora," he said,—his Spanish matched his other assimilations of travel— "Señora. Allow me."

Lulu rose. On his arm she entered the parlour. Dwight was narrating and did not observe that entrance. To the Plows it was sufficiently normal. But Ina looked up and said:

"Well!"—in two notes, descending, curving.

Lulu did not look at her. Lulu sat in a low rocker. Her starched white skirt, throwing her chally in ugly lines, revealed a peeping rim of white embroidery. Her lace front wrinkled when she sat, and perpetually she adjusted it. She curled her feet sidewise beneath her chair, her long wrists and veined hands lay along her lap in no relation to her. She was tense. She rocked.

When Dwight had finished his narration, there was a pause, broken at last by Mrs. Bett:

"You tell that better than you used to when you started in telling it," she observed. "You got in some things I guess you used to clean forget about. Monona, get off my rocker."

Monona made a little whimpering sound, in pretence to tears. Ina said "Darling—quiet!"—chin a little lifted, lower lip revealing lower teeth for the word's completion; and she held it.

The Plows were asking something about Mexico. Dwight was wondering if it would let up raining *at all*. Di and Jenny came whispering into the room. But all these distractions Ninian Deacon swept aside.

"Miss Lulu," he said, "I wanted you to hear about my trip up the Amazon, because I knew how interested you are in travels."

He talked, according to his lights, about the Amazon. But the person who most enjoyed the recital could not afterward have told two words that he said. Lulu kept the position which she had taken at first, and she dare not change. She saw the blood in the veins of her hands and wanted to hide them. She wondered if she might fold her arms, or have one hand to support her chin, gave it all up and sat motionless, save for the rocking.

Then she forgot everything. For the first time in years some one was talking and looking not only at Ina and Dwight and their guests, but at her.

III

June

On a June morning Dwight Herbert Deacon looked at the sky, and said with his manner of originating it:

"How about a picnic this afternoon?"

Ina, with her blank, upward look, exclaimed: "To-*day?*"

"First class day, it looks like to me."

Come to think of it, Ina didn't know that there was anything to prevent, but mercy, Herbert was so sudden. Lulu began to recite the resources of the house for a lunch. Meanwhile, since the first mention of picnic, the child Monona had been dancing stiffly about the room, knees stiff, elbows stiff, shoulders immovable, her straight hair flapping about her face. The sad dance of the child who cannot dance because she never has danced. Di gave a conservative assent—she was at that age—and then took advantage of the family softness incident to a guest and demanded that Bobby go too. Ina hesitated, partly because she always hesitated, partly because she was tribal in the extreme. "Just our little family and Uncle Ninian would have been so nice," she sighed, with her consent.

When, at six o'clock, Ina and Dwight and Ninian assembled on the porch and Lulu came out with the basket, it was seen that she was in a blue-cotton house-gown.

"Look here," said Ninian, "aren't you going?"

"Me?" said Lulu. "Oh, no."

"Why not?"

"Oh, I haven't been to a picnic since I can remember."

"But why not?"

"Oh, I never think of such a thing."

Ninian waited for the family to speak. They did speak. Dwight said:

"Lulu's a regular home body."

And Ina advanced kindly with: "Come with us, Lulu, if you like."

"No," said Lulu, and flushed. "Thank you," she added, formally.

Mrs. Bett's voice shrilled from within the house, startlingly close—just beyond the blind, in fact:

"Go on, Lulie. It'll do you good. You mind me and go on."

"Well," said Ninian, "that's what I say. You hustle for your hat and you come along."

For the first time this course presented itself to Lulu as a possibility. She stared up at Ninian.

"You can slip on my linen duster, over," Ina said graciously.

"Your new one?" Dwight incredulously wished to know.

"Oh, no!" Ina laughed at the idea. "The old one."

They were having to wait for Di in any case—they always had to wait for Di—and at last, hardly believing in her own motions, Lulu was running to make ready. Mrs. Bett hurried to help her, but she took down the wrong things and they were both irritated. Lulu reappeared in the linen duster and a wide hat. There had been no time to "tighten up" her hair; she was flushed at the adventure; she had never looked so well.

They started. Lulu, falling in with Monona, heard for the first time in her life, the step of the pursuing male, choosing to walk beside her and the little girl. Oh, would Ina like that? And what did Lulu care what Ina liked? Monona, making a silly, semi-articulate observation, was enchanted to have Lulu burst into laughter and squeeze her hand.

Di contributed her bright presence, and Bobby Larkin appeared from nowhere, running, with a gigantic bag of fruit.

"Bullylujah!" he shouted, and Lulu could have shouted with him.

She sought for some utterance. She wanted to talk with Ninian.

"I do hope we've brought sandwiches enough," was all that she could get to say.

They chose a spot, that is to say Dwight Herbert chose a spot, across the river and up the shore where there was at that season a strip of warm beach. Dwight Herbert declared himself the builder of incomparable fires, and made a bad smudge. Ninian, who was a camper neither by birth nor by adoption, kept offering brightly to help, could think of nothing to do, and presently, bethinking himself of skipping stones, went and tried to skip them on the flowing river. Ina cut her hand opening the condensed milk and was obliged to sit under a tree and nurse the wound. Monona spilled all the salt and sought diligently to recover it. So Lulu did all the work. As for Di and Bobby, they had taken the pail and gone for water, discouraging Monona from accompanying them, discouraging her to the point of tears. But the two were gone for so long that on their return Dwight was hungry and cross and majestic.

"Those who disregard the comfort of other people," he enunciated, "can not expect consideration for themselves in the future."

He did not say on what ethical tenet this dictum was based, but he delivered it with extreme authority. Ina caught her lower lip with her teeth, dipped her head, and looked at Di. And Monona laughed like a little demon.

As soon as Lulu had all in readiness, and cold corned beef and salad had begun their orderly progression, Dwight became the immemorial dweller in green fastnesses. He began:

"This is ideal. I tell you, people don't half know life if they don't get out and eat in the open. It's better than any tonic at a dollar the bottle. Nature's tonic—eh? Free as the air. Look at that sky. See that water. Could anything be more pleasant?"

He smiled at his wife. This man's face was glowing with simple pleasure. He loved the out-of-doors with a love which could not explain itself. But he now lost a definite climax when his wife's comment was heard to be:

"Monona! Now it's all over both ruffles. And mamma does try so hard…"

After supper some boys arrived with a boat which they beached, and Dwight, with enthusiasm, gave the boys ten cents for a half hour's use of that boat and invited to the waters his wife, his brother and his younger daughter. Ina was timid—not because she was afraid but because she was congenitally timid— with her this was not a belief or an emotion, it was a disease.

"Dwight darling, are you sure there's no danger?"

Why, none. None in the world. Whoever heard of drowning in a river.

"But you're not so very used—"

Oh, wasn't he? Who was it that had lived in a boat throughout youth if not he?

Ninian refused out-of-hand, lighted a cigar, and sat on a log in a permanent fashion. Ina's plump figure was fitted in the stern, the child Monona affixed, and the boat put off, bow well out of water. On this pleasure ride the face of the wife was as the face of the damned. It was true that she revered her husband's opinions above those of all other men. In politics, in science, in religion, in dentistry she looked up to his dicta as to revelation. And was he not a magistrate? But let him take oars in hand, or shake lines or a whip above the back of any horse, and this woman would trust any other woman's husband by preference. It was a phenomenon.

Lulu was making the work last, so that she should be out of everybody's way. When the boat put off without Ninian, she felt a kind of terror and wished that he had gone. He had sat down near her, and she pretended not to see. At last Lulu understood that Ninian was deliberately choosing to remain with her. The languor of his bulk after the evening meal made no explanation for Lulu. She asked for no explanation. He had stayed.

And they were alone. For Di, on a pretext of examining the flocks and herds, was leading Bobby away to the pastures, a little at a time.

The sun, now fallen, had left an even, waxen sky. Leaves and ferns appeared drenched with the light just withdrawn. The hush, the warmth, the colour, were charged with some influence. The air of the time communicated itself to Lulu as intense and quiet happiness. She had not yet felt quiet with Ninian. For the first time her blind excitement in his presence ceased, and she felt curiously accustomed to him. To him the air of the time imparted itself in a deepening of his facile sympathy.

"Do you know something?" he began. "I think you have it pretty hard around here."

"I?" Lulu was genuinely astonished.

"Yes, sir. Do you have to work like this all the time? I guess you won't mind my asking."

"Well, I ought to work. I have a home with them. Mother too."

"Yes, but glory. You ought to have some kind of a life of your own. You want it, too. You told me you did—that first day."

She was silent. Again he was investing her with a longing which she had never really had, until he had planted that longing. She had wanted she knew not what. Now she accepted the dim, the romantic interest of this rôle.

"I guess you don't see how it seems," he said, "to me, coming along—a stranger so. I don't like it."

He frowned, regarded the river, flicked away ashes, his diamond obediently shining. Lulu's look, her head drooping, had the liquid air of the look of a young girl. For the first time in her life she was feeling her helplessness. It intoxicated her.

"They're very good to me," she said.

He turned. "Do you know why you think that? Because you've never had anybody really good to you. That's why."

"But they treat me good."

"They make a slave of you. Regular slave." He puffed, frowning. "Damned shame, *I* call it," he said.

Her loyalty stirred Lulu. "We have our whole living—"

"And you earn it. I been watching you since I been here. Don't you ever go anywheres?"

She said: "This is the first place in—in years."

"Lord. Don't you want to? Of course you do!"

"Not so much places like this—"

"I see. What you want is to get away—like you'd ought to." He regarded her. "You've been a blamed fine-looking woman," he said.

She did not flush, but that faint, unsuspected Lulu spoke for her:

"You must have been a good-looking man once yourself."

His laugh went ringing across the water. "You're pretty good," he said. He regarded her approvingly. "I don't see how you do it," he mused, "blamed if I do."

"How I do what?"

"Why come back, quick like that, with what you say."

Lulu's heart was beating painfully. The effort to hold her own in talk like this was terrifying. She had never talked in this fashion to any one. It was as if some matter of life or death hung on her ability to speak an alien tongue. And yet, when she was most at loss, that other Lulu, whom she had never known anything about, seemed suddenly to speak for her. As now:

"It's my grand education," she said.

She sat humped on the log, her beautiful hair shining in the light of the warm sky. She had thrown off her hat and the linen duster, and was in her blue gingham gown against the sky and leaves. But she sat stiffly, her feet carefully covered, her hands ill at ease, her eyes rather piteous in their hope somehow to hold her vague own. Yet from her came these sufficient, insouciant replies.

"Education," he said laughing heartily. "That's mine, too." He spoke a creed. "I ain't never had it and I ain't never missed it."

"Most folks are happy without an education," said Lulu.

"You're not very happy, though."

"Oh, no," she said.

"Well, sir," said Ninian, "I'll tell you what we'll do. While I'm here I'm going to take you and Ina and Dwight up to the city."

"To the city?"

"To a show. Dinner and a show. I'll give you *one* good time."

"Oh!" Lulu leaned forward. "Ina and Dwight go sometimes. I never been."

"Well, just you come with me. I'll look up what's good. You tell me just what you like to eat, and we'll get it—"

She said: "I haven't had anything to eat in years that I haven't cooked myself."

He planned for that time to come, and Lulu listened as one intensely experiencing every word that he uttered. Yet it was not in that future merry-making that she found her joy, but in the consciousness that he—some one—any one—was planning like this for her.

Meanwhile Di and Bobby had rounded the corner by an old hop-house and kept on down the levee. Now that the presence of the others was withdrawn, the two looked about them differently and began themselves to give off an influence instead of being pressed upon by overpowering personalities. Frogs were chorusing in the near swamp, and Bobby wanted one. He was off after it. But Di eventually drew him back, reluctant, frogless. He entered upon an exhaustive account of the use of frogs for bait, and as he talked he constantly flung stones. Di grew restless. There was, she had found, a certain amount of this to be gone through before Bobby would focus on the personal. At length she was obliged to say, "Like me to-day?" And then he entered upon personal talk with the same zest with which he had discussed bait.

"Bobby," said Di, "sometimes I think we might be married, and not wait for any old money."

They had now come that far. It was partly an authentic attraction, grown from out the old repulsion, and partly it was that they both—and especially Di—so much wanted the experiences of attraction that they assumed its ways. And then each cared enough to assume the pretty rôle required by the other, and by the occasion, and by the air of the time.

"Would you?" asked Bobby—but in the subjunctive.

She said: "Yes. I will."

"It would mean running away, wouldn't it?" said Bobby, still subjunctive.

"I suppose so. Mamma and papa are so unreasonable."

"Di," said Bobby, "I don't believe you could ever be happy with me."

"The idea! I can too. You're going to be a great man—you know you are."

Bobby was silent. Of course he knew it—but he passed it over.

"Wouldn't it be fun to elope and surprise the whole school?" said Di, sparkling.

Bobby grinned appreciatively. He was good to look at, with his big frame, his head of rough dark hair, the sky warm upon his clear skin and full mouth. Di suddenly announced that she would be willing to elope *now*.

"I've planned eloping lots of times," she said ambiguously.

It flashed across the mind of Bobby that in these plans of hers he may not always have been the principal, and he could not be sure… But she talked in nothings, and he answered her so.

Soft cries sounded in the centre of the stream. The boat, well out of the strong current, was seen to have its oars shipped; and there sat Dwight Herbert gently rocking the boat. Dwight Herbert would.

"Bertie, Bertie—please!" you heard his Ina say.

Monona began to cry, and her father was irritated, felt that it would be ignominious to desist, and did not know that he felt this. But he knew that he was annoyed, and he took refuge in this, and picked up the oars with: "Some folks never can enjoy anything without spoiling it."

"That's what I was thinking," said Ina, with a flash of anger.

They glided toward the shore in a huff. Monona found that she enjoyed crying across the water and kept it up. It was almost as good as an echo. Ina, stepping safe to the sands, cried ungratefully that this was the last time that she would ever, ever go with her husband anywhere. Ever. Dwight Herbert, recovering, gauged the moment to require of him humour, and observed that his wedded wife was as skittish as a colt. Ina kept silence, head poised so that her full little chin showed double. Monona, who had previously hidden a cooky in her frock, now remembered it and crunched sidewise, the eyes ruminant.

Moving toward them, with Di, Bobby was suddenly overtaken by the sense of disliking them all. He never had liked Dwight Herbert, his employer. Mrs. Deacon seemed to him so overwhelmingly mature that he had no idea how to treat her. And the child Monona he would like to roll in the river. Even Di... He fell silent, was silent on the walk home which was the signal for Di to tease him steadily. The little being was afraid of silence. It was too vast for her. She was like a butterfly in a dome.

But against that background of ruined occasion, Lulu walked homeward beside Ninian. And all that night, beside her mother who groaned in her sleep, Lulu lay tense and awake. He had walked home with her. He had told Ina and Herbert about going to the city. What did it mean? Suppose... oh no; oh no!

"Either lay still or get up and set up," Mrs. Bett directed her at length.

IV

July

When, on a warm evening a fortnight later, Lulu
descended the stairs dressed for her incredible trip to the city,
she wore the white waist which she had often thought they
would "use" for her if she died. And really, the waist looked as
if it had been planned for the purpose, and its wide, upstanding
plaited lace at throat and wrist made her neck look thinner,
her forearm sharp and veined. Her hair she had "crimped" and
parted in the middle, puffed high—it was so that hair had been
worn in Lulu's girlhood.

"*Well!*" said Ina, when she saw this coiffure, and frankly
examined it, head well back, tongue meditatively teasing at her
lower lip.

For travel Lulu was again wearing Ina's linen duster—the
old one.

Ninian appeared, in a sack coat—and his diamond. His
distinctly convex face, its thick, rosy flesh, thick mouth and
cleft chin gave Lulu once more that bold sense of looking—not
at him, for then she was shy and averted her eyes—but at his
photograph at which she could gaze as much as she would. She

looked up at him openly, fell in step beside him. Was he not taking her to the city? Ina and Dwight themselves were going because she, Lulu, had brought about this party.

"Act as good as you look, Lulie," Mrs. Bett called after them. She gave no instructions to Ina who was married and able to shine in her conduct, it seemed.

Dwight was cross. On the way to the station he might have been heard to take it up again, whatever it was, and his Ina unmistakably said: "Well, now don't keep it going all the way there"; and turned back to the others with some elaborate comment about the dust, thus cutting off her so-called lord from his legitimate retort. A mean advantage.

The city was two hours' distant, and they were to spend the night. On the train, in the double seat, Ninian beside her among the bags, Lulu sat in the simple consciousness that the people all knew that she too had been chosen. A man and a woman were opposite, with their little boy between them. Lulu felt this woman's superiority of experience over her own, and smiled at her from a world of fellowship. But the woman lifted her eyebrows and stared and turned away, with slow and insolent winking.

Ninian had a boyish pride in his knowledge of places to eat in many cities—as if he were leading certain of the tribe to a deer-run in a strange wood. Ninian took his party to a downtown café, then popular among business and newspaper men. The place was below the sidewalk, was reached by a dozen marble steps, and the odour of its griddle-cakes took the air of the street. Ninian made a great show of selecting a table, changed once, called the waiter "my man" and rubbed soft hands on "What do you say? Shall it be lobster?" He ordered the dinner, instructing the waiter with painstaking gruffness.

"Not that they can touch *your* cooking here, Miss Lulu," he said, settling himself to wait, and crumbling a crust.

Dwight, expanding a bit in the aura of the food, observed that Lulu was a regular chef, that was what Lulu was. He still would not look at his wife, who now remarked:

"Sheff, Dwightie. Not cheff."

This was a mean advantage, which he pretended not to hear—another mean advantage.

"Ina," said Lulu, "your hat's just a little mite—no, over the other way."

"Was there anything to prevent your speaking of that before?" Ina inquired acidly.

"I started to and then somebody always said something," said Lulu humbly.

Nothing could so much as cloud Lulu's hour. She was proof against any shadow.

"Say, but you look tremendous to-night," Dwight observed to her.

Understanding perfectly that this was said to tease his wife, Lulu yet flushed with pleasure. She saw two women watching, and she thought: "They're feeling sorry for Ina—nobody talking to her." She laughed at everything that the men said. She passionately wanted to talk herself. "How many folks keep going past," she said, many times.

At length, having noted the details of all the clothes in range, Ina's isolation palled upon her and she set herself to take Ninian's attention. She therefore talked with him about himself.

"Curious you've never married, Nin," she said.

"Don't say it like that," he begged. "I might yet."

Ina laughed enjoyably. "Yes, you might!" she met this.

"She wants everybody to get married, but she wishes I hadn't," Dwight threw in with exceeding rancour.

They developed this theme exhaustively, Dwight usually speaking in the third person and always with his shoulder turned a bit from his wife. It was inconceivable, the gusto with which they proceeded. Ina had assumed for the purpose an air distrait, casual, attentive to the scene about them. But gradually her cheeks began to burn.

"She'll cry," Lulu thought in alarm, and said at random: "Ina, that hat is so pretty—ever so much prettier than the old one." But Ina said frostily that she never saw anything the matter with the old one.

"Let us talk," said Ninian low, to Lulu. "Then they'll simmer down."

He went on, in an undertone, about nothing in particular. Lulu hardly heard what he said, it was so pleasant to have him talking to her in this confidential fashion; and she was pleasantly aware that his manner was open to misinterpretation.

In the nick of time, the lobster was served.

Dinner and the play—the show, as Ninian called it. This show was "Peter Pan," chosen by Ninian because the seats cost the most of those at any theatre. It was almost indecent to see how Dwight Herbert, the immortal soul, had warmed and melted at these contacts. By the time that all was over, and they were at the hotel for supper, such was his pleasurable excitement that he was once more playful, teasing, once more the irrepressible. But now his Ina was to be won back, made it evident that she was not one lightly to overlook, and a fine firmness sat upon the little doubling chin.

They discussed the play. Not one of them had understood the story. The dog-kennel part—wasn't that the queerest thing? Nothing to do with the rest of the play.

"I was for the pirates. The one with the hook—he was my style," said Dwight.

"Well, there it is again," Ina cried. "They didn't belong to the real play, either."

"Oh, well," Ninian said, "they have to put in parts, I suppose, to catch everybody. Instead of a song and dance, they do that."

"And I didn't understand," said Ina, "why they all clapped when the principal character ran down front and said something to the audience that time. But they all did."

Ninian thought this might have been out of compliment. Ina wished that Monona might have seen, confessed that the last part was so pretty that she herself would not look; and into Ina's eyes came their loveliest light.

Lulu sat there, hearing the talk about the play. "Why couldn't I have said that?" she thought as the others spoke.

All that they said seemed to her apropos, but she could think of nothing to add. The evening had been to her a light from heaven—how could she find anything to say? She sat in a daze of happiness, her mind hardly operative, her look moving from one to another. At last Ninian looked at her.

"Sure you liked it, Miss Lulu?"

"Oh, yes! I think they all took their parts real well."

It was not enough. She looked at them appealingly, knowing that she had not said enough.

"You could hear everything they said," she added. "It was—" she dwindled to silence.

Dwight Herbert savoured his rarebit with a great show of long wrinkled dimples.

"Excellent sauces they make here—excellent," he said, with the frown of an epicure. "A tiny wee bit more Athabasca," he added, and they all laughed and told him that Athabasca was a lake, of course. Of course he meant tobasco, Ina said. Their entertainment and their talk was of this sort, for an hour.

"Well, now," said Dwight Herbert when it was finished, "somebody dance on the table."

"Dwightie!"

"Got to amuse ourselves somehow. Come, liven up. They'll begin to read the funeral service over us."

"Why not say the wedding service?" asked Ninian.

In the mention of wedlock there was always something stimulating to Dwight, something of overwhelming humour. He shouted a derisive endorsement of this proposal.

"I shouldn't object," said Ninian. "Should you, Miss Lulu?"

Lulu now burned the slow red of her torture. They were all looking at her. She made an anguished effort to defend herself.

"I don't know it," she said, "so I can't say it."

Ninian leaned toward her.

"I, Ninian, take thee, Lulu, to be my wedded wife," he pronounced. "That's the way it goes!"

"Lulu daren't say it!" cried Dwight. He laughed so loudly that those at the near tables turned. And, from the fastness of her wifehood and motherhood, Ina laughed. Really, it was ridiculous to think of Lulu that way…

Ninian laughed too. "Course she don't dare say it," he challenged.

From within Lulu, that strange Lulu, that other Lulu who sometimes fought her battles, suddenly spoke out:

"I, Lulu, take thee, Ninian, to be my wedded husband."

"You will?" Ninian cried.

"I will," she said, laughing tremulously, to prove that she too could join in, could be as merry as the rest.

"And I will. There, by Jove, now have we entertained you, or haven't we?" Ninian laughed and pounded his soft fist on the table.

"Oh, say, honestly!" Ina was shocked. "I don't think you ought to—holy things—what's the *matter*, Dwightie?"

Dwight Herbert Deacon's eyes were staring and his face was scarlet.

"Say, by George," he said, "a civil wedding is binding in this state."

"A civil wedding? Oh, well—" Ninian dismissed it.

"But I," said Dwight, "happen to be a magistrate."

They looked at one another foolishly. Dwight sprang up with the indeterminate idea of inquiring something of some one, circled about and returned. Ina had taken his chair and sat clasping Lulu's hand. Ninian continued to laugh.

"I never saw one done so offhand," said Dwight. "But what you've said is all you have to say according to law. And there don't have to be witnesses… say!" he said, and sat down again.

Above that shroud-like plaited lace, the veins of Lulu's throat showed dark as she swallowed, cleared her throat, swallowed again.

"Don't you let Dwight scare you," she besought Ninian.

"Scare me!" cried Ninian. "Why, I think it's a good job done, if you ask me."

Lulu's eyes flew to his face. As he laughed, he was looking at her, and now he nodded and shut and opened his eyes several times very fast. Their points of light flickered. With a pang of wonder which pierced her and left her shaken, Lulu looked. His eyes continued to meet her own. It was exactly like looking at his photograph.

Dwight had recovered his authentic air.

"Oh, well," he said, "we can inquire at our leisure. If it is necessary, I should say we can have it set aside quietly up here in the city—no one'll be the wiser."

"Set aside nothing!" said Ninian. "I'd like to see it stand."

"Are you serious, Nin?"

"Sure I'm serious."

Ina jerked gently at her sister's arm.

"Lulu! You hear him? What you going to say to that?"

Lulu shook her head. "He isn't in earnest," she said.

"I am in earnest—hope to die," Ninian declared. He was on two legs of his chair and was slightly tilting, so that the effect of his earnestness was impaired. But he was obviously in earnest.

They were looking at Lulu again. And now she looked at Ninian, and there was something terrible in that look which tried to ask him, alone, about this thing.

Dwight exploded. "There was a fellow I know there in the theatre," he cried. "I'll get him on the line. He could tell me if there's any way—" and was off.

Ina inexplicably began touching away tears. "Oh," she said, "what will mamma say?"

Lulu hardly heard her. Mrs. Bett was incalculably distant.

"You sure?" Lulu said low to Ninian.

For the first time, something in her exceeding isolation really touched him.

"Say," he said, "you come on with me. We'll have it done over again somewhere, if you say so."

"Oh," said Lulu, "if I thought—"

He leaned and patted her hand.

"Good girl," he said.

They sat silent, Ninian padding on the cloth with the flat of his plump hands.

Dwight returned. "It's a go all right," he said. He sat down, laughed weakly, rubbed at his face. "You two are tied as tight as the church could tie you."

"Good enough," said Ninian. "Eh, Lulu?"

"It's—it's all right, I guess," Lulu said.

"Well, I'll be dished," said Dwight.

"Sister!" said Ina.

Ninian meditated, his lips set tight and high. It is impossible to trace the processes of this man. Perhaps they were all compact of the devil-may-care attitude engendered in any persistent traveller. Perhaps the incomparable cookery of Lulu played its part.

"I was going to make a trip south this month," he said, "on my way home from here. Suppose we get married again by somebody or other, and start right off. You'd like that, wouldn't you—going South?"

"Yes," said Lulu only.

"It's July," said Ina, with her sense of fitness, but no one heard.

It was arranged that their trunks should follow them—Ina would see to that, though she was scandalised that they were not first to return to Warbleton for the blessing of Mrs. Bett.

"Mamma won't mind," said Lulu. "Mamma can't stand a fuss any more."

They left the table. The men and women still sitting at the other tables saw nothing unusual about these four, indifferently dressed, indifferently conditioned. The hotel orchestra, playing ragtime in deafening concord, made Lulu's wedding march.

It was still early next day—a hot Sunday—when Ina and Dwight reached home. Mrs. Bett was standing on the porch.

"Where's Lulie?" asked Mrs. Bett.

They told.

Mrs. Bett took it in, a bit at a time. Her pale eyes searched their faces, she shook her head, heard it again, grasped it. Her first question was:

"Who's going to do your work?"

Ina had thought of that, and this was manifest.

"Oh," she said, "you and I'll have to manage."

Mrs. Bett meditated, frowning.

"I left the bacon for her to cook for your breakfasts," she said. "I can't cook bacon fit to eat. Neither can you."

"We've had our breakfasts," Ina escaped from this dilemma.

"Had it up in the city, on expense?"

"Well, we didn't have much."

In Mrs. Bett's eyes tears gathered, but they were not for Lulu.

"I should think," she said, "I should think Lulie might have had a little more gratitude to her than this."

On their way to church Ina and Dwight encountered Di, who had left the house some time earlier, stepping sedately to church in company with Bobby Larkin. Di was in white, and her face was the face of an angel, so young, so questioning, so utterly devoid of her sophistication.

"That child," said Ina, "*must* not see so much of that Larkin boy. She's just a little, little girl."

"Of course she mustn't," said Dwight sharply, "and if *I* was her mother—"

"Oh stop that!" said Ina, sotto voce, at the church steps.

To every one with whom they spoke in the aisle after church, Ina announced their news: Had they heard? Lulu married Dwight's brother Ninian in the city yesterday. Oh, sudden, yes! And ro*man*tic... spoken with that upward inflection to which Ina was a prey.

V

August

Mrs. Bett had been having a "tantrim," brought on by nothing definable. Abruptly as she and Ina were getting supper, Mrs. Bett had fallen silent, had in fact refused to reply when addressed. When all was ready and Dwight was entering, hair wetly brushed, she had withdrawn from the room and closed her bedroom door until it echoed.

"She's got one again," said Ina, grieving; "Dwight, you go."

He went, showing no sign of annoyance, and stood outside his mother-in-law's door and knocked.

No answer.

"Mother, come and have some supper."

No answer.

"Looks to me like your muffins was just about the best ever."

No answer.

"Come on—I had something funny to tell you and Ina."

He retreated, knowing nothing of the admirable control exercised by this woman for her own passionate satisfaction in sending him away unsatisfied. He showed nothing but anxious concern, touched with regret, at his failure. Ina, too, returned from that door discomfited. Dwight made a gallant effort to retrieve the fallen fortunes of their evening meal, and turned upon Di, who had just entered, and with exceeding facetiousness inquired how Bobby was.

Di looked hunted. She could never tell whether her parents were going to tease her about Bobby, or rebuke her for being seen with him. It depended on mood, and this mood Di had not the experience to gauge. She now groped for some neutral fact, and mentioned that he was going to take her and Jenny for ice cream that night.

Ina's irritation found just expression in her office of motherhood.

"I won't have you downtown in the evening," she said.

"But you let me go last night."

"All the better reason why you should not go to-night."

"I tell you," cried Dwight. "Why not all walk down? Why not all have ice cream…" He was all gentleness and propitiation, the reconciling element in his home.

"Me too?" Monona's ardent hope, her terrible fear were in her eyebrows, her parted lips.

"You too, certainly." Dwight could not do enough for every one.

Monona clapped her hands. "Goody! goody! Last time you wouldn't let me go."

"That's why papa's going to take you this time," Ina said.

These ethical balances having been nicely struck, Ina proposed another:

"But," she said, "but, you must eat more supper or you can *not* go."

"I don't want any more." Monona's look was honest and piteous.

"Makes no difference. You must eat or you'll get sick."

"No!"

"Very well, then. No ice cream soda for such a little girl."

Monona began to cry quietly. But she passed her plate. She ate, chewing high, and slowly.

"See? She can eat if she will eat," Ina said to Dwight. "The only trouble is, she will *not* take the time."

"She don't put her mind on her meals," Dwight Herbert diagnosed it. "Oh, bigger bites than that!" he encouraged his little daughter.

Di's mind had been proceeding along its own paths.

"Are you going to take Jenny and Bobby too?" she inquired.

"Certainly. The whole party."

"Bobby'll want to pay for Jenny and I."

"Me, darling," said Ina patiently, punctiliously—and less punctiliously added: "Nonsense. This is going to be papa's little party."

"But we had the engagement with Bobby. It was an engagement."

"Well," said Ina, "I think we'll just set that aside—that important engagement. I think we just will."

"Papa! Bobby'll want to be the one to pay for Jenny and I—"

"Di!" Ina's voice dominated all. "Will you be more careful of your grammar or shall I speak to you again?"

"Well, I'd rather use bad grammar than—than—than—" she looked resentfully at her mother, her father. Their moral defection was evident to her, but it was indefinable. They told her that she ought to be ashamed when papa wanted to give them all a treat. She sat silent, frowning, put-upon.

"Look, mamma!" cried Monona, swallowing a third of an egg at one impulse. Ina saw only the empty plate.

"Mamma's nice little girl!" cried she, shining upon her child.

The rules of the ordinary sports of the playground, scrupulously applied, would have clarified the ethical atmosphere of this little family. But there was no one to apply them.

When Di and Monona had been excused, Dwight asked: "Nothing new from the bride and groom?"

"No. And, Dwight, it's been a week since the last."

"See—where were they then?"

He knew perfectly well that they were in Savannah, Georgia, but Ina played his game, told him, and retold bits that the letter had said.

"I don't understand," she added, "why they should go straight to Oregon without coming here first."

Dwight hazarded that Nin probably had to get back, and shone pleasantly in the reflected importance of a brother filled with affairs.

"I don't know what to make of Lulu's letters," Ina proceeded. "They're so—so—"

"You haven't had but two, have you?"

"That's all—well, of course it's only been a month. But both letters have been so—"

Ina was never really articulate. Whatever corner of her brain had the blood in it at the moment seemed to be operative, and she let the matter go at that.

"I don't think it's fair to mamma—going off that way. Leaving her own mother. Why, she may never see mamma again—" Ina's breath caught. Into her face came something of the lovely tenderness with which she sometimes looked at Monona and Di. She sprang up. She had forgotten to put some supper to warm for mamma. The lovely light was still in her face as she bustled about against the time of mamma's recovery from her tantrim. Dwight's face was like this when he spoke of his foster-mother. In both these beings there was something which functioned as pure love.

Mamma had recovered and was eating cold scrambled eggs on the corner of the kitchen table when the ice cream soda party was ready to set out. Dwight threw her a casual "Better come, too, Mother Bett," but she shook her head. She wished to go, wished it with violence, but she contrived to give to her arbitrary refusal a quality of contempt. When Jenny arrived with Bobby, she had brought a sheaf of gladioli for Mrs. Bett, and took them to her in the kitchen, and as she laid the flowers beside her, the young girl stopped and kissed her. "You little darling!" cried Mrs. Bett, and clung to her, her lifted eyes lit by something intense and living. But when the ice cream party had set off at last, Mrs. Bett left her supper, gathered up the flowers, and crossed the lawn to the old cripple, Grandma Gates.

"Inie sha'n't have 'em," the old woman thought.

And then it was quite beautiful to watch her with Grandma Gates, whom she tended and petted, to whose complainings she listened, and to whom she tried to tell the small events of her day. When her neighbour had gone, Grandma Gates said that it was as good as a dose of medicine to have her come in.

Mrs. Bett sat on the porch restored and pleasant when the family returned. Di and Bobby had walked home with Jenny.

"Look here," said Dwight Herbert, "who is it sits home and has *ice* cream put in her lap, like a queen?"

"Vanilly or chocolate?" Mrs. Bett demanded.

"Chocolate, mamma!" Ina cried, with the breeze in her voice.

"Vanilly sets better," Mrs. Bett said.

They sat with her on the porch while she ate. Ina rocked on a creaking board. Dwight swung a leg over the railing. Monona sat pulling her skirt over her feet, and humming all on one note. There was no moon, but the warm dusk had a quality of transparency as if it were lit in all its particles.

The gate opened, and some one came up the walk. They looked, and it was Lulu.

"Well, if it ain't Miss Lulu Bett!" Dwight cried involuntarily, and Ina cried out something.

"How did you know?" Lulu asked.

"Know! Know what?"

"That it ain't Lulu Deacon. Hello, mamma."

She passed the others, and kissed her mother.

"Say," said Mrs. Bett placidly. "And I just ate up the last spoonful o' cream."

"Ain't Lulu Deacon!" Ina's voice rose and swelled richly. "What you talking?"

"Didn't he write to you?" Lulu asked.

"Not a word." Dwight answered this. "All we've had we had from you—the last from Savannah, Georgia."

"Savannah, Georgia," said Lulu, and laughed.

They could see that she was dressed well, in dark red cloth, with a little tilting hat and a drooping veil. She did not seem in any wise upset, nor, save for that nervous laughter, did she show her excitement.

"Well, but he's here with you, isn't he?" Dwight demanded. "Isn't he here? Where is he?"

"Must be 'most to Oregon by this time," Lulu said.

"Oregon!"

"You see," said Lulu, "he had another wife."

"Why, he had not!" exclaimed Dwight absurdly.

"Yes. He hasn't seen her for fifteen years and he thinks she's dead. But he isn't sure."

"Nonsense," said Dwight. "Why, of course she's dead if he thinks so."

"I had to be sure," said Lulu.

At first dumb before this, Ina now cried out: "Monona! Go upstairs to bed at once."

"It's only quarter to," said Monona, with assurance.

"Do as mamma tells you."

"But—"

"Monona!"

She went, kissing them all good-night and taking her time about it. Everything was suspended while she kissed them and departed, walking slowly backward.

"Married?" said Mrs. Bett with tardy apprehension. "Lulie, was your husband married?"

"Yes," Lulu said, "my husband was married, mother."

"Mercy," said Ina. "Think of anything like that in our family."

"Well, go on—go on!" Dwight cried. "Tell us about it."

Lulu spoke in a monotone, with her old manner of hesitation:

"We were going to Oregon. First down to New Orleans and then out to California and up the coast." On this she paused and sighed. "Well, then at Savannah, Georgia, he said he thought I better know, first. So he told me."

"Yes—well, what did he *say?*" Dwight demanded irritably.

"Cora Waters," said Lulu. "Cora Waters. She married him down in San Diego, eighteen years ago. She went to South America with him."

"Well, he never let us know of it, if she did," said Dwight.

"No. She married him just before he went. Then in South America, after two years, she ran away again. That's all he knows."

"That's a pretty story," said Dwight contemptuously.

"He says if she'd been alive, she'd been after him for a divorce. And she never has been, so he thinks she must be dead. The trouble is," Lulu said again, "he wasn't sure. And I had to be sure."

"Well, but mercy," said Ina, "couldn't he find out now?"

"It might take a long time," said Lulu simply, "and I didn't want to stay and not know."

"Well, then, why didn't he say so here?" Ina's indignation mounted.

"He would have. But you know how sudden everything was. He said he thought about telling us right there in the restaurant, but of course that'd been hard—wouldn't it? And then he felt so sure she was dead."

"Why did he tell you at all, then?" demanded Ina, whose processes were simple.

"Yes. Well! Why indeed?" Dwight Herbert brought out these words with a curious emphasis.

"I thought that, just at first," Lulu said, "but only just at first. Of course that wouldn't have been right. And then, you see, he gave me my choice."

"Gave you your choice?" Dwight echoed.

"Yes. About going on and taking the chances. He gave me my choice when he told me, there in Savannah, Georgia."

"What made him conclude, by then, that you ought to be told?" Dwight asked.

"Why, he'd got to thinking about it," she answered.

A silence fell. Lulu sat looking out toward the street.

"The only thing," she said, "as long as it happened, I kind of wish he hadn't told me till we got to Oregon."

"Lulu!" said Ina. Ina began to cry. "You poor thing!" she said.

Her tears were a signal to Mrs. Bett, who had been striving to understand all. Now she too wept, tossing up her hands and rocking her body. Her saucer and spoon clattered on her knee.

"He felt bad too," Lulu said.

"He!" said Dwight. "He must have."

"It's you," Ina sobbed. "It's you. *My* sister!"

"Well," said Lulu, "but I never thought of it making you both feel bad, or I wouldn't have come home. I knew," she added, "it'd make Dwight feel bad. I mean, it was his brother—"

"Thank goodness," Ina broke in, "nobody need know about it."

Lulu regarded her, without change.

"Oh, yes," she said in her monotone. "People will have to know."

"I do not see the necessity." Dwight's voice was an edge. Then too he said "do not," always with Dwight betokening the finalities.

"Why, what would they think?" Lulu asked, troubled.

"What difference does it make what they think?"

"Why," said Lulu slowly, "I shouldn't like—you see they might—why, Dwight, I think we'll have to tell them."

"You do! You think the disgrace of bigamy in this family is something the whole town will have to know about?"

Lulu looked at him with parted lips.

"Say," she said, "I never thought about it being that."

Dwight laughed. "What did you think it was? And whose disgrace is it, pray?"

"Ninian's," said Lulu.

"Ninian's! Well, he's gone. But you're here. And I'm here. Folks'll feel sorry for you. But the disgrace—that'd reflect on me. See?"

"But if we don't tell, what'll they think then?"

Said Dwight: "They'll think what they always think when a wife leaves her husband. They'll think you couldn't get along. That's all."

"I should hate that," said Lulu.

"Well, I should hate the other, let me tell you."

"Dwight, Dwight," said Ina. "Let's go in the house. I'm afraid they'll hear—"

As they rose, Mrs. Bett plucked at her returned daughter's sleeve.

"Lulie," she said, "was his other wife—was she *there?*"

"No, no, mother. She wasn't there."

Mrs. Bett's lips moved, repeating the words. "Then that ain't so bad," she said. "I was afraid maybe she turned you out."

"No," Lulu said, "it wasn't that bad, mother."

Mrs. Bett brightened. In little matters, she quarrelled and resented, but the large issues left her blank.

Through some indeterminate sense of the importance due this crisis, the Deacons entered their parlour. Dwight lighted that high, central burner and faced about, saying:

"In fact, I simply will not have it, Lulu! You expect, I take it, to make your home with us in the future, on the old terms."

"Well—"

"I mean, did Ninian give you any money?"

"No. He didn't give me any money—only enough to get home on. And I kept my suit—why!" she flung her head back, "I wouldn't have taken any money!"

"That means," said Dwight, "that you will have to continue to live here—on the old terms, and of course I'm quite willing that you should. Let me tell you, however, that this is on condition—on condition that this disgraceful business is kept to ourselves."

She made no attempt to combat him now. She looked back at him, quivering, and in a great surprise, but she said nothing.

"Truly, Lulu," said Ina, "wouldn't that be best? They'll talk anyway. But this way they'll only talk about you, and the other way it'd be about all of us."

Lulu said only: "But the other way would be the truth."

Dwight's eyes narrowed: "My dear Lulu," he said, "are you *sure* of that?"

"Sure?"

"Yes. Did he give you any proofs?"

"Proofs?"

"Letters—documents of any sort? Any sort of assurance that he was speaking the truth?"

"Why, no," said Lulu. "Proofs—no. He told me."

"He told you!"

"Why, that was hard enough to have to do. It was terrible for him to have to do. What proofs—" She stopped, puzzled.

"Didn't it occur to you," said Dwight, "that he might have told you that because he didn't want to have to go on with it?"

As she met his look, some power seemed to go from Lulu. She sat down, looked weakly at them, and within her closed lips her jaw was slightly fallen. She said nothing. And seeing on her skirt a spot of dust she began to rub at that.

"Why, Dwight!" Ina cried, and moved to her sister's side.

"I may as well tell you," he said, "that I myself have no idea that Ninian told you the truth. He was always imagining things—you saw that. I know him pretty well—have been more or less in touch with him the whole time. In short, I haven't the least idea he was ever married before."

Lulu continued to rub at her skirt.

"I never thought of that," she said.

"Look here," Dwight went on persuasively, "hadn't you and he had some little tiff when he told you?"

"No—no! Why, not once. Why, we weren't a bit like you and Ina."

She spoke simply and from her heart and without guile.

"Evidently not," Dwight said drily.

Lulu went on: "He was very good to me. This dress—and my shoes—and my hat. And another dress, too." She found the pins and took off her hat. "He liked the red wing," she said. "I wanted black—oh, Dwight! He did tell me the truth!" It was as if the red wing had abruptly borne mute witness.

Dwight's tone now mounted. His manner, it mounted too.

"Even if it is true," said he, "I desire that you should keep silent and protect my family from this scandal. I merely mention my doubts to you for your own profit."

"My own profit!"

She said no more, but rose and moved to the door.

"Lulu—you see! With Di and all!" Ina begged. "We just couldn't have this known—even if it was so."

"You have it in your hands," said Dwight, "to repay me, Lulu, for anything that you feel I may have done for you in the past. You also have it in your hands to decide whether your home here continues. That is not a pleasant position for me to find myself in. It is distinctly unpleasant, I may say. But you see for yourself."

Lulu went on, into the passage.

"Wasn't she married when she thought she was?" Mrs. Bett cried shrilly.

"Mamma," said Ina. "Do, please, remember Monona. Yes—Dwight thinks she's married all right now—and that it's all right, all the time."

"Well, I hope so, for pity sakes," said Mrs. Bett, and left the room with her daughter.

Hearing the stir, Monona upstairs lifted her voice:

"Mamma! Come on and hear my prayers, why don't you?"

When they came downstairs next morning, Lulu had breakfast ready.

"Well!" cried Ina in her curving tone, "if this isn't like old times."

Lulu said yes, that it was like old times, and brought the bacon to the table.

"Lulu's the only one in *this* house can cook the bacon so's it'll chew," Mrs. Bett volunteered. She was wholly affable, and held contentedly to Ina's last word that Dwight thought now it was all right.

"Ho!" said Dwight. "The happy family, once more about the festive toaster." He gauged the moment to call for good cheer. Ina, too, became breezy, blithe. Monona caught their spirit and laughed, head thrown well back and gently shaken.

Di came in. She had been told that Auntie Lulu was at home, and that she, Di, wasn't to say anything to her about anything, nor anything to anybody else about Auntie Lulu being back. Under these prohibitions, which loosed a thousand speculations, Di was very nearly paralysed. She stared at her Aunt Lulu incessantly.

Not one of them had even a talent for the casual, save Lulu herself. Lulu was amazingly herself. She took her old place, assumed her old offices. When Monona declared against bacon, it was Lulu who suggested milk toast and went to make it.

"Mamma," Di whispered then, like escaping steam, "isn't Uncle Ninian coming too?"

"Hush. No. Now don't ask any more questions."

"Well, can't I tell Bobby and Jenny she's here?"

"*No.* Don't say anything at all about her."

"But, mamma. What has she done?"

"Di! Do as mamma tells you. Don't you think mamma knows best?"

Di of course did not think so, had not thought so for a long time. But now Dwight said:

"Daughter! Are you a little girl or are you our grown-up young lady?"

"I don't know," said Di reasonably, "but I think you're treating me like a little girl now."

"Shame, Di," said Ina, unabashed by the accident of reason being on the side of Di.

"I'm eighteen," Di reminded them forlornly, "and through high school."

"Then act so," boomed her father.

Baffled, thwarted, bewildered, Di went over to Jenny Plow's and there imparted understanding by the simple process of letting Jenny guess, to questions skilfully shaped.

When Dwight said, "Look at my beautiful handkerchief," displayed a hole, sent his Ina for a better, Lulu, with a manner of haste, addressed him:

"Dwight. It's a funny thing, but I haven't Ninian's Oregon address."

"Well?"

"Well, I wish you'd give it to me."

Dwight tightened and lifted his lips. "It would seem," he said, "that you have no real use for that particular address, Lulu."

"Yes, I have. I want it. You have it, haven't you, Dwight?"

"Certainly I have it."

"Won't you please write it down for me?" She had ready a bit of paper and a pencil stump.

"My dear Lulu, now why revive anything? Why not he sensible and leave this alone? No good can come by——"

"But why shouldn't I have his address?"

"If everything is over between you, why should you?"

"But you say he's still my husband."

Dwight flushed. "If my brother has shown his inclination as plainly as I judge that he has, it is certainly not my place to put you in touch with him again."

"You won't give it to me?"

"My dear Lulu, in all kindness—no."

His Ina came running back, bearing handkerchiefs with different coloured borders for him to choose from. He chose the initial that she had embroidered, and had not the good taste not to kiss her.

They were all on the porch that evening, when Lulu came downstairs.

"*Where* are you going?" Ina demanded, sisterly. And on hearing that Lulu had an errand, added still more sisterly; "Well, but mercy, what you so dressed up for?"

Lulu was in a thin black and white gown which they had never seen, and wore the tilting hat with the red wing.

"Ninian bought me this," said Lulu only.

"But, Lulu, don't you think it might be better to keep, well—out of sight for a few days?" Ina's lifted look besought her.

"Why?" Lulu asked.

"Why set people wondering till we have to?"

"They don't have to wonder, far as I'm concerned," said Lulu, and went down the walk.

Ina looked at Dwight. "She never spoke to me like that in her life before," she said.

She watched her sister's black and white figure going erectly down the street.

"That gives me the funniest feeling," said Ina, "as if Lulu had on clothes bought for her by some one that wasn't—that was—"

"By her husband who has left her," said Dwight sadly.

"Is that what it is, papa?" Di asked alertly. For a wonder, she was there; had been there the greater part of the day—most of the time staring, fascinated, at her Aunt Lulu.

"That's what it is, my little girl," said Dwight, and shook his head.

"Well, I think it's a shame," said Di stoutly. "And I think Uncle Ninian is a slunge."

"Di!"

"I do. And I'd be ashamed to think anything else. I'd like to tell everybody."

"There is," said Dwight, "no need for secrecy—now."

"Dwight!" said Ina—Ina's eyes always remained expressionless, but it must have been her lashes that looked so startled.

"No need whatever for secrecy," he repeated with firmness. "The truth is, Lulu's husband has tired of her and sent her home. We must face it."

"But, Dwight—how awful for Lulu..."

"Lulu," said Dwight, "has us to stand by her."

Lulu, walking down the main street, thought:

"Now Mis' Chambers is seeing me. Now Mis' Curtis. There's somebody behind the vines at Mis' Martin's. Here comes Mis' Grove and I've got to speak to her..."

One and another and another met her, and every one cried out at her some version of:

"Lulu Bett!" Or, "W-well, it *isn't* Lulu Bett any more, is it? Well, what are you doing here? I thought…"

"I'm back to stay," she said.

"The idea! Well, where you hiding that handsome husband of yours? Say, but we were surprised! You're the sly one—"

"My—Mr. Deacon isn't here."

"Oh."

"No. He's West."

"Oh, I see."

Having no arts, she must needs let the conversation die like this, could invent nothing concealing or gracious on which to move away.

She went to the post-office. It was early, there were few at the post-office—with only one or two there had she to go through her examination. Then she went to the general delivery window, tense for a new ordeal.

To her relief, the face which was shown there was one strange to her, a slim youth, reading a letter of his own, and smiling.

"Excuse me," said Lulu faintly.

The youth looked up, with eyes warmed by the words on the pink paper which he held.

"Could you give me the address of Mr. Ninian Deacon?"

"Let's see—you mean Dwight Deacon, I guess?"

"No. It's his brother. He's been here. From Oregon. I thought he might have given you his address—" she dwindled away.

"Wait a minute," said the youth. "Nope. No address here. Say, why don't you send it to his brother? He'd know. Dwight Deacon, the dentist."

"I'll do that," Lulu said absurdly, and turned away.

She went back up the street, walking fast now to get away from them all. Once or twice she pretended not to see a familiar face. But when she passed the mirror in an insurance office window, she saw her reflection and at its appearance she felt surprise and pleasure.

"Well!" she thought, almost in Ina's own manner.

Abruptly her confidence rose.

Something of this confidence was still upon her when she returned. They were in the dining-room now, all save Di, who was on the porch with Bobby, and Monona, who was in bed and might be heard extravagantly singing.

Lulu sat down with her hat on. When Dwight inquired playfully, "Don't we look like company?" she did not reply. He looked at her speculatively. Where had she gone, with whom had she talked, what had she told? Ina looked at her rather fearfully. But Mrs. Bett rocked contentedly and ate cardamom seeds.

"Whom did you see?" Ina asked.

Lulu named them.

"See them to talk to?" from Dwight.

Oh, yes. They had all stopped.

"What did they say?" Ina burst out.

They had inquired for Ninian, Lulu said; and said no more.

Dwight mulled this. Lulu might have told every one of these women that cock-and-bull story with which she had come home. It might be all over town. Of course, in that case he could turn Lulu out—should do so, in fact. Still the story would be all over town.

"Dwight," said Lulu, "I want Ninian's address."

"Going to write to him!" Ina cried incredulously.

"I want to ask him for the proofs that Dwight wanted."

"My dear Lulu," Dwight said impatiently, "you are not the one to write. Have you no delicacy?"

Lulu smiled—a strange smile, originating and dying in one corner of her mouth.

"Yes," she said. "So much delicacy that I want to be sure whether I'm married or not."

Dwight cleared his throat with a movement which seemed to use his shoulders for the purpose.

"I myself will take this up with my brother," he said. "I will write to him about it."

Lulu sprang to her feet. "Write to him *now!*" she cried.

"Really," said Dwight, lifting his brows.

"Now—now!" Lulu said. She moved about, collecting writing materials from their casual lodgments on shelf and table. She set all before him and stood by him. "Write to him now," she said again.

"My dear Lulu, don't be absurd."

She said: "Ina. Help me. If it was Dwight—and they didn't know whether he had another wife, or not, and you wanted to ask him—oh, don't you see? Help me."

Ina was not yet the woman to cry for justice for its own sake, nor even to stand by another woman. She was primitive, and her instinct was to look to her own male merely.

"Well," she said, "of course. But why not let Dwight do it in his own way? Wouldn't that be better?"

She put it to her sister fairly: Now, no matter what Dwight's way was, wouldn't that be better?

"Mother!" said Lulu. She looked irresolutely toward her mother. But Mrs. Bett was eating cardamom seeds with exceeding gusto, and Lulu looked away. Caught by the gesture, Mrs. Bett voiced her grievance.

"Lulie," she said, "Set down. Take off your hat, why don't you?"

Lulu turned upon Dwight a quiet face which he had never seen before.

"You write that letter to Ninian," she said, "and you make him tell you so you'll understand. *I* know he spoke the truth. But I want you to know."

"M—m," said Dwight. "And then I suppose you're going to tell it all over town—as soon as you have the proofs."

"I'm going to tell it all over town," said Lulu, "just as it is—unless you write to him now."

"Lulu!" cried Ina. "Oh, you wouldn't."

"I would," said Lulu. "I will."

Dwight was sobered. This unimagined Lulu looked capable of it. But then he sneered.

"And get turned out of this house, as you would be?"

"Dwight!" cried his Ina. "Oh, you wouldn't!"

"I would," said Dwight. "I will. Lulu knows it."

"I shall tell what I know and then leave your house anyway," said Lulu, "unless you get Ninian's word. And I want you should write him now."

"Leave your mother? And Ina?" he asked.

"Leave everything," said Lulu.

"Oh, Dwight," said Ina, "we can't get along without Lulu." She did not say in what particulars, but Dwight knew.

Dwight looked at Lulu, an upward, sidewise look, with a manner of peering out to see if she meant it. And he saw.

He shrugged, pursed his lips crookedly, rolled his head to signify the inexpressible. "Isn't that like a woman?" he demanded. He rose. "Rather than let you in for a show of temper," he said grandly, "I'd do anything."

He wrote the letter, addressed it, his hand elaborately curved in secrecy about the envelope, pocketed it.

"Ina and I'll walk down with you to mail it," said Lulu.

Dwight hesitated, frowned. His Ina watched him with consulting brows.

"I was going," said Dwight, "to propose a little stroll before bedtime." He roved about the room. "Where's my beautiful straw hat? There's nothing like a brisk walk to induce sound, restful sleep," he told them. He hummed a bar.

"You'll be all right, mother?" Lulu asked.

Mrs. Bett did not look up. "These cardamon hev got a little mite too dry," she said.

In their room, Ina and Dwight discussed the incredible actions of Lulu.

"I saw," said Dwight, "I saw she wasn't herself. I'd do anything to avoid having a scene—you know that." His glance swept a little anxiously his Ina. "You know that, don't you?" he sharply inquired.

"But I really think you ought to have written to Ninian about it," she now dared to say. "It's—it's not a nice position for Lulu."

"Nice? Well, but whom has she got to blame for it?"

"Why, Ninian," said Ina.

Dwight threw out his hands. "Herself," he said. "To tell you the truth, I was perfectly amazed at the way she snapped him up there in that restaurant."

"Why, but, Dwight—"

"Brazen," he said. "Oh, it was brazen."

"It was just fun, in the first place."

"But no really nice woman—" he shook his head.

"Dwight! Lulu *is* nice. The idea!"

He regarded her. "Would you have done that?" he would know.

Under his fond look, she softened, took his homage, accepted everything, was silent.

"Certainly not," he said. "Lulu's tastes are not fine like yours. I should never think of you as sisters."

"She's awfully good," Ina said feebly. Fifteen years of married life behind her—but this was sweet and she could not resist.

"She has excellent qualities." He admitted it. "But look at the position she's in—married to a man who tells her he has another wife in order to get free. Now, no really nice woman—"

"No really nice man—" Ina did say that much.

"Ah," said Dwight, "but *you* could never be in such a position. No, no. Lulu is sadly lacking somewhere."

Ina sighed, threw back her head, caught her lower lip with her upper, as might be in a hem. "What if it was Di?" she supposed.

"Di!" Dwight's look rebuked his wife. "Di," he said, "was born with ladylike feelings."

It was not yet ten o'clock. Bobby Larkin was permitted to stay until ten. From the veranda came the indistinguishable murmur of those young voices.

"Bobby," Di was saying within that murmur, "Bobby, you don't kiss me as if you really wanted to kiss me, to-night."

VI

September

The office of Dwight Herbert Deacon, Dentist, Gold Work
a Speciality (sic) in black lettering, and Justice of the Peace in
gold, was above a store which had been occupied by one unlucky
tenant after another, and had suffered long periods of vacancy
when ladies' aid societies served lunches there, under great white
signs, badly lettered. Some months of disuse were now broken
by the news that the store had been let to a music man. A music
man, what on earth was that, Warbleton inquired.

The music man arrived, installed three pianos, and filled
his window with sheet music, as sung by many ladies who swung
in hammocks or kissed their hands on the music covers. While
he was still moving in, Dwight Herbert Deacon wandered
downstairs and stood informally in the door of the new store.
The music man, a pleasant-faced chap of thirty-odd, was rubbing
at the face of a piano.

"Hello, there!" he said. "Can I sell you an upright?"

"If I can take it out in pulling your teeth, you can,"
Dwight replied. "Or," said he, "I might marry you free, either
one."

On this their friendship began. Thenceforth, when business was dull, the idle hours of both men were beguiled with idle gossip.

"How the dickens did you think of pianos for a line?" Dwight asked him once. "Now, my father was a dentist, so I came by it natural—never entered my head to be anything else. But *pianos*—"

The music man—his name was Neil Cornish—threw up his chin in a boyish fashion, and said he'd be jiggered if he knew. All up and down the Warbleton main street, the chances are that the answer would sound the same. "I'm studying law when I get the chance," said Cornish, as one who makes a bid to be thought of more highly.

"I see," said Dwight, respectfully dwelling on the verb.

Later on Cornish confided more to Dwight: He was to come by a little inheritance some day—not much, but something. Yes, it made a man feel a certain confidence....

"*Don't* it?" said Dwight heartily, as if he knew.

Every one liked Cornish. He told funny stories, and he never compared Warbleton save to its advantage. So at last Dwight said tentatively at lunch:

"What if I brought that Neil Cornish up for supper, one of these nights?"

"Oh, Dwightie, do," said Ina. "If there's a man in town, let's know it."

"What if I brought him up to-night?"

Up went Ina's eyebrows. *To-night?*

"'Scalloped potatoes and meat loaf and sauce and bread and butter," Lulu contributed.

Cornish came to supper. He was what is known in Warbleton as dapper. This Ina saw as she emerged on the veranda in response to Dwight's informal halloo on his way upstairs. She herself was in white muslin, now much too snug, and a blue ribbon. To her greeting their guest replied in that engaging shyness which is not awkwardness. He moved in some pleasant web of gentleness and friendliness.

They asked him the usual questions, and he replied, rocking all the time with a faint undulating motion of head and shoulders: Warbleton was one of the prettiest little towns that he had ever seen. He liked the people—they seemed different. He was sure to like the place, already liked it. Lulu came to the door in Ninian's thin black-and-white gown. She shook hands with the stranger, not looking at him, and said, "Come to supper, all." Monona was already in her place, singing under-breath. Mrs. Bett, after hovering in the kitchen door, entered; but they forgot to introduce her.

"Where's Di?" asked Ina. "I declare that daughter of mine is never anywhere."

A brief silence ensued as they were seated. There being a guest, grace was to come, and Dwight said unintelligibly and like lightning a generic appeal to bless this food, forgive all our sins and finally save us. And there was something tremendous, in this ancient form whereby all stages of men bow in some now unrecognized recognition of the ceremonial of taking food to nourish life—and more.

At "Amen" Di flashed in, her offices at the mirror fresh upon her—perfect hair, silk dress turned up at the hem. She met Cornish, crimsoned, fluttered to her seat, joggled the table and, "Oh, dear," she said audibly to her mother, "I forgot my ring."

The talk was saved alive by a frank effort. Dwight served, making jests about everybody coming back for more. They went on with Warbleton happenings, improvements and openings; and the runaway. Cornish tried hard to make himself agreeable, not ingratiatingly but good-naturedly. He wished profoundly that before coming he had looked up some more stories in the back of the Musical Gazettes. Lulu surreptitiously pinched off an ant that was running at large upon the cloth and thereafter kept her eyes steadfastly on the sugar-bowl to see if it could be from *that*. Dwight pretended that those whom he was helping a second time were getting more than their share and facetiously landed on Di about eating so much that she would grow up and be married, first thing she knew. At the word "married" Di turned scarlet, laughed heartily and lifted her glass of water.

"And what instruments do you play?" Ina asked Cornish, in an unrelated effort to lift the talk to musical levels.

"Well, do you know," said the music man, "I can't play a thing. Don't know a black note from a white one."

"You don't? Why, Di plays very prettily," said Di's mother. "But then how can you tell what songs to order?" Ina cried.

"Oh, by the music houses. You go by the sales." For the first time it occurred to Cornish that this was ridiculous. "You know, I'm really studying law," he said, shyly and proudly. Law! How very interesting, from Ina. Oh, but won't he bring up some songs some evening, for them to try over? Her and Di? At this Di laughed and said that she was out of practice and lifted her glass of water. In the presence of adults Di made one weep, she was so slender, so young, so without defences, so intolerably sensitive to every contact, so in agony lest she be found wanting. It was amazing how unlike was this Di to the Di who had ensnared Bobby Larkin. What was one to think?

Cornish paid very little attention to her. To Lulu he said kindly, "Don't you play, Miss——?" He had not caught her name—no stranger ever did catch it. But Dwight now supplied it: "Miss Lulu Bett," he explained with loud emphasis, and Lulu burned her slow red. This question Lulu had usually answered by telling how a felon had interrupted her lessons and she had stopped "taking"—a participle sacred to music, in Warbleton. This vignette had been a kind of epitome of Lulu's biography. But now Lulu was heard to say serenely:

"No, but I'm quite fond of it. I went to a lovely concert— two weeks ago."

They all listened. Strange indeed to think of Lulu as having had experiences of which they did not know.

"Yes," she said. "It was in Savannah, Georgia." She flushed, and lifted her eyes in a manner of faint defiance. "Of course," she said, "I don't know the names of all the different instruments they played, but there were a good many." She laughed pleasantly as a part of her sentence. "They had some lovely tunes," she said.

She knew that the subject was not exhausted and she hurried on. "The hall was real large," she superadded, "and there were quite a good many people there. And it was too warm."

"I see," said Cornish, and said what he had been waiting to say: That he too had been in Savannah, Georgia.

Lulu lit with pleasure. "Well!" she said. And her mind worked and she caught at the moment before it had escaped. "Isn't it a pretty city?" she asked. And Cornish assented with the intense heartiness of the provincial. He, too, it seemed, had a conversational appearance to maintain by its own effort. He said that he had enjoyed being in that town and that he was there for two hours.

"I was there for a week." Lulu's superiority was really pretty.

"Have good weather?" Cornish selected next.

Oh, yes. And they saw all the different buildings—but at her "we" she flushed and was silenced. She was colouring and breathing quickly. This was the first bit of conversation of this sort of Lulu's life.

After supper Ina inevitably proposed croquet, Dwight pretended to try to escape and, with his irrepressible mien, talked about Ina, elaborate in his insistence on the third person—"She loves it, we have to humour her, you know how it is. Or no! You don't know! But you will"—and more of the same sort, everybody laughing heartily, save Lulu, who looked uncomfortable and wished that Dwight wouldn't, and Mrs. Bett, who paid no attention to anybody that night, not because she had not been introduced, an omission, which she had not even noticed, but merely as another form of "tantrim." A self-indulgence.

They emerged for croquet. And there on the porch sat Jenny Plow and Bobby, waiting for Di to keep an old engagement, which Di pretended to have forgotten, and to be frightfully annoyed to have to keep. She met the objections of her parents with all the batteries of her coquetry, set for both Bobby and Cornish and, bold in the presence of "company," at last went laughing away. And in the minute areas of her consciousness she said to herself that Bobby would be more in love with her than ever because she had risked all to go with him; and that Cornish ought to be distinctly attracted to her because she had not stayed. She was as primitive as pollen.

Ina was vexed. She said so, pouting in a fashion which she should have outgrown with white muslin and blue ribbons, and she had outgrown none of these things.

"That just spoils croquet," she said. "I'm vexed. Now we can't have a real game."

From the side-door, where she must have been lingering among the waterproofs, Lulu stepped forth.

"I'll play a game," she said.

When Cornish actually proposed to bring some music to the Deacons', Ina turned toward Dwight Herbert all the facets of her responsibility. And Ina's sense of responsibility toward Di was enormous, oppressive, primitive, amounting, in fact, toward this daughter of Dwight Herbert's late wife, to an ability to compress the offices of stepmotherhood into the functions of the lecture platform. Ina was a fountain of admonition. Her idea of a daughter, step or not, was that of a manufactured product, strictly, which you constantly pinched and moulded. She thought that a moral preceptor had the right to secrete precepts. Di got them all. But of course the crest of Ina's responsibility was to marry Di. This verb should be transitive only when lovers are speaking of each other, or the minister or magistrate is speaking of lovers. It should never be transitive when predicated of parents or any other third party. But it is. Ina was quite agitated by its transitiveness as she took to her husband her incredible responsibility.

"You know, Herbert," said Ina, "if this Mr. Cornish comes here *very* much, what we may expect."

"What may we expect?" demanded Dwight Herbert, crisply.

Ina always played his games, answered what he expected her to answer, pretended to be intuitive when she was not so, said "I know" when she didn't know at all. Dwight Herbert,

on the other hand, did not even play her games when he knew
perfectly what she meant, but pretended not to understand,
made her repeat, made her explain. It was as if Ina *had* to
please him for, say, a living; but as for that dentist, he had to
please nobody. In the conversations of Dwight and Ina you saw
the historical home forming in clots in the fluid wash of the
community.

"He'll fall in love with Di," said Ina.

"And what of that? Little daughter will have many a man
fall in love with her, *I* should say."

"Yes, but, Dwight, what do you think of him?"

"What do I think of him? My dear Ina, I have other things
to think of."

"But we don't know anything about him, Dwight—a
stranger so."

"On the other hand," said Dwight with dignity, "I know a
good deal about him."

With a great air of having done the fatherly and found
out about this stranger before bringing him into the home,
Dwight now related a number of stray circumstances dropped
by Cornish in their chance talks.

"He has a little inheritance coming to him—shortly,"
Dwight wound up.

"An inheritance—really? How much, Dwight?"

"Now isn't that like a woman. Isn't it?"

"I *thought* he was from a good family," said Ina.

"My mercenary little pussy!"

"Well," she said with a sigh, "I shouldn't be surprised if Di
did really accept him. A young girl is awfully flattered when a
good-looking older man pays her attention. Haven't you noticed
that?"

Dwight informed her, with an air of immense abstraction,
that he left all such matters to her. Being married to Dwight
was like a perpetual rehearsal, with Dwight's self-importance for
audience.

A few evenings later, Cornish brought up the music. There
was something overpowering in this brown-haired chap against

the background of his negligible little shop, his whole capital in
his few pianos. For he looked hopefully ahead, woke with plans,
regarded the children in the street as if, conceivably, children
might come within the confines of his life as he imagined it.
A preposterous little man. And a preposterous store, empty,
echoing, bare of wall, the three pianos near the front, the
remainder of the floor stretching away like the corridors of
the lost. He was going to get a dark curtain, he explained, and
furnish the back part of the store as his own room. What dignity
in phrasing, but how mean that little room would look—cot
bed, washbowl and pitcher, and little mirror—almost certainly a
mirror with a wavy surface, almost certainly that.

"And then, you know," he always added, "I'm reading law."

The Plows had been asked in that evening. Bobby was
there. They were, Dwight Herbert said, going to have a sing.

Di was to play. And Di was now embarked on the most
difficult feat of her emotional life, the feat of remaining to
Bobby Larkin the lure, the beloved lure, the while to Cornish
she instinctively played the rôle of womanly little girl.

"Up by the festive lamp, everybody!" Dwight Herbert
cried.

As they gathered about the upright piano, that startled,
Dwightish instrument, standing in its attitude of unrest, Lulu
came in with another lamp.

"Do you need this?" she asked.

They did not need it, there was, in fact, no place to set it,
and this Lulu must have known. But Dwight found a place. He
swept Ninian's photograph from the marble shelf of the mirror,
and when Lulu had placed the lamp there, Dwight thrust the
photograph into her hands.

"You take care of that," he said, with a droop of lid
discernible only to those who—presumably—loved him. His
old attitude toward Lulu had shown a terrible sharpening in
these ten days since her return.

She stood uncertainly, in the thin black and white gown
which Ninian had bought for her, and held Ninian's photograph

and looked helplessly about. She was moving toward the door
when Cornish called:

"See here! Aren't *you* going to sing?"

"What?" Dwight used the falsetto, "Lulu sing? *Lulu?*"

She stood awkwardly. She had a piteous recrudescence of
her old agony at being spoken to in the presence of others. But
Di had opened the "Album of Old Favourites," which Cornish
had elected to bring, and now she struck the opening chords
of "Bonny Eloise." Lulu stood still, looking rather piteously at
Cornish. Dwight offered his arm, absurdly crooked. The Plows
and Ina and Di began to sing. Lulu moved forward, and stood
a little away from them, and sang, too. She was still holding
Ninian's picture. Dwight did not sing. He lifted his shoulders
and his eyebrows and watched Lulu.

When they had finished, "Lulu the mocking bird!" Dwight
cried. He said "ba-ird."

"Fine!" cried Cornish. "Why, Miss Lulu, you have a good
voice!"

"Miss Lulu Bett, the mocking ba-ird!" Dwight insisted.

Lulu was excited, and in some accession of faint power. She
turned to him now, quietly, and with a look of appraisal.

"Lulu the dove," she then surprisingly said, "to put up
with you."

It was her first bit of conscious repartee to her brother-in-
law.

Cornish was bending over Di.

"What next do you say?" he asked.

She lifted her eyes, met his own, held them. "There's such a
lovely, lovely sacred song here," she suggested, and looked down.

"You like sacred music?"

She turned to him her pure profile, her eyelids fluttering
up, and said: "I love it."

"That's it. So do I. Nothing like a nice sacred piece,"
Cornish declared.

Bobby Larkin, at the end of the piano, looked directly
into Di's face.

"Give *me* ragtime," he said now, with the effect of bursting out of somewhere. "Don't you like ragtime?" he put it to her directly.

Di's eyes danced into his, they sparkled for him, her smile was a smile for him alone, all their store of common memories was in their look.

"Let's try 'My Rock, My Refuge,'" Cornish suggested. "That's got up real attractive."

Di's profile again, and her pleased voice saying that this was the very one she had been hoping to hear him sing.

They gathered for "My Rock, My Refuge."

"Oh," cried Ina, at the conclusion of this number, "I'm having such a perfectly beautiful time. Isn't everybody?" everybody's hostess put it.

"Lulu is," said Dwight, and added softly to Lulu: "She don't have to hear herself sing."

It was incredible. He was like a bad boy with a frog. About that photograph of Ninian he found a dozen ways to torture her, called attention to it, showed it to Cornish, set it on the piano facing them all. Everybody must have understood—excepting the Plows. These two gentle souls sang placidly through the Album of Old Favourites, and at the melodies smiled happily upon each other with an air from another world. Always it was as if the Plows walked some fair, inter-penetrating plane, from which they looked out as do other things not quite of earth, say, flowers and fire and music.

Strolling home that night, the Plows were overtaken by some one who ran badly, and as if she were unaccustomed to running.

"Mis' Plow, Mis' Plow!" this one called, and Lulu stood beside them.

"Say!" she said. "Do you know of any job that I could get me? I mean that I'd know how to do? A job for money…. I mean a job…."

She burst into passionate crying. They drew her home with them.

Lying awake sometime after midnight, Lulu heard the telephone ring. She heard Dwight's concerned "Is that so?" And his cheerful "Be right there."

Grandma Gates was sick, she heard him tell Ina. In a few moments he ran down the stairs. Next day they told how Dwight had sat for hours that night, holding Grandma Gates so that her back would rest easily and she could fight for her faint breath. The kind fellow had only about two hours of sleep the whole night long.

Next day there came a message from that woman who had brought up Dwight—"made him what he was," he often complacently accused her. It was a note on a postal card—she had often written a few lines on a postal card to say that she had sent the maple sugar, or could Ina get her some samples. Now she wrote a few lines on a postal card to say that she was going to die with cancer. Could Dwight and Ina come to her while she was still able to visit? If he was not too busy....

Nobody saw the pity and the terror of that postal card. They stuck it up by the kitchen clock to read over from time to time, and before they left, Dwight lifted the griddle of the cooking-stove and burned the postal card.

And before they left Lulu said: "Dwight—you can't tell how long you'll be gone?"

"Of course not. How should I tell?"

"No. And that letter might come while you're away."

"Conceivably. Letters do come while a man's away!"

"Dwight—I thought if you wouldn't mind if I opened it—"

"Opened it?"

"Yes. You see, it'll be about me mostly—"

"I should have said that it'll be about my brother mostly."

"But you know what I mean. You wouldn't mind if I did open it?"

"But you say you know what'll be in it."

"So I did know—till you—I've got to see that letter, Dwight."

"And so you shall. But not till I show it to you. My dear Lulu, you know how I hate having my mail interfered with."

She might have said: "Small souls always make a point of that." She said nothing. She watched them set off, and kept her mind on Ina's thousand injunctions.

"Don't let Di see much of Bobby Larkin. And, Lulu—if it occurs to her to have Mr. Cornish come up to sing, of course you ask him. You might ask him to supper. And don't let mother overdo. And, Lulu, now do watch Monona's handkerchief—the child will never take a clean one if I'm not here to tell her...."

She breathed injunctions to the very step of the 'bus.

In the 'bus Dwight leaned forward:

"See that you play post-office squarely, Lulu!" he called, and threw back his head and lifted his eyebrows.

In the train he turned tragic eyes to his wife.

"Ina," he said. "It's *ma*. And she's going to die. It can't be...."

Ina said: "But you're going to help her, Dwight, just being there with her."

It was true that the mere presence of the man would bring a kind of fresh life to that worn frame. Tact and wisdom and love would speak through him and minister.

Toward the end of their week's absence the letter from Ninian came.

Lulu took it from the post-office when she went for the mail that evening, dressed in her dark red gown. There was no other letter, and she carried that one letter in her hand all through the streets. She passed those who were surmising what her story might be, who were telling one another what they had heard. But she knew hardly more than they. She passed Cornish in the doorway of his little music shop, and spoke with him; and there was the letter. It was so that Dwight's foster mother's postal card might have looked on its way to be mailed.

Cornish stepped down and overtook her.

"Oh, Miss Lulu. I've got a new song or two—"

She said abstractedly: "Do. Any night. To-morrow night—could you—" It was as if Lulu were too preoccupied to remember to be ill at ease.

Cornish flushed with pleasure, said that he could indeed.

"Come for supper," Lulu said.

Oh, could he? Wouldn't that be…. Well, say! Such was his acceptance.

He came for supper. And Di was not at home. She had gone off in the country with Jenny and Bobby, and they merely did not return.

Mrs. Bett and Lulu and Cornish and Monona supped alone. All were at ease, now that they were alone. Especially Mrs. Bett was at ease. It became one of her young nights, her alive and lucid nights. She was *there*. She sat in Dwight's chair and Lulu sat in Ina's chair. Lulu had picked flowers for the table—a task coveted by her but usually performed by Ina. Lulu had now picked Sweet William and had filled a vase of silver gilt taken from the parlour. Also, Lulu had made ice-cream.

"I don't see what Di can be thinking of," Lulu said. "It seems like asking you under false—" She was afraid of "pretences" and ended without it.

Cornish savoured his steaming beef pie, with sage. "Oh, well!" he said contentedly.

"Kind of a relief, *I* think, to have her gone," said Mrs. Bett, from the fulness of something or other.

"Mother!" Lulu said, twisting her smile.

"Why, my land, I love her," Mrs. Bett explained, "but she wiggles and chitters."

Cornish never made the slightest effort, at any time, to keep a straight face. The honest fellow now laughed loudly.

"Well!" Lulu thought. "He can't be so *very* much in love." And again she thought: "He doesn't know anything about the letter. He thinks Ninian got tired of me." Deep in her heart there abode her certainty that this was not so.

By some etiquette of consent, Mrs. Bett cleared the table and Lulu and Cornish went into the parlour. There lay the letter on the drop-leaf side-table, among the shells. Lulu had carried it there, where she need not see it at her work. The letter looked no more than the advertisement of dental office furniture beneath it. Monona stood indifferently fingering both.

"Monona," Lulu said sharply, "leave them be!"

Cornish was displaying his music. "Got up quite attractive," he said—it was his formula of praise for his music.

"But we can't try it over," Lulu said, "if Di doesn't come."

"Well, say," said Cornish shyly, "you know I left that Album of Old Favourites here. Some of them we know by heart."

Lulu looked. "I'll tell you something," she said, "there's some of these I can play with one hand—by ear. Maybe—"

"Why sure!" said Cornish.

Lulu sat at the piano. She had on the wool chally, long sacred to the nights when she must combine her servant's estate with the quality of being Ina's sister. She wore her coral beads and her cameo cross. In her absence she had caught the trick of dressing her hair so that it looked even more abundant—but she had not dared to try it so until to-night, when Dwight was gone. Her long wrist was curved high, her thin hand pressed and fingered awkwardly, and at her mistakes her head dipped and strove to make all right. Her foot continuously touched the loud pedal—the blurred sound seemed to accomplish more. So she played "How Can I Leave Thee," and they managed to sing it. So she played "Long, Long Ago," and "Little Nell of Narragansett Bay." Beyond open doors, Mrs. Bett listened, sang, it may be, with them; for when the singers ceased, her voice might be heard still humming a loud closing bar.

"Well!" Cornish cried to Lulu; and then, in the formal village phrase: "You're quite a musician."

"Oh, no!" Lulu disclaimed it. She looked up, flushed, smiling. "I've never done this in front of anybody," she owned. "I don't know what Dwight and Ina'd say...." She drooped.

They rested, and, miraculously, the air of the place had stirred and quickened, as if the crippled, halting melody had some power of its own, and poured this forth, even thus trampled.

"I guess you could do 'most anything you set your hand to," said Cornish.

"Oh, no," Lulu said again.

"Sing and play and cook—"

"But I can't earn anything. I'd like to earn something." But this she had not meant to say. She stopped, rather frightened.

"You would! Why, you have it fine here, I thought."

"Oh, fine, yes. Dwight gives me what I have. And I do their work."

"I see," said Cornish. "I never thought of that, "he added. She caught his speculative look—he had heard a tale or two concerning her return, as who in Warbleton had not heard?

"You're wondering why I didn't stay with him!" Lulu said recklessly. This was no less than wrung from her, but its utterance occasioned in her an unspeakable relief.

"Oh, no," Cornish disclaimed, and coloured and rocked.

"Yes, you are," she swept on. "The whole town's wondering. Well, I'd like 'em to know, but Dwight won't let me tell."

Cornish frowned, trying to understand.

"'Won't let you!'" he repeated. "I should say that was your own affair."

"No. Not when Dwight gives me all I have."

"Oh, that—" said Cornish. "That's not right."

"No. But there it is. It puts me—you see what it does to me. They think—they all think my—husband left me."

It was curious to hear her bring out that word— tentatively, deprecatingly, like some one daring a foreign phrase without warrant.

Cornish said feebly: "Oh, well...."

Before she willed it, she was telling him:

"He didn't. He didn't leave me," she cried with passion. "He had another wife." Incredibly it was as if she were defending both him and herself.

"Lord sakes!" said Cornish.

She poured it out, in her passion to tell some one, to share her news of her state where there would be neither hardness nor censure.

"We were in Savannah, Georgia," she said. "We were going to leave for Oregon—going to go through California. We were in the hotel, and he was going out to get the tickets. He started to go. Then he came back. I was sitting the same as there. He opened the door again—the same as here. I saw he looked different—and he said quick: 'There's something you'd ought to know before we go.' And of course I said, 'What?' And he said it right out—how he was married eighteen years ago and in two years she ran away and she must be dead but he wasn't sure. He hadn't the proofs. So of course I came home. But it wasn't him left me."

"No, no. Of course he didn't," Cornish said earnestly. "But Lord sakes—" he said again. He rose to walk about, found it impracticable and sat down.

"That's what Dwight don't want me to tell—he thinks it isn't true. He thinks—he didn't have any other wife. He thinks he wanted—" Lulu looked up at him. "You see," she said, "Dwight thinks he didn't want me."

"But why don't you make your—husband—I mean, why doesn't he write to Mr. Deacon here, and tell him the truth—" Cornish burst out.

Under this implied belief, she relaxed and into her face came its rare sweetness.

"He has written," she said. "The letter's there."

He followed her look, scowled at the two letters.

"What'd he say?"

"Dwight don't like me to touch his mail. I'll have to wait till he comes back."

"Lord sakes!" said Cornish.

This time he did rise and walk about. He wanted to say something, wanted it with passion. He paused beside Lulu and stammered:

"You—you—you're too nice a girl to get a deal like this. Darned if you aren't."

To her own complete surprise Lulu's eyes filled with tears, and she could not speak. She was by no means above self-sympathy.

"And there ain't," said Cornish sorrowfully, "there ain't a thing I can do."

And yet he was doing much. He was gentle, he was listening, and on his face a frown of concern. His face continually surprised her, it was so fine and alive and near, by comparison with Ninian's loose-lipped, ruddy, impersonal look and Dwight's thin, high-boned hardness. All the time Cornish gave her something, instead of drawing upon her. Above all, he was there, and she could talk to him.

"It's—it's funny," Lulu said. "I'd be awful glad if I just *could* know for sure that the other woman was alive—if I couldn't know she's dead."

This surprising admission Cornish seemed to understand.

"Sure you would," he said briefly.

"Cora Waters," Lulu said. "Cora Waters, of San Diego, California. And she never heard of me."

"No," Cornish admitted. They stared at each other as across some abyss.

In the doorway Mrs. Bett appeared.

"I scraped up everything," she remarked, "and left the dishes set."

"That's right, mamma," Lulu said. "Come and sit down."

Mrs. Bett entered with a leisurely air of doing the thing next expected of her.

"I don't hear any more playin' and singin'," she remarked. "It sounded real nice."

"We—we sung all I knew how to play, I guess, mamma."

"I use' to play on the melodeon," Mrs. Bett volunteered, and spread and examined her right hand.

"Well!" said Cornish.

She now told them about her log-house in a New England clearing, when she was a bride. All her store of drama and life came from her. She rehearsed it with far eyes. She laughed at old delights, drooped at old fears. She told about her little daughter

who had died at sixteen—a tragedy such as once would have
been renewed in a vital ballad. At the end she yawned frankly as
if, in some terrible sophistication, she had been telling the story
of some one else.

"Give us one more piece," she said.

"Can we?" Cornish asked.

"I can play 'I Think When I Read That Sweet Story of
Old,'" Lulu said.

"That's the ticket!" cried Cornish.

They sang it, to Lulu's right hand.

"That's the one you picked out when you was a little girl,
Lulie," cried, Mrs. Bett.

Lulu had played it now as she must have played it then.

Half after nine and Di had not returned. But nobody
thought of Di. Cornish rose to go.

"What's them?" Mrs. Bett demanded.

"Dwight's letters, mamma. You mustn't touch them!"
Lulu's voice was sharp.

"Say!" Cornish, at the door, dropped his voice "If there was
anything I could do at any time, you'd let me know, wouldn't
you?"

That past tense, those subjunctives, unconsciously called
upon her to feel no intrusion.

"Oh, thank you," she said. "You don't know how good it is
to feel—"

"Of course it is," said Cornish heartily.

They stood for a moment on the porch. The night was one
of low clamour from the grass, tiny voices, insisting.

"Of course," said Lulu, "of course you won't—you
wouldn't—"

"Say anything?" he divined. "Not for dollars. Not," he
repeated, "for dollars."

"But I knew you wouldn't," she told him.

He took her hand. "Good-night," he said. "I've had an
awful nice time singing and listening to you talk—well, of
course—I mean, " he cried, "the supper was just fine. And so
was the music."

"Oh, no," she said.

Mrs. Bett came into the hall.

"Lulie," she said, "I guess you didn't notice—this one's from Ninian."

"Mother—"

"I opened it—why, of course I did. It's from Ninian."

Mrs. Bett held out the opened envelope, the unfolded letter, and a yellowed newspaper clipping.

"See," said the old woman, "says, 'Corie Waters, music hall singer—married last night to Ninian Deacon—' Say, Lulie, that must be her...."

Lulu threw out her hands.

"There!" she cried triumphantly. "He *was* married to her, just like he said!"

The Plows were at breakfast next morning when Lulu came in casually at the side-door. Yes, she said, she had had breakfast. She merely wanted to see them about something. Then she said nothing, but sat looking with a troubled frown at Jenny. Jenny's hair was about her neck, like the hair of a little girl, a south window poured light upon her, the fruit and honey upon the table seemed her only possible food.

"You look troubled, Lulu," Mrs. Plow said. "Is it about getting work?"

"No," said Lulu, "no. I've been places to ask—quite a lot of places. I guess the bakery is going to let me make cake."

"I knew it would come to you," Mrs. Plow said, and Lulu thought that this was a strange way to speak, when she herself had gone after the cakes. But she kept on looking about the room. It was so bright and quiet. As she came in, Mr. Plow had been reading from a book. Dwight never read from a book at table.

"I wish—" said Lulu, as she looked at them. But she did not know what she wished. Certainly it was for no moral excellence, for she perceived none.

"What is it, Lulu?" Mr. Plow asked, and he was bright and quiet too, Lulu thought.

"Well," said Lulu, "it's not much. But I wanted Jenny to tell me about last night."

"Last night?"

"Yes. Would you—" Hesitation was her only way of apology. "Where did you go?" She turned to Jenny.

Jenny looked up in her clear and ardent fashion: "We went across the river and carried supper and then we came home."

"What time did you get home?"

"Oh, it was still light. Long before eight, it was."

Lulu hesitated and flushed, asked how long Di and Bobby had stayed there at Jenny's; whereupon she heard that Di had to be home early on account of Mr. Cornish, so that she and Bobby had not stayed at all. To which Lulu said an "of course," but first she stared at Jenny and so impaired the strength of her assent. Almost at once she rose to go.

"Nothing else?" said Mrs. Plow, catching that look of hers.

Lulu wanted to say: "My husband *was* married before, just as he said he was." But she said nothing more, and went home. There she put it to Di, and with her terrible bluntness reviewed to Di the testimony.

"You were not with Jenny after eight o'clock. Where were you?" Lulu spoke formally and her rehearsals were evident.

Di said: "When mamma comes home, I'll tell her."

With this Lulu had no idea how to deal, and merely looked at her helplessly. Mrs. Bett, who was lacing her shoes, now said casually:

"No need to wait till then. Her and Bobby were out in the side yard sitting in the hammock till all hours."

Di had no answer save her furious flush, and Mrs. Bett went on:

"Didn't I tell you? I knew it before the company left, but I didn't say a word. Thinks I, 'She's wiggles and chitters.' So I left her stay where she was."

"But, mother!" Lulu cried. "You didn't even tell me after he'd gone."

"I forgot it," Mrs. Bett said, "finding Ninian's letter and all—" She talked of Ninian's letter.

Di was bright and alert and firm of flesh and erect before Lulu's softness and laxness.

"I don't know what your mother'll say," said Lulu, "and I don't know what people'll think."

"They won't think Bobby and I are tired of each other, anyway," said Di, and left the room.

Through the day Lulu tried to think what she must do. About Di she was anxious and felt without power. She thought of the indignation of Dwight and Ina that Di had not been more scrupulously guarded. She thought of Di's girlish folly, her irritating independence—"and there," Lulu thought, "just the other day I was teaching her to sew." Her mind dwelt too on Dwight's furious anger at the opening of Ninian's letter. But when all this had spent itself, what was she herself to do? She must leave his house before he ordered her to do so, when she told him that she had confided in Cornish, as tell she must. But what was she to *do?* The bakery cake-making would not give her a roof.

Stepping about the kitchen in her blue cotton gown, her hair tight and flat as seemed proper when one was not dressed, she thought about these things. And it was strange: Lulu bore no physical appearance of one in distress or any anxiety. Her head was erect, her movements were strong and swift, her eyes were interested. She was no drooping Lulu with dragging step. She was more intent, she was somehow more operative than she had ever been.

Mrs. Bett was working contentedly beside her, and now and then humming an air of that music of the night before. The sun surged through the kitchen door and east window, a returned oriole swung and fluted on the elm above the gable. Wagons clattered by over the rattling wooden block pavement.

"Ain't it nice with nobody home?" Mrs. Bett remarked at intervals, like the burden of a comic song.

"Hush, mother," Lulu said, troubled, her ethical refinements conflicting with her honesty.

"Speak the truth and shame the devil," Mrs. Bett contended.

When dinner was ready at noon, Di did not appear. A little earlier Lulu had heard her moving about her room, and she served her in expectation that she would join them.

"Di must be having the 'tantrim' this time," she thought, and for a time said nothing. But at length she did say: "Why doesn't Di come? I'd better put her plate in the oven."

Rising to do so, she was arrested by her mother. Mrs. Bett was eating a baked potato, holding her fork close to the tines, and presenting a profile of passionate absorption.

"Why, Di went off," she said.

"Went off!"

"Down the walk. Down the sidewalk."

"She must have gone to Jenny's," said Lulu. "I wish she wouldn't do that without telling me."

Monona laughed out and shook her straight hair. "She'll catch it!" she cried in sisterly enjoyment.

It was when Lulu had come back from the kitchen and was seated at the table that Mrs. Bett observed:

"I didn't think Inie'd want her to take her nice new satchel."

"Her satchel?"

"Yes. Inie wouldn't take it north herself, but Di had it."

"Mother," said Lulu, "when Di went away just now, was she carrying a satchel?"

"Didn't I just tell you?" Mrs. Bett demanded, aggrieved. "I said I didn't think Inie—"

"Mother! Which way did she go?"

Monona pointed with her spoon. "She went that way, "she said. "I seen her."

Lulu looked at the clock. For Monona had pointed toward the railway station. The twelve-thirty train, which every one took to the city for shopping, would be just about leaving.

"Monona," said Lulu, "don't you go out of the yard while I'm gone. Mother, you keep her—"

Lulu ran from the house and up the street. She was in her blue cotton dress, her old shoes, she was hatless and without money. When she was still two or three blocks from the station, she heard the twelve-thirty "pulling out."

She ran badly, her ankles in their low, loose shoes continually turning, her arms held taut at her sides. So she came down the platform, and to the ticket window. The contained ticket man, wonted to lost trains and perturbed faces, yet actually ceased counting when he saw her:

"Lenny! Did Di Deacon take that train?"

"Sure she did," said Lenny.

"And Bobby Larkin?" Lulu cared nothing for appearances now.

"He went in on the Local," said Lenny, and his eyes widened.

"Where?"

"See." Lenny thought it through. "Millton," he said. "Yes, sure. Millton. Both of 'em."

"How long till another train?"

"Well, sir," said the ticket man, "you're in luck, if you was goin' too. Seventeen was late this morning—she'll be along, jerk of a lamb's tail."

"Then," said Lulu, "you got to give me a ticket to Millton, without me paying till after—and you got to lend me two dollars."

"Sure thing," said Lenny, with a manner of laying the entire railway system at her feet.

"Seventeen" would rather not have stopped at Warbleton, but Lenny's signal was law on the time card, and the magnificent yellow express slowed down for Lulu. Hatless and in her blue cotton gown, she climbed aboard.

Then her old inefficiency seized upon her. What was she going to do? Millton! She had been there but once, years ago—how could she ever find anybody? Why had she not stayed in Warbleton and asked the sheriff or somebody—no, not the sheriff. Cornish, perhaps. Oh, and Dwight and Ina were going to be angry now! And Di—little Di. As Lulu thought of her she began to cry. She said to herself that she had taught Di to sew.

In sight of Millton, Lulu was seized with trembling and physical nausea. She had never been alone in any unfamiliar town. She put her hands to her hair and for the first time realized her rolled-up sleeves. She was pulling down these sleeves when the conductor came through the train.

"Could you tell me," she said timidly, "the name of the principal hotel in Millton?"

Ninian had asked this as they neared Savannah, Georgia.

The conductor looked curiously at her.

"Why, the Hess House," he said. "Wasn't you expecting anybody to meet you?" he asked, kindly.

"No," said Lulu, "but I'm going to find my folks—" Her voice trailed away.

"Beats all," thought the conductor, using his utility formula for the universe.

In Millton Lulu's inquiry for the Hess House produced no consternation. Nobody paid any attention to her. She was almost certainly taken to be a new servant there.

"You stop feeling so!" she said to herself angrily at the lobby entrance. "Ain't you been to that big hotel in Savannah, Georgia?"

The Hess House, Millton, had a tradition of its own to maintain, it seemed, and they sent her to the rear basement door. She obeyed meekly, but she lost a good deal of time before she found herself at the end of the office desk. It was still longer before any one attended her.

"Please, sir!" she burst out. "See if Di Deacon has put her name on your book."

Her appeal was tremendous, compelling. The young clerk listened to her, showed her where to look in the register. When only strange names and strange writing presented themselves there, he said:

"Tried the parlour?"

And directed her kindly and with his thumb, and in the other hand a pen divorced from his ear for the express purpose.

In crossing the lobby in the hotel at Savannah, Georgia, Lulu's most pressing problem had been to know where to look.

But now the idlers in the Hess House lobby did not exist. In time she found the door of the intensely rose-coloured reception room. There, in a fat, rose-coloured chair, beside a cataract of lace curtain, sat Di, alone.

Lulu entered. She had no idea what to say. When Di looked up, started up, frowned, Lulu felt as if she herself were the culprit. She said the first thing that occurred to her:

"I don't believe mamma'll like your taking her nice satchel."

"Well!" said Di, exactly as if she had been at home. And superadded: "My goodness!" And then cried rudely: "What are you here for?"

"For you," said Lulu. "You—you—you'd ought not to be here, Di."

"What's that to you?" Di cried.

"Why, Di, you're just a little girl—"

Lulu saw that this was all wrong, and stopped miserably. How was she to go on? "Di," she said, "if you and Bobby want to get married, why not let us get you up a nice wedding at home?" And she saw that this sounded as if she were talking about a tea-party.

"Who said we wanted to be married?"

"Well, he's here."

"Who said he's here?"

"Isn't he?"

Di sprang up. "Aunt Lulu," she said, "you're a funny person to be telling *me* what to do."

Lulu said, flushing: "I love you just the same as if I was married happy, in a home."

"Well, you aren't!" cried Di cruelly, "and I'm going to do just as I think best."

Lulu thought this over, her look grave and sad. She tried to find something to say. "What do people say to people," she wondered, "when it's like this?"

"Getting married is for your whole life," was all that came to her.

"Yours wasn't," Di flashed at her.

Lulu's colour deepened, but there seemed to be no resentment in her. She must deal with this right—that was what her manner seemed to say. And how should she deal?

"Di," she cried, "come back with me—and wait till mamma and papa get home."

"That's likely. They say I'm not to be married till I'm twenty-one."

"Well, but how young that is!"

"It is to you."

"Di! This is wrong—it *is* wrong."

"There's nothing wrong about getting married—if you stay married."

"Well, then it can't be wrong to let them know."

"It isn't. But they'd treat me wrong. They'd make me stay at home. And I won't stay at home—I won't stay there. They act as if I was ten years old."

Abruptly in Lulu's face there came a light of understanding.

"Why, Di," she said, "do you feel that way too?"

Di missed this. She went on:

"I'm grown up. I feel just as grown up as they do. And I'm not allowed to do a thing I feel. I want to be away—I will be away!"

"I know about that part," Lulu said.

She now looked at Di with attention. Was it possible that Di was suffering in the air of that home as she herself suffered? She had not thought of that. There Di had seemed so young, so dependent, so—asquirm. Here, by herself, waiting for Bobby, in the Hess House at Millton, she was curiously adult. Would she be adult if she were let alone?

"You don't know what it's like, " Di cried, "to be hushed up and laughed at and paid no attention to, everything you say."

"Don't I?" said Lulu. "Don't I?"

She was breathing quickly and looking at Di. If *this* was why Di was leaving home....

"But, Di," she cried, "do you love Bobby Larkin?"

By this Di was embarrassed. "I've got to marry somebody," she said, "and it might as well be him."

"But is it him?"

"Yes, it is," said Di. "But," she added, "I know I could love almost anybody real nice that was nice to me." And this she said, not in her own right, but either she had picked it up somewhere and adopted it, or else the terrible modernity and honesty of her day somehow spoke through her, for its own. But to Lulu it was as if something familiar turned its face to be recognised.

"Di!" she cried.

"It's true. You ought to know that." She waited for a moment. "You did it," she added. "Mamma said so."

At this onslaught Lulu was stupefied. For she began to perceive its truth.

"I know what I want to do, I guess," Di muttered, as if to try to cover what she had said.

Up to that moment, Lulu had been feeling intensely that she understood Di, but that Di did not know this. Now Lulu felt that she and Di actually shared some unsuspected sisterhood. It was not only that they were both badgered by Dwight. It was more than that. They were two women. And she must make Di know that she understood her.

"Di," Lulu said, breathing hard, "what you just said is true, I guess. Don't you think I don't know. And now I'm going to tell you—"

She might have poured it all out, claimed her kinship with Di by virtue of that which had happened in Savannah, Georgia. But Di said:

"Here come some ladies. And goodness, look at the way you look!"

Lulu glanced down. "I know," she said, "but I guess you'll have to put up with me."

The two women entered, looked about with the complaisance of those who examine a hotel property, find criticism incumbent, and have no errand. These two women had outdressed their occasion. In their presence Di kept silence, turned away her head, gave them to know that she had nothing to do with this blue cotton person beside her. When they had gone on, "What do you mean by my having to put up with you?" Di asked sharply.

"I mean I'm going to stay with you."

Di laughed scornfully—she was again the rebellious child. "I guess Bobby'll have something to say about that," she said insolently.

"They left you in my charge."

"But I'm not a baby—the idea, Aunt Lulu!"

"I'm going to stay right with you," said Lulu. She wondered what she should do if Di suddenly marched away from her, through that bright lobby and into the street. She thought miserably that she must follow. And then her whole concern for the ethics of Di's course was lost in her agonised memory of her terrible, broken shoes.

Di did not march away. She turned her back squarely upon Lulu, and looked out of the window. For her life Lulu could think of nothing more to say. She was now feeling miserably on the defensive.

They were sitting in silence when Bobby Larkin came into the room.

Four Bobby Larkins there were, in immediate succession.

The Bobby who had just come down the street was distinctly perturbed, came hurrying, now and then turned to the left when he met folk, glanced sidewise here and there, was altogether anxious and ill at ease.

The Bobby who came through the hotel was a Bobby who had on an importance assumed for the crisis of threading the lobby—a Bobby who wished it to be understood that here he was, a man among men, in the Hess House at Millton.

The Bobby who entered the little rose room was the Bobby who was no less than overwhelmed with the stupendous character of the adventure upon which he found himself.

The Bobby who incredibly came face to face with Lulu was the real Bobby into whose eyes leaped instant, unmistakable relief.

Di flew to meet him. She assumed all the pretty agitations of her rôle, ignored Lulu.

"Bobby! Is it all right?"

Bobby looked over her head.

"Miss Lulu," he said fatuously. "If it ain't Miss Lulu."

He looked from her to Di, and did not take in Di's resigned shrug.

"Bobby," said Di, "she's come to stop us getting married, but she can't. I've told her so."

"She don't have to stop us," quoth Bobby gloomily, "we're stopped."

"What do you mean?" Di laid one hand flatly along her cheek, instinctive in her melodrama.

Bobby drew down his brows, set his hand on his leg, elbow out.

"We're minors," said he.

"Well, gracious, you didn't have to tell them that."

"No. They knew *I* was."

"But, Silly! Why didn't you tell them you're not?"

"But I am."

Di stared. "For pity sakes," she said, "don't you know how to do anything?"

"What would you have me do?" he inquired indignantly, with his head held very stiff, and with a boyish, admirable lift of chin.

"Why, tell them we're both twenty-one. We look it. We know we're responsible—that's all they care for. Well, you are a funny...."

"You wanted me to lie?" he said.

"Oh, don't make out you never told a fib."

"Well, but this—" he stared at her.

"I never heard of such a thing," Di cried accusingly.

"Anyhow," he said, "there's nothing to do now. The cat's out. I've told our ages. We've got to have our folks in on it."

"Is that all you can think of?" she demanded.

"What else?"

"Why, come on to Bainbridge or Holt, and tell them we're of age, and be married there."

"Di," said Bobby, "why, that'd be a rotten go."

Di said, oh very well, if he didn't want to marry her. He replied stonily that of course he wanted to marry her. Di stuck out her little hand. She was at a disadvantage. She could use no arts, with Lulu sitting there, looking on. "Well, then, come on to Bainbridge," Di cried, and rose.

Lulu was thinking: "What shall I say? I don't know what to say. I don't know what I can say." Now she also rose, and laughed awkwardly. "I've told Di," she said to Bobby, "that wherever you two go, I'm going too. Di's folks left her in my care, you know. So you'll have to take me along, I guess." She spoke in a manner of distinct apology.

At this Bobby had no idea what to reply. He looked down miserably at the carpet. His whole manner was a mute testimony to his participation in the eternal query: How did I get into it?

"Bobby," said Di, "are you going to let her lead you home?"

This of course nettled him, but not in the manner on which Di had counted. He said loudly:

"I'm not going to Bainbridge or Holt or any town and lie, to get you or any other girl."

Di's head lifted, tossed, turned from him. "You're about as much like a man in a story," she said, "as—as papa is."

The two idly inspecting women again entered the rose room, this time to stay. They inspected Lulu too. And Lulu rose and stood between the lovers.

"Hadn't we all better get the four-thirty to Warbleton?" she said, and swallowed.

"Oh, if Bobby wants to back out—" said Di.

"I don't want to back out," Bobby contended furiously, "b-b-but I won't—"

"Come on, Aunt Lulu," said Di grandly.

Bobby led the way through the lobby, Di followed, and Lulu brought up the rear. She walked awkwardly, eyes down, her hands stiffly held. Heads turned to look at her. They passed into the street.

"You two go ahead," said Lulu, "so they won't think—"

They did so, and she followed, and did not know where to look, and thought of her broken shoes.

At the station, Bobby put them on the train and stepped back. He had, he said, something to see to there in Millton. Di did not look at him. And Lulu's good-bye spoke her genuine regret for all.

"Aunt Lulu," said Di, "you needn't think I'm going to sit with you. You look as if you were crazy. I'll sit back here."

"All right, Di," said Lulu humbly.

It was nearly six o'clock when they arrived at the Deacons'. Mrs. Bett stood on the porch, her hands rolled in her apron.

"Surprise for you!" she called brightly.

Before they had reached the door, Ina bounded from the hall.

"Darling!"

She seized upon Di, kissed her loudly, drew back from her, saw the travelling bag.

"My new bag!" she cried. "Di! What have you got that for?"

In any embarrassment Di's instinctive defence was hearty laughter. She now laughed heartily, kissed her mother again, and ran up the stairs.

Lulu slipped by her sister, and into the kitchen.

"Well, where have *you,* been?" cried Ina. "I declare, I never saw such a family. Mamma don't know anything and neither of you will tell anything."

"Mamma knows a-plenty," snapped Mrs. Bett.

Monona, who was eating a sticky gift, jumped stiffly up and down.

"You'll catch it—you'll catch it!" she sent out her shrill general warning.

Mrs. Bett followed Lulu to the kitchen; "I didn't tell Inie about her bag and now she says I don't know nothing," she complained. "There I knew about the bag the hull time, but I wasn't going to tell her and spoil her gettin' home." She banged the stove-griddle. "I've a good notion not to eat a mouthful o' supper," she announced.

"Mother, please!" said Lulu passionately. "Stay here. Help me. I've got enough to get through to-night."

Dwight had come home. Lulu could hear Ina pouring out to him the mysterious circumstance of the bag, could hear the exaggerated air of the casual with which he always received the excitement of another, and especially of his Ina. Then she heard Ina's feet padding up the stairs, and after that Di's shrill, nervous laughter. Lulu felt a pang of pity for Di, as if she herself were about to face them.

There was not time both to prepare supper and to change the blue cotton dress. In that dress Lulu was pouring water when Dwight entered the dining-room.

"Ah!" said he. "Our festive ball-gown."

She gave him her hand, with her peculiar sweetness of expression—almost as if she were sorry for him or were bidding him good-bye.

"*That* shows who you dress for!" he cried. "You dress for me; Ina, aren't you jealous? Lulu dresses for me!"

Ina had come in with Di, and both were excited, and Ina's head was moving stiffly, as in all her indignations. Mrs. Bett had thought better of it and had given her presence. Already Monona was singing.

"Lulu," said Dwight, "really? Can't you run up and slip on another dress?"

Lulu sat down in her place. "No," she said. "I'm too tired. I'm sorry, Dwight."

"It seems to me—" he began.

"I don't want any," said Monona.

But no one noticed Monona, and Ina did not defer even to Dwight. She, who measured delicate, troy occasions by avoirdupois, said brightly:

"Now, Di. You must tell us all about it. Where had you and Aunt Lulu been with mamma's new bag?"

"Aunt Lulu!" cried Dwight. "A-ha! So Aunt Lulu was along. Well now, that alters it."

"How does it?" asked his Ina crossly.

"Why, when Aunt Lulu goes on a jaunt," said Dwight Herbert, "events begin to event."

"Come, Di, let's hear," said Ina.

"Ina," said Lulu, "first can't we hear something about your visit? How is—"

Her eyes consulted Dwight. His features dropped, the lines of his face dropped, its muscles seemed to sag. A look of suffering was in his eyes.

"She'll never be any better," he said. "I know we've said good-bye to her for the last time."

"Oh, Dwight!" said Lulu.

"She knew it too," he said. "It—it put me out of business, I can tell you. She gave me my start—she took all the care of me—taught me to read—she's the only mother I ever knew—" He stopped, and opened his eyes wide on account of their dimness.

"They said she was like another person while Dwight was there," said Ina, and entered upon a length of particulars, and details of the journey. These details Dwight interrupted: Couldn't Lulu remember that he liked sage on the chops? He could hardly taste it. He had, he said, told her this thirty-seven times. And when she said that she was sorry, "Perhaps you think I'm sage enough," said the witty fellow.

"Dwightie!" said Ina. "Mercy." She shook her head at him. "Now, Di," she went on, keeping the thread all this time. "Tell us your story. About the bag."

"Oh, mamma," said Di, "let me eat my supper."

"And so you shall, darling. Tell it in your own way. Tell us first what you've done since we've been away. Did Mr. Cornish come to see you?"

"Yes," said Di, and flashed a look at Lulu.

But eventually they were back again before that new black bag. And Di would say nothing. She laughed, squirmed, grew irritable, laughed again.

"Lulu!" Ina demanded. "You were with her—where in the world had you been? Why, but you couldn't have been with her—in that dress. And yet I saw you come in the gate together."

"What!" cried Dwight Herbert, drawing down his brows. "You certainly did not so far forget us, Lulu, as to go on the street in that dress?"

"It's a good dress," Mrs. Bett now said positively. "Of course it's a good dress. Lulie wore it on the street—of course she did. She was gone a long time. I made me a cup o' tea, and *then* she hadn't come."

"Well," said Ina, "I never heard anything like this before. Where were you both?"

One would say that Ina had entered into the family and been born again, identified with each one. Nothing escaped her. Dwight, too, his intimacy was incredible.

"Put an end to this, Lulu," he commanded. "Where were you two—since you make such a mystery?"

Di's look at Lulu was piteous, terrified. Di's fear of her father was now clear to Lulu. And Lulu feared him too. Abruptly she heard herself temporising, for the moment making common cause with Di.

"Oh," she said, "we have a little secret. Can't we have a secret if we want one?"

"Upon my word," Dwight commented, "she has a beautiful secret. I don't know about your secrets, Lulu."

Every time that he did this, that fleet, lifted look of Lulu's seemed to bleed.

"I'm glad for my dinner," remarked Monona at last. "Please excuse me." On that they all rose. Lulu stayed in the kitchen and did her best to make her tasks indefinitely last. She had nearly finished when Di burst in.

"Aunt Lulu, Aunt Lulu!" she cried. "Come in there—come. I can't stand it. What am I going to do?"

"Di, dear," said Lulu. "Tell your mother—you must tell her."

"She'll cry," Di sobbed. "Then she'll tell papa—and he'll never stop talking about it. I know him—every day he'll keep it going. After he scolds me it'll be a joke for months. I'll die—I'll die, Aunt Lulu."

Ina's voice sounded in the kitchen. "What are you two whispering about? I declare, mamma's hurt, Di, at the way you're acting...."

"Let's go out on the porch," said Lulu, and when Di would have escaped, Ina drew her with them, and handled the situation in the only way that she knew how to handle it, by complaining: Well, but what in this world....

Lulu threw a white shawl about her blue cotton dress.

"A bridal robe," said Dwight. "How's that, Lulu—what are *you* wearing a bridal robe for—eh?"

She smiled dutifully. There was no need to make him angry, she reflected, before she must. He had not yet gone into the parlour—had not yet asked for his mail.

It was a warm dusk, moonless, windless. The sounds of the village street came in—laughter, a touch at a piano, a chiming clock. Lights starred and quickened in the blurred houses. Footsteps echoed on the board walks. The gate opened. The gloom yielded up Cornish.

Lulu was inordinately glad to see him. To have the strain of the time broken by him was like hearing, on a lonely whiter wakening, the clock strike reassuring dawn.

"Lulu," said Dwight low, "your dress. Do go!"

Lulu laughed. "The bridal shawl takes off the curse," she said.

Cornish, in his gentle way, asked about the journey, about the sick woman—and Dwight talked of her again, and this time his voice broke. Di was curiously silent. When Cornish addressed her, she replied simply and directly—the rarest of Di's manners, in fact not Di's manner at all. Lulu spoke not at all— it was enough to have this respite.

After a little the gate opened again. It was Bobby. In the besetting fear that he was leaving Di to face something alone, Bobby had arrived.

And now Di's spirits rose. To her his presence meant repentance, recapitulation. Her laugh rang out, her replies came archly. But Bobby was plainly not playing up. Bobby was, in fact, hardly less than glum. It was Dwight, the irrepressible fellow, who kept the talk going. And it was no less than deft, his continuously displayed ability playfully to pierce Lulu. Some one had "married at the drop of the hat. You know the kind of girl?" And some one "made up a likely story to soothe her own pride—you know how they do that?"

"Well," said Ina, "my part, I think *the* most awful thing is to have somebody one loves keep secrets from one. No wonder folks get crabbed and spiteful with such treatment."

"Mamma!" Monona shouted from her room. "Come and hear me say my prayers!"

Monona entered this request with precision on Ina's nastiest moments, but she always rose, unabashed, and went, motherly and dutiful, to hear devotions, as if that function and the process of living ran their two divided channels.

She had dispatched this errand and was returning when Mrs. Bett crossed the lawn from Grandma Gates's, where the old lady had taken comfort in Mrs. Bett's ministrations for an hour.

"Don't you help me," Mrs. Bett warned them away sharply. "I guess I can help myself yet awhile."

She gained her chair. And still in her momentary rule of attention, she said clearly:

"I got a joke. Grandma Gates says it's all over town Di and Bobby Larkin eloped off together to-day. *He!*" The last was a single note of laughter, high and brief.

The silence fell.

"What nonsense!" Dwight Herbert said angrily.

But Ina said tensely: "*Is* it nonsense? Haven't I been trying and trying to find out where the black satchel went? Di!"

Di's laughter rose, but it sounded thin and false.

"Listen to that, Bobby," she said. "Listen!"

"That won't do, Di," said Ina. "You can't deceive mamma and don't you try!" Her voice trembled, she was frantic with loving and authentic anxiety, but she was without power, she overshadowed the real gravity of the moment by her indignation.

"Mrs. Deacon—" began Bobby, and stood up, very straight and manly before them all.

But Dwight intervened, Dwight, the father, the master of his house. Here was something requiring him to act. So the father set his face like a mask and brought down his hand on the rail of the porch. It was as if the sound shattered a thousand filaments—where?

"Diana!" his voice was terrible, demanded a response, ravened among them.

"Yes, papa," said Di, very small.

"Answer your mother. Answer *me*. Is there anything to this absurd tale?"

"No, papa," said Di, trembling.

"Nothing whatever?"

"Nothing whatever."

"Can you imagine how such a ridiculous report started?"

"No, papa."

"Very well. Now we know where we are. If anyone hears this report repeated, send them to *me*."

"Well, but that satchel—" said Ina, to whom an idea manifested less as a function than as a leech.

"One moment," said Dwight. "Lulu will of course verify what the child has said."

There had never been an adult moment until that day when Lulu had not instinctively taken the part of the parents, of all parents. Now she saw Dwight's cruelty to her as his cruelty to Di; she saw Ina, herself a child in maternity, as ignorant of how to deal with the moment as was Dwight. She saw Di's falseness partly parented by these parents. She burned at the enormity of Dwight's appeal to her for verification. She threw up her head and no one had ever seen Lulu look like this.

"If you cannot settle this with Di," said Lulu, "you cannot settle it with me."

"A shifty answer," said Dwight. "You have a genius at misrepresenting facts, you know, Lulu."

"Bobby wanted to say something," said Ina, still troubled.

"No, Mrs. Deacon," said Bobby, low. "I have nothing—more to say."

In a little while, when Bobby went away, Di walked with him to the gate. It was as if, the worst having happened to her, she dared everything now.

"Bobby," she said, "you hate a lie. But what else could I do?"

He could not see her, could see only the little moon of her face, blurring.

"And anyhow," said Di, "it wasn't a lie. We *didn't* elope, did we?"

"What do you think I came for to-night?" asked Bobby.

The day had aged him; he spoke like a man. His very voice came gruffly. But she saw nothing, softened to him, yielded, was ready to take his regret that they had not gone on.

"Well, I came for one thing," said Bobby, "to tell you that I couldn't stand for your wanting me to lie to-day. Why, Di—I hate a lie. And now to-night—" He spoke his code almost beautifully "I'd rather," he said, "they had never let us see each other again than to lose you the way I've lost you now."

"Bobby!"

"It's true. We mustn't talk about it."

"Bobby! I'll go back and tell them all."

"You can't go back," said Bobby. "Not out of a thing like that."

She stood staring after him. She heard some one coming and she turned toward the house, and met Cornish leaving.

"Miss Di," he cried, "if you're going to elope with anybody, remember it's with me!"

Her defence was ready—her laughter rang out so that the departing Bobby might hear.

She came back to the steps and mounted slowly in the lamplight, a little white thing with whom birth had taken exquisite pains.

"If," she said, "if you have any fear that I may ever elope with Bobby Larkin, let it rest. I shall never marry him if he asks me fifty times a day."

"Really, darling?" cried Ina.

"Really and truly," said Di, "and he knows it, too."

Lulu listened and read all.

"I wondered," said Ina pensively, "I wondered if you wouldn't see that Bobby isn't much beside that nice Mr. Cornish!"

When Di had gone upstairs, Ina said to Lulu in a manner of cajoling confidence:

"Sister—" she rarely called her that, "*why* did you and Di have the black bag?"

So that after all it was a relief to Lulu to hear Dwight ask casually: "By the way, Lulu, haven't I got some mail somewhere about?"

"There are two letters on the parlour table," Lulu answered. To Ina she added: "Let's go in the parlour."

As they passed through the hall, Mrs. Bett was going up the stairs to bed—when she mounted stairs she stooped her shoulders, bunched her extremities, and bent her head. Lulu looked after her, as if she were half minded to claim the protection so long lost.

Dwight lighted the gas. "Better turn down the gas jest a little," said he, tirelessly.

Lulu handed him the two letters. He saw Ninian's writing and looked up, said "A-ha!" and held it while he leisurely read the advertisement of dental furniture, his Ina reading over his shoulder. "A-ha!" he said again, and with designed deliberation turned to Ninian's letter. "An epistle from my dear brother Ninian." The words failed, as he saw the unsealed flap.

"You opened the letter?" he inquired incredulously. Fortunately he had no climaxes of furious calm for high occasions. All had been used on small occasions. "You opened the letter" came in a tone of no deeper horror than "You picked the flower"—once put to Lulu.

She said nothing. As it is impossible to continue looking indignantly at some one who is not looking at you, Dwight turned to Ina, who was horror and sympathy, a nice half and half.

"Your sister has been opening my mail," he said.

"But, Dwight, if it's from Ninian—"

"It is *my* mail," he reminded her. "She had asked me if she might open it. Of course I told her no."

"Well," said Ina practically, "what does he say?"

"I shall open the letter in my own time. My present concern is this disregard of my wishes." His self-control was perfect, ridiculous, devilish. He was self-controlled because thus he could be more effectively cruel than in temper. "What excuse have you to offer?"

Lulu was not looking at him. "None," she said—not defiantly, or ingratiatingly, or fearfully. Merely, "None."

"Why did you do it?"

She smiled faintly and shook her head.

"Dwight," said Ina, reasonably, "she knows what's in it and we don't. Hurry up."

"She is," said Dwight, after a pause, "an ungrateful woman."

He opened the letter, saw the clipping, the avowal, with its facts.

"A-ha!" said he. "So after having been absent with my brother for a month, you find that you were *not* married to him."

Lulu spoke her exceeding triumph.

"You see, Dwight," she said, "he told the truth. He had another wife. He didn't just leave me."

Dwight instantly cried: "But this seems to me to make you considerably worse off than if he had."

"Oh, no," Lulu said serenely. "No. Why," she said, "you know how it all came about. He—he was used to thinking of his wife as dead. If he hadn't—hadn't liked me, he wouldn't have told me. You see that, don't you?"

Dwight laughed. "That your apology?" he asked.

She said nothing.

"Look here, Lulu," he went on, "this is a bad business. The less you say about it the better, for all our sakes—*you* see that, don't you?"

"See that? Why, no. I wanted you to write to him so I could tell the truth. You said I mustn't tell the truth till I had the proofs..."

"Tell who?"

"Tell everybody. I want them to know."

"Then you care nothing for our feelings in this matter?"

She looked at him now. "Your feeling?"

"It's nothing to you that we have a brother who's a bigamist?"

"But it's me—it's me."

"You! You're completely out of it. Just let it rest as it is and it'll drop."

"I want the people to know the truth," Lulu said.

"But it's nobody's business but our business! I take it you don't intend to sue Ninian?"

"Sue him? Oh no!"

"Then, for all our sakes, let's drop the matter."

Lulu had fallen in one of her old attitudes, tense, awkward, her hands awkwardly placed, her feet twisted. She kept putting a lock back of her ear, she kept swallowing.

"Tell you, Lulu," said Dwight. "Here are three of us. Our interests are the same in this thing—only Ninian is our relative and he's nothing to you now. Is he?"

"Why, no," said Lulu in surprise.

"Very well. Let's have a vote. Your snap judgment is to tell this disgraceful fact broadcast. Mine is, least said, soonest mended. What do you say, Ina—considering Di and all?"

"Oh, goodness," said Ina, "if we get mixed up with bigamy, we'll never get away from it. Why, I wouldn't have it told for worlds."

Still in that twisted position, Lulu looked up at her. Her straying hair, her parted lips, her lifted eyes were singularly pathetic.

"My poor, poor sister!" Ina said. She struck together her little plump hands. "Oh, Dwight—when I think of it: What have I done—what have *we* done that I should have a good, kind, loving husband—be so protected, so loved, when other women.... Darling!" she sobbed, and drew near to Lulu. "You *know* how sorry I am—we all are...."

Lulu stood up. The white shawl slipped to the floor. Her hands were stiffly joined.

"Then," she said, "give me the only thing I've got—that's my pride. My pride—that he didn't want to get rid of me."

They stared at her. "What about *my* pride?" Dwight called to her, as across great distances. "Do you think I want everybody to know my brother did a thing like that?"

"You can't help that," said Lulu.

"But I want you to help it. I want you to promise me that you won't shame us like this before all our friends."

"You want me to promise what?"

"I want you—I ask you," Dwight said with an effort, "to promise me that you will keep this, with us—a family secret."

"No!" Lulu cried. "No. I won't do it! I won't do it! I won't do it!"

It was like some crude chant, knowing only two tones. She threw out her hands, her wrists long and dark on her blue skirt. "Can't you understand anything?" she asked. "I've lived here all my life—on your money. I've not been strong enough to work, they say—well, but I've been strong enough to be a hired girl in your house—and I've been glad to pay for my keep…. But there wasn't anything about it I liked. Nothing about being here that I liked…. Well, then I got a little something, same as other folks. I thought I was married and I went off on the train and he bought me things and I saw the different towns. And then it was all a mistake. I didn't have any of it. I came back here and went into your kitchen again—I don't know why I came back. I s'pose because I'm most thirty-four and new things ain't so easy any more—but what have I got or what'll I ever have? And now you want to put on to me having folks look at me and think he run off and left me, and having 'em all wonder…. I can't stand it. I can't stand it. I can't…."

"You'd rather they'd know he fooled you, when he had another wife?" Dwight sneered.

"Yes! Because he wanted me. How do I know—maybe he wanted me only just because he was lonesome, the way I was. I don't care why! And I won't have folks think he went and left me."

"That," said Dwight, "is a wicked vanity."

"That's the truth. Well, why can't they know the truth?"

"And bring disgrace on us all."

"It's me—it's me—" Lulu's individualism strove against that terrible tribal sense, was shattered by it.

"It's all of us!" Dwight boomed. "It's Di."

"*Di?*" He had Lulu's eyes now.

"Why, it's chiefly on Di's account that I'm talking," said Dwight.

"How would it hurt Di?"

"To have a thing like that in the family? Well, can't you see how it'd hurt her?"

"Would it, Ina? Would it hurt Di?"

"Why, it would shame her—embarrass her—make people wonder what kind of stock she came from—oh, " Ina sobbed, "my pure little girl!"

"Hurt her prospects, of course," said Dwight. "Anybody could see that."

"I s'pose it would," said Lulu.

She clasped her arms tightly, awkwardly, and stepped about the floor, her broken shoes showing beneath her cotton skirt.

"When a family once gets talked about for any reason—" said Ina and shuddered.

"I'm talked about now!"

"But nothing that you could help. If he got tired of you, you couldn't help that." This misstep was Dwight's.

"No," Lulu said, "I couldn't help that. And I couldn't help his other wife, either."

"Bigamy," said Dwight, "that's a crime."

"I've done no crime," said Lulu.

"Bigamy," said Dwight, "disgraces everybody it touches."

"Even Di," Lulu said.

"Lulu," said Dwight, "on Di's account will you promise us to let this thing rest with us three?"

"I s'pose so," said Lulu quietly.

"You will?"

"I s'pose so."

Ina sobbed: "Thank you, thank you, Lulu. This makes up for everything."

Lulu was thinking: "Di has a hard enough time as it is." Aloud she said: "I told Mr. Cornish, but he won't tell."

"I'll see to that," Dwight graciously offered.

"Goodness," Ina said, "so he knows. Well, that settles—" She said no more.

"You'll be happy to think you've done this for us, Lulu," said Dwight.

"I s'pose so," said Lulu.

Ina, pink from her little gust of sobbing, went to her, kissed her, her trim tan tailor suit against Lulu's blue cotton.

"My sweet, self-sacrificing sister," she murmured.

"Oh stop that!" Lulu said.

Dwight took her hand, lying limply in his. "I can now," he said, "overlook the matter of the letter."

Lulu drew back. She put her hair behind her ears, swallowed, and cried out.

"Don't you go around pitying me! I'll have you know I'm glad the whole thing happened!"

Cornish had ordered six new copies of a popular song. He knew that it was popular because it was called so in a Chicago paper. When the six copies arrived with a danseuse on the covers he read the "words," looked wistfully at the symbols which shut him out, and felt well pleased.

"Got up quite attractive," he thought, and fastened the six copies in the window of his music store.

It was not yet nine o'clock of a vivid morning. Cornish had his floor and sidewalk sprinkled, his red and blue plush piano spreads dusted. He sat at a folding table well back in the store, and opened a law book.

For half an hour he read. Then he found himself looking off the page, stabbed by a reflection which always stabbed him anew: Was he really getting anywhere with his law? And where did he really hope to get? Of late when he awoke at night this question had stood by the cot, waiting.

The cot had appeared there in the back of the music-store, behind a dark sateen curtain with too few rings on the wire. How little else was in there, nobody knew. But those passing in the late evening saw the blur of his kerosene lamp behind that curtain and were smitten by a realistic illusion of personal loneliness.

It was behind that curtain that these unreasoning questions usually attacked him, when his giant, wavering shadow had died upon the wall and the faint smell of the extinguished lamp went with him to his bed; or when he waked before any sign of dawn. In the mornings all was cheerful and wonted—the question had not before attacked him among his red and blue plush spreads, his golden oak and ebony cases, of a sunshiny morning.

A step at his door set him flying. He wanted passionately to sell a piano.

"Well!" he cried, when he saw his visitor.

It was Lulu, in her dark red suit and her tilted hat.

"Well!" she also said, and seemed to have no idea of saying anything else. Her excitement was so obscure that he did not discern it.

"You're out early," said he, participating in the village chorus of this bright challenge at this hour.

"Oh, no," said Lulu.

He looked out the window, pretending to be caught by something passing, leaned to see it the better.

"Oh, how'd you get along last night?" he asked, and wondered why he had not thought to say it before.

"All right, thank you," said Lulu.

"Was he—about the letter, you know?"

"Yes," she said, "but that didn't matter. You'll be sure," she added, "not to say anything about what was in the letter?"

"Why, not till you tell me I can," said Cornish, "but won't everybody know now?"

"No," Lulu said.

At this he had no more to say, and feeling his speculation in his eyes, dropped them to a piano scarf from which he began flicking invisible specks.

"I came to tell you good-bye," Lulu said.

"*Good-bye!*"

"Yes. I'm going off—for a while. My satchel's in the bakery—I had my breakfast in the bakery."

"Say!" Cornish cried warmly, "then everything *wasn't* all right last night?"

"As right as it can ever be with me," she told him. "Oh, yes. Dwight forgave me."

"Forgave you!"

She smiled, and trembled.

"Look here," said Cornish, "you come here and sit down and tell me about this."

He led her to the folding table, as the only social spot in that vast area of his, seated her in the one chair, and for himself brought up a piano stool. But after all she told him nothing. She merely took the comfort of his kindly indignation.

"It came out all right," she said only. "But I won't stay there any more. I can't do that."

"Then what are you going to do?"

"In Millton yesterday," she said, "I saw an advertisement in the hotel—they wanted a chambermaid."

"Oh, Miss Bett!" he cried. At that name she flushed. "Why," said Cornish, "you must have been coming from Millton yesterday when I saw you. I noticed Miss Di had her bag—" He stopped, stared.

"You brought her back!" he deduced everything.

"Oh!" said Lulu. "Oh, no—I mean—"

"I heard about the eloping again this morning," he said. "That's just what you did—you brought her back."

"You mustn't tell that! You won't? You won't!"

"No. 'Course not." He mulled it. "You tell me this: Do they know? I mean about your going after her?"

"No."

"You never told!"

"They don't know she went."

"That's a funny thing," he blurted out, "for you not to tell her folks—I mean, right off. Before last night...."

"You don't know them. Dwight'd never let up on that—he'd *joke* her about it after a while."

"But it seems—"

"Ina'd talk about disgracing *her*. They wouldn't know what to do. There's no sense in telling them. They aren't a mother and father," Lulu said.

Cornish was not accustomed to deal with so much reality. But Lulu's reality he could grasp.

"You're a trump anyhow," he affirmed.

"Oh, no," said Lulu modestly.

Yes, she was. He insisted upon it.

"By George," he exclaimed, "you don't find very many *married* women with as good sense as you've got."

At this, just as he was agonising because he had seemed to refer to the truth that she was, after all, not married, at this Lulu laughed in some amusement, and said nothing.

"You've been a jewel in their home all right," said Cornish "I bet they'll miss you if you do go."

"They'll miss my cooking," Lulu said without bitterness.

"They'll miss more than that, I know. I've often watched you there—"

"You have?" It was not so much pleasure as passionate gratitude which lighted her eyes.

"You made the whole place," said Cornish.

"You don't mean just the cooking?"

"No, no. I mean—well, that first night when you played croquet. I felt at home when you came out."

That look of hers, rarely seen, which was no less than a look of loveliness, came now to Lulu's face. After a pause she said: "I never had but one compliment before that wasn't for my cooking." She seemed to feel that she must confess to that one. "He told me I done my hair up nice." She added conscientiously: "That was after I took notice how the ladies in Savannah, Georgia, done up theirs."

"Well, well," said Cornish only.

"Well," said Lulu, "I must be going now. I wanted to say good-bye to you—and there's one or two other places...."

"I hate to have you go," said Cornish, and tried to add something. "I hate to have you go," was all that he could find to add.

Lulu rose. "Oh, well," was all that she could find.

They shook hands, Lulu laughing a little. Cornish followed her to the door. He had begun on "Look here, I wish…" when Lulu said "good-bye," and paused, wishing intensely to know what he would have said. But all that he said was: "Good-bye. I wish you weren't going."

"So do I," said Lulu, and went, still laughing.

Cornish saw her red dress vanish from his door, flash by his window, her head averted. And there settled upon him a depression out of all proportion to the slow depression of his days. This was more—it assailed him, absorbed him.

He stood staring out the window. Some one passed with a greeting of which he was conscious too late to return. He wandered back down the store and his pianos looked back at him like strangers. Down there was the green curtain which screened his home life. He suddenly hated that green curtain. He hated this whole place. For the first time it occurred to him that he hated Warbleton.

He came back to his table, and sat down before his lawbook. But he sat, chin on chest, regarding it. No…no escape that way….

A step at the door and he sprang up. It was Lulu, coming toward him, her face unsmiling but somehow quite lighted. In her hand was a letter.

"See," she said. "At the office was this…."

She thrust in his hand the single sheet. He read:

"… Just wanted you to know you're actually rid of me. I've heard from her, in Brazil. She ran out of money and thought of me, and her lawyer wrote to me…. I've never been any good— Dwight would tell you that if his pride would let him tell the truth once in a while. But there ain't anything in my life makes me feel as bad as this…. I s'pose you couldn't understand and I don't myself…. Only the sixteen years keeping still made me think she was gone sure... but you were so downright good, that's what was the worst... do you see what I want to say..."

Cornish read it all and looked at Lulu. She was grave and in her eyes there was a look of dignity such as he had never seen them wear. Incredible dignity.

"He didn't lie to get rid of me—and she was alive, just as he thought she might be," she said.

"I'm glad," said Cornish.

"Yes," said Lulu. "He isn't quite so bad as Dwight tried to make him out."

It was not of this that Cornish had been thinking.

"Now you're free," he said.

"Oh, that..." said Lulu.

She replaced her letter in its envelope.

"Now I'm really going," she said. "Good-bye for sure this time...."

Her words trailed away. Cornish had laid his hand on her arm.

"Don't say good-bye," he said.

"It's late," she said, "I—"

"Don't you go," said Cornish.

She looked at him mutely.

"Do you think you could possibly stay here with me?"

"Oh!" said Lulu, like no word.

He went on, not looking at her. "I haven't got anything. I guess maybe you've heard something about a little something I'm supposed to inherit. Well, it's only five hundred dollars."

His look searched her face, but she hardly heard what he was saying.

"That little Warden house—it don't cost much—you'd be surprised. Rent, I mean. I can get it now. I went and looked at it the other day, but then I didn't think—" he caught himself on that. "It don't cost near as much as this store. We could furnish up the parlour with pianos—"

He was startled by that "we, " and began again:

"That is, if you could ever think of such a thing as marrying me."

"But," said Lulu. "You *know!* Why, don't the disgrace—"

"What disgrace?" asked Cornish.

"Oh," she said, "you—you—"

"There's only this about that," said he. "Of course, if you loved him very much, then I'd ought not to be talking this way to you. But I didn't think—"

"You didn't think what?"

"That you did care so very much—about him. I don't know why."

She said: "I wanted somebody of my own. That's the reason I done what I done. I know that now."

"I figured that way," said Cornish.

They dismissed it. But now he brought to bear something which he saw that she should know.

"Look here," he said, "I'd ought to tell you. I'm—I'm awful lonesome myself. This is no place to live. And I guess living so is one reason why I want to get married. I want some kind of a home."

He said it as a confession. She accepted it as a reason.

"Of course," she said.

"I ain't never lived what you might say private," said Cornish.

"I've lived too private," Lulu said.

"Then there's another thing." This was harder to tell her. "I—I don't believe I'm ever going to be able to do a thing with law."

"I don't see," said Lulu, "how anybody does."

"I'm not much good in a business way," he owned, with a faint laugh. "Sometimes I think," he drew down his brows, "that I may never be able to make any money."

She said: "Lots of men don't."

"Could you risk it with me?" Cornish asked her. "There's nobody I've seen," he went on gently, "that I like as much as I do you. I—I was engaged to a girl once, but we didn't get along. I guess if you'd be willing to try me, we would get along."

Lulu said: "I thought it was Di that you—"

"Miss Di? Why," said Cornish, "she's a little kid. And," he added, "she's a little liar."

"But I'm going on thirty-four."

"So am I!"

"Isn't there somebody—"

"Look here. Do you like me?"

"Oh, yes!"

"Well enough—"

"It's you I was thinking of," said Lulu. "I'd be all right."

"Then!" Cornish cried, and he kissed her.

"And now," said Dwight, "nobody must mind if I hurry a little wee bit. I've got something on."

He and Ina and Monona were at dinner. Mrs. Bett was in her room. Di was not there.

"Anything about Lulu?" Ina asked.

"Lulu?" Dwight stared. "Why should I have anything to do about Lulu?"

"Well, but, Dwight—we've got to do something."

"As I told you this morning," he observed, "we shall do nothing. Your sister is of age—I don't know about the sound mind, but she is certainly of age. If she chooses to go away, she is free to go where she will."

"Yes, but, Dwight, where has she gone? Where could she go? Where—"

"You are a question-box," said Dwight playfully. "A question-box."

Ina had burned her plump wrist on the oven. She lifted her arm and nursed it.

"I'm certainly going to miss her if she stays away very long," she remarked.

"You should be sufficient unto your little self," said Dwight.

"That's all right," said Ina, "except when you're getting dinner."

"I want some crust coffee," announced Monona firmly.

"You'll have nothing of the sort," said Ina. "Drink your milk."

"As I remarked," Dwight went on, "I'm in a tiny wee bit of a hurry."

"Well, why don't you say what for?" his Ina asked.

She knew that he wanted to be asked, and she was sufficiently willing to play his games, and besides she wanted to know. But she *was* hot.

"I am going," said Dwight, "to take Grandma Gates out in a wheel-chair, for an hour."

"Where did you get a wheel-chair, for mercy sakes?"

"Borrowed it from the railroad company," said Dwight, with the triumph peculiar to the resourceful man. "Why I never did it before, I can't imagine. There that chair's been in the depot ever since I can remember—saw it every time I took the train— and yet I never once thought of grandma."

"My, Dwight," said Ina, "how good you are!"

"Nonsense!" said he.

"Well, you are. Why don't I send her over a baked apple? Monona, you take Grandma Gates a baked apple—no. You shan't go till you drink your milk."

"I don't want it."

"Drink it or mamma won't let you go."

Monona drank it, made a piteous face, took the baked apple, ran.

"The apple isn't very good," said Ina, "but it shows my good will."

"Also," said Dwight, "it teaches Monona a life of thoughtfulness for others."

"That's what I always think," his Ina said.

"Can't you get mother to come out?" Dwight inquired.

"I had so much to do getting dinner onto the table, I didn't try," Ina confessed.

"You didn't have to try," Mrs. Bett's voice sounded. "I was coming when I got rested up."

She entered, looking vaguely about. "I want Lulie," she said, and the corners of her mouth drew down. She ate her dinner cold, appeased in vague areas by such martyrdom. They were still at table when the front door opened.

"Monona hadn't ought to use the front door so common," Mrs. Bett complained.

But it was not Monona. It was Lulu and Cornish.

"Well!" said Dwight, tone curving downward.

"Well!" said Ina, in replica.

"Lulie!" said Mrs. Bett, and left her dinner, and went to her daughter and put her hands upon her.

"We wanted to tell you first," Cornish said. "We've just got married."

"For*ever*more!" said Ina.

"What's this?" Dwight sprang to his feet. "You're joking!" he cried with hope.

"No," Cornish said soberly. "We're married—just now. Methodist parsonage. We've had our dinner," he added hastily.

"Where'd you have it?" Ina demanded, for no known reason.

"The bakery," Cornish replied, and flushed.

"In the dining-room part," Lulu added.

Dwight's sole emotion was his indignation.

"What on earth did you do it for?" he put it to them. "Married in a bakery—"

No, no. They explained it again. Neither of them, they said, wanted the fuss of a wedding.

Dwight recovered himself in a measure. "I'm not surprised, after all," he said. "Lulu usually marries in this way."

Mrs. Bett patted her daughter's arm. "Lulie," she said, "why, Lulie. You ain't been and got married twice, have you? After waitin' so long?"

"Don't be disturbed, Mother Bett," Dwight cried. "She wasn't married that first time, if you remember. No marriage about it!"

Ina's little shriek sounded.

"Dwight!" she cried. "Now everybody'll have to know that. You'll have to tell about Ninian now—and his other wife!"

Standing between her mother and Cornish, an arm of each about her, Lulu looked across at Ina and Dwight, and they all saw in her face a horrified realisation.

"Ina!" she said. "Dwight! You *will* have to tell now, won't you? Why I never thought of that."

At this Dwight sneered, was sneering still as he went to give Grandma Gates her ride in the wheel-chair and as he stooped with patient kindness to tuck her in.

The street door was closed. If Mrs. Bett was peeping through the blind, no one saw her. In the pleasant mid-day light under the maples, Mr. and Mrs. Neil Cornish were hurrying toward the railway station.

Miss Lulu Bett
An American
Comedy of Errors

An Open Letter

August 5, 1921

Dear Miss Gale,

Any foreword that I can write to your play, *Miss Lulu Bett*, must be addressed to you, and others must read it, if at all, over your shoulder. As an artist you are, of course, not interested in definitions, being absorbed rather in always nearer and nearer approximations; but I shall not, on that account, forbear to remark how much your novel, and the play that followed it, have widened the practice of the arts that they represent.

As a matter of fact, if one would understand your novel, one must think of it in terms of dramatic art. It is a commonplace to say that this novel marks a turning point in your art. But perhaps it is not a commonplace to say that if we look back over the road you have traveled we shall find a theater at the crossroads.

Are we then to consider the play in the light of the technique of fiction? By no means! Rather one is filled with wonder that you, an artist heretofore of the more discursive type, should have out-theatred the theater when you come to practice on its narrow stage. If the theater is an art of condensation here is condensation distilled; if of form, here is form refined and simplified; if of discourse, here is discourse summarized to shorthand. We are told that a true play is like a score for an orchestra; that it is a series of expert notes directed to the conductor and his players. Of no play of recent years is this so truly the case as of *Miss Lulu Bett*. Not here are the spacious character analyses, the circumstantial prescriptions of movements from right to left. And yet in what recent play are characters so silhouette-clear, or are actions so genuinely of the fabric of the fable? Let him who thinks your play a "comedy

1 3 1

of words" skip a page or even a speech and see where he finds himself.

As for your two endings,—that is for you to say. Frankly the matter doesn't interest me greatly, for it goes back to the consideration of the drama as a social art, while I, forgetting its dependent state, would prefer to think of it as the product of the free spirit of the writer. I know that I may not so think of a play any more than that you may so write one. But I will not admit that the matter has anything to do with happy versus drab endings, or with the variations in inclination of the curve of Lulu Bett's career. Nor has it anything to do with the relative excellence of this or that. It is concerned entirely with the fact that while as practiced to-day the art of fiction permits to the artist more or less independence in the use of his imagination, in writing a play he can rarely forget that he is working with a collaborator who at the best perplexes him and at the worst strikes terror to his heart.

Granting, as I do, that you may have two endings I see no reason why you should not have half a dozen if you wish and if circumstances require them. All I ask is that one of these be the ending of your choice. If one of these endings be the artist's own I care not what ending he writes in collaboration. The best thing you have done in offering to the reader your two endings is to show him the documents in the case. To this extent you have taken another step toward that declaration of the independence of dramatic authorship that is sorely needed.

For the craftmanship of your play, for the combined burden and opportunity you give to your producer and to the actors (admirably carried in every respect), for the courage of its refusals, not less than of its manifest innovations, I, with thousands of others, well-wishers for the American theater, am profoundly grateful to you.

Thomas H. Dickinson
Milton, Conn.

Foreword

For centuries people in plays have been abnormally distinguished. Theirs has been a peculiar facility for cleverness, virility, or personal charm, which has raised them above the individuals in the audience and made of the theater a place where one goes to experience vicariously the warm glow of uttering an epigram through the mouth of "Lord Goring," the deep satisfaction of romantic relations with a beautiful lady ("Prince Rudolpho" acting as our agent), or the inexpressible relief of having a mortgage lifted through the efforts of young "Tom Cartwright."

If Art is to be held down to one of the many indefinite definitions given to it throughout the ages—that of reflecting life—then the theater has contained but little of Art, for it has been peopled by unnaturally brilliant characters living preposterous lives in a manner so totally removed from life as it is known by the honored members of the public that they have been willing to pay money to witness it as a curiosity.

Especially in its dialogue has the stage clung to an artificiality which even the best of playwrights seem unable to shake off once the blood mounts to their temples and they feel the resiliency of the second act beneath their feet. Statistics could be brought out to prove that, in an average gathering, the proportion of clever conversationalists to dull though voluble talkers is one to three hundred and twenty-four thousand. And yet almost every play contains at least three in a cast of ten whose repartee is unquestionably intended to be classed as "entertaining."

Even the "old-home" talk of our rural dramas, the line, "Land sakes, ain't them pies done yet?" with which the first act opens, has become, in spite of its affectation of naturalness, so theatrical that whenever we hear a genuine housewife say it in a real kitchen we suspect her of trying to talk like an actress.

Into this babel of artificial dialogue came *Miss Lulu Bett* bearing the revolutionary banner of banality. And under this banner march ninety-nine one-hundredths of American conversationalists. First in her book, and then in her play, Zona Gale discarded the ideal held by writers since Plutarch that their characters must say something unusual, and gave us "Dwight Herbert Deacon" to say the gorgeously conventional thing with epoch-making dullness.

"The baked potato contains more nourishment than potatoes prepared any other way. Roasting retains it," he asserts in the first act.

To which his wife replies: "That's what I always think."

And the white light of truth which bursts forth from this conversational sally discovers Oscar Wilde to be a shining collection of tinsel.

Zona Gale is the first author, to my knowledge, who has dared to write genuinely dull dialogue. Many writers have achieved dull dialogue under a misapprehension on their parts, and still others have started out with the honest intention of making their characters dull in the interests of veracity. But these latter have sooner or later succumbed to the temptation either of enlarging upon the dullness until it became burlesque or of capitulating entirely and throwing in a clever line simply to keep up the tone of the play.

But Miss Gale saw the truth and has kept it whole. She was depicting uninspired American family life (almost for the first time in our literature) and she held fast to the ideals of American family conversation. In the opening scene of the first act of *Miss Lulu Bett* there is not a single redeeming feature in the remarks made by the Deacon family across the creamed salmon. It is nothing short of magnificent.

"Dwight Herbert" is, of course, the high priest of this elaborate banality, and in his creation Miss Gale has given to America a man made in its own image, something rarely done on our native stage. And, as if this were not enough, she has also brought, whining and scuffling before the footlights, our first normal stage-child, in the unpleasing person of the recalcitrant "Monona." For years we have seen no small children on the stage who did not spend their time coming downstairs in their nighties to reunite uncongenial parents or bringing tears to the hard eyes of adventuresses by telling them that they looked "des like muvver." It was with the full force of an original dramatic creation therefore that "Monona Deacon," the world's most disagreeable stage-child, came swimming petulantly into our ken. She and her disillusioned "Grandma Bett" (a character somewhat more generic as acted but no less vivid), with their joint and articulate hatred of the rest of the family, constitute a refreshing rearrangement of the hitherto idyllic characters of Childhood and Old Age.

In the interests of truth, then, Miss Gale has violated many sacred dramatic rules. She has given us characters who talk as people really talk and who therefore are dull. She has given us an old lady who is not sweet, and a child who is not cute. And, on the technical side, she has begun two successive scenes with practically the same dialogue, so that for several minutes one is scarcely distinct from the other. And in this last deviation from established custom she has at one stroke succeeded in creating an atmosphere of monotony and domestic routine in home life which stands unique among theatrical effects.

The result of such adherence to uninspiring reality might well have been expected to be a failure in its appeal to an uninspiring nation of theater-goers. But Miss Gale took the chance. She wrote the play, as she had written the book, without compromise, and was rewarded by an enthusiastic public.

Robert C. Benchley

The Cast

As produced and staged by Mr. Brock Pemberton beginning December 27, 1920, at the Belmont Theatre, New York.

Monona Deacon.....................Lois Shore
Dwight Herbert Deacon........William Holden
Ina Deacon...........................Catherine Calhoun Doucet
Lulu Bett.............................Carroll McComas
Bobby Larkin.........................Jack Bohn
Mrs. Bett.............................Louis Closser Hale
Diana Deacon ....Beth Varden
Neil Cornish.........................Willard Robertson
Ninian Deacon ....Brigham Royce

Time: .... The Present

Place: .... The Middle Class

Act I.
 Scene 1. The Deacon's dining-room.
 Scene 2. The same; ten days later.

Act II.
 Scene 1. The Deacon's front porch; a month later.
 Scene 2. The same; the following evening.
 Scene 3. The same; a fortnight later.

Act III (2nd version). The Deacon's front porch. A
 morning later.
Act III (1st version). Cornish's music store; the following
 morning.

Between the scenes in Acts I and II the curtain will be lowered a half a minute to indicate the lapse of time.

Act I

Scene i

The Deacon dining room: Plain rose paper, oak sideboard, straight chairs, a soft old brown divan, table laid for supper. Large pictures of, say, "Paul and Virginia" and Abbott Thayer's "Motherhood." A door left leads to kitchen; a door right front leads to the passage and the "other" room. Back are two windows with lace curtains, revealing shrubbery or blossoming plants; and a shelf with a clock and a photograph of Ninian Deacon. Over the table is a gas burner in a glass globe. In the center of the table is a pink tulip in a pot. The stage is empty.

[*Enter* **Monona.** *She tiptoes to the table, tastes a dish or two, hides a cooky in her frock; begins a terrible little chant on miscellaneous notes.*]

[*Enter* **Dwight Deacon.**]

Dwight
What! You don't mean you're in time for supper, baby?

Monona
I ain't a baby.

Dwight
Ain't. Ain't. Ain't.

Monona
Well, I ain't.

Dwight
We shall have to take you in hand, mama and I. We shall-have-to-take-you in hand.

Monona

I ain't such a bad girl.

Dwight

Ain't. Ain't. Ain't.

[*Enter* **Ina**, *Door R. E.*]

Ina

Dwightie! Have I kept you waiting?

Dwight

It's all right, my pet. Bear and forbear. Bear and forbear.

Ina

Everything's on the table. I didn't hear Lulu call us, though. She's fearfully careless. And Dwight, she looks so bad—when there's company I hate to have her around.

[*They seat themselves.*]

Dwight

My dear Ina, your sister is very different from you.

Ina

Well, Lulu certainly is a trial. Come Monona.

Dwight

Live and let live, my dear. We have to overlook, you know. What have we on the festive board to-night?

Ina

We have creamed salmon. On toast.

Monona

I don't want any.

Dwight

What's this? *No* salmon?

Monona

No.

Ina

Oh now, pet! You liked it before.

Monona

I don't want any.

Dwight

Just a little? A very little? What is this? Progeny will not eat?

Ina

She can eat if she will eat. The trouble is, she will *not* take the time.

Dwight

She don't put her mind on her meals.

Ina

Now, pettie, you must eat or you'll get sick.

Monona

I don't want any.

Ina

Well, pettie—then how would you like a nice egg?

Monona

No.

Ina

Some bread and milk?

Monona

No.

[*Enter* **Lulu Bett.** *She carries a plate of muffins.*]

Ina

Lulu, Monona won't eat a thing. I should think you might think of something to fix for her.

Lulu

Can't I make her a little milk toast?

Monona

Yes!

Ina

Well now, sister. Don't toast it too much. That last was too— and it's no use, she will *not* eat it if it's burned.

Lulu

I won't burn it on purpose.

Ina

Well, see that you don't… Lulu! Which milk are you going to take?

Lulu

The bottle that sets in front, won't I?

Ina

But that's yesterday's milk. No, take the fresh bottle from over back. Monona must be nourished.

Lulu

But then the yesterday's'll sour and I can't make a custard pie—

Dwight

Kindly settle these domestic matters without bringing them to my attention at meal time.

[*Observes the tulip.*]

Flowers! Who's been having flowers sent in?

Ina

Ask Lulu.

Dwight

Suitors?

Lulu

It was a quarter. There'll be five flowers.

Dwight

You bought it?

Lulu

Yes. Five flowers. That's a nickel apiece.

Dwight

Yet we give you a home on the supposition that you have no money to spend, even for the necessities.

Ina

Well, but Dwightie. Lulu isn't strong enough to work. What's the use—

Dwight

The justice business and the dental profession do not warrant the purchase of spring flowers in my home.

Ina

Well, but Dwightie—

Dwight

No more. Lulu meant no harm.

Ina

The back bottle, Lulu. And be as quick as you can. Remember, the back bottle. She has a terrible will, hangs on to her own ideas, and hangs on—

[*Exit* **Lulu.**]

Dwight

Forbearance my pet, forbearance. Baked potatoes. That's good—
that's good. The baked potato contains more nourishment than
potatoes prepared in any other way. Roasting retains it.

Ina

That's what I always think.

Dwight

Where's your mother? Isn't she coming to supper?

Ina

No. Tantrim.

Dwight

Oh ho, mama has a tantrim, eh? My dear Ina, your mother is
getting old. She don't have as many clear-headed days as she did.

Ina

Mama's mind is just as good as it ever was, sometimes.

Dwight

Hadn't I better call her up?

Ina

You know how mama is.

[*Enter* **Lulu**. *She takes flowerpot from table and throws it out the
window. Exit* **Lulu**.]

Dwight

I'd better see.

[*Goes to door and opens it.*]

Mother Bett!… Come and have some supper. Looks to
me Lulu's muffins'd go down pretty easy! Come on—I had
something funny to tell you and Ina….

[*Returns.*]

No use. She's got a tall one on to-night, evidently. What's the matter with her?

Ina

Well, I told Lulu to put the creamed salmon on the new blue platter, and mama thought I ought to use the old deep dish.

Dwight

You reminded her that you are mistress here in your own home? But gently, I hope?

Ina

Well—I reminded her. She said if I kept on using the best dishes I wouldn't have a cup left for my own wake.

Dwight

And my little puss insisted?

Ina

Why of course. I wanted to have the table look nice for you, didn't I?

Dwight

My precious pussy.

Ina

So then she walked off to her room.

[**Monona** *sings her terrible little chant.*]

Quiet, pettie, quiet!

Dwight

Softly, softly, *softly*, SOFTLY!… Well, here we are, aren't we? I tell you people don't know what living is if they don't belong in a little family circle.

Ina

That's what I always think.

Dwight

Just coming home here and sort of settling down—it's worth more than a tonic at a dollar the bottle. Look at this room. See this table. Could anything be pleasanter?

Ina

Monona! Now, it's all over both ruffles. And mama does try so hard....

Dwight

My dear. Can't you put your mind on the occasion?

Ina

Well, but Monona *is* so messy.

Dwight

Women cannot generalize.

[*Clock strikes half hour.*]

Curious how that clock loses. It must be fully quarter to. It is quarter to! I'm pretty good at guessing time.

Ina

I've often noticed that.

Dwight

That clock is a terrible trial. Last night it was only twenty-three after when the half hour struck.

Ina

Twenty-one I thought.

Dwight

Twenty-three. My dear Ina, didn't I particularly notice. It was twenty-three.

Monona

[*Like lightning.*]

I want my milk toast, I want my milk toast, I want my milk toast.

Ina

Do hurry, sister. She's going to get nervous.

[**Monona** *chants her chant. Enter* **Lulu**.]

Lulu

I've got the toast here.

Ina

Did you burn it?

Lulu

Not black.

Dwight

There we are. Milk toast like a ku-ween. Where is our young lady daughter to-night?

Ina

She's at Jenny Plows, at a teaparty.

Dwight

Oh ho, teaparty, is it?

Lulu

We told you that this noon.

Dwight

[*Frowning at* **Lulu**.]

How much is salmon the can now, Ina?

Ina

How much is it, Lulu?

Lulu

The large ones are forty, that used to be twenty-five. And the small ones that were ten, they're twenty-five. The butter's about all gone. Shall I wait for the butter woman or get some creamery?

Dwight

Not at meal time, if you please, Lulu. The conversation at my table must not deal with domestic matters.

Lulu

I suppose salmon made me think of butter.

Dwight

There is not the remotest connection. Salmon comes from a river. Butter comes from a cow. A cow bears no relation to a river. A cow may drink from a river, she may do that, but I doubt if that was in your mind when you spoke—you're not that subtle.

Lulu

No, that wasn't in my mind.

[*Enter* **Mother Bett**.]

Dwight

Well, Mama Bett, hungry now?

Mrs. Bett

No, I'm not hungry.

Ina

We put a potato in the oven for you, mama.

Mrs. Bett

No, I thank you.

Dwight

And a muffin, Mama Bett.

Mrs. Bett

No, I thank you.

Lulu

Mama, can't I fix you some fresh tea?

Mrs. Bett

That's right, Lulie. You're a good girl. And see that you put in enough tea so as a body can taste tea part of the way down.

Ina

Sit here with us, mama.

Mrs. Bett

No, I thank you. I'll stand and keep my figger.

Dwight

You know you look like a queen when you stand up, straight back, high head, a regular wonder for your years, you are.

Mrs. Bett

Sometimes I think you try to flatter me.

[*Sits.*]

[*Doorbell.*]

Monona

I'll go. I'll go. Let me go.

Dwight

Now what can anybody be thinking of to call just at meal time. Can't I even have a quiet supper with my family without the outside world clamoring?

Lulu

Maybe that's the butter woman.

Dwight

Lulu, no more about the butter, please.

Monona

Come on in. Here's Bobby to see you, papa, let's feed him.

Dwight

Oh ho! So I'm the favored one. Then draw up to the festive board, Robert. A baked potato?

Bobby

No, sir. I—I wanted something else.

Dwight

What's this? Came to see the justice about getting married, did you? Or the dentist to have your tooth pulled—eh? Same thing—eh, Ina? Ha! ha! ha!

Bobby

I—I wondered whether—I thought if you would give me job....

Dwight

So that's it.

Bobby

I thought maybe I might cut the grass or cut—cut something.

Dwight

My boy, every man should cut his own grass. Every man should come home at night, throw off his coat and, in his vigor, cut his own grass.

Bobby

Yes, sir.

Dwight

Exercise, exercise is next to bread—next to gluten. Hold on, though—hold on. After dental hours I want to begin presently to work my garden. I have two lots. Property is a burden. Suppose you cut the grass on the one lot through the spring.

Bobby

Good enough, sir. Can I start right in now? It isn't dark yet.

Dwight

That's right, that's right. Energy—it's the driving power of the nation.

[*They rise,* **Dwight** *goes toward the door with* **Bobby.**]

Start right in, by all means. You'll find the mower in the shed, oiled and ready. Tools always ready—that's my motto, my boy.

[*Enter* **Di** *and* **Cornish**. **Cornish** *carries many favors.*]

Ah ha!

Di

Where is everybody? Oh, hullo, Bobby! You came to see me?

Bobby

Oh, hullo! No. I came to see your father.

Di

Did you? Well, there he is. Look at him.

Bobby

You don't need to tell me where to look or what to do. Good-by. I'll find the mower, Mr. Deacon.

[*Exit.*]

Dwight

Mama! What do you s'pose? Di thought she had a beau—How are you, Cornish?

Di

Oh, papa! Why, I just hate Bobby Larkin, and the whole school knows it. Mama, wasn't Mr. Cornish nice to help carry my favors?

Ina
Ah, Mr. Cornish! You see what a popular little girl we have.

Cornish
Yes, I suppose so. That is—isn't that remarkable, Mrs. Deacon?

[*He tries to greet* **Lulu***, who is clearing the table.*]

Di
Oh, papa, the sweetest party—and the dearest supper and the darlingest decorations and the georgeousest—Monona, let go of me!

Dwight
Children, children, can't we have peace in this house?

Monona
Ah, you'll catch it for talking so smarty.

Di
Oh, will I?

Ina
Monona, don't stand listening to older people. Run around and play.

[**Monona** *runs a swift circle and returns to her attitude of listener.*]

Cornish
Pardon me—this is Miss Bett, isn't it?

Lulu
I—Lulu Bett, yes.

Cornish
I had the pleasure of meeting you the night I was here for supper.

Lulu
I didn't think you'd remember.

Cornish

Don't you think I'd remember that meat pie?

Lulu

Oh, yes. The meat pie. You might remember the meat pie.

[*Exit, carrying plates.*]

Cornish

What in the dickens did I say that for?

Ina

Oh, Lulu likes it. She's a wonderful cook. I don't know what we should do without her.

Dwight

A most exemplary woman is Lulu.

Ina

That's eggsemplary, Dwightie.

Dwight

My darling little dictionary.

Di

Mama, Mr. Cornish and I have promised to go back to help Jenny.

Ina

How nice! And Mr. Cornish, do let us see you oftener.

Dwight

Yes, yes, Cornish. Drop in. Any time, you know.

Cornish

I'll be glad to come. I do get pretty lonesome evenings.

[*Enter **Lulu**, clearing table.*]

I eat out around. I guess that's why your cooking made such an impression on me, Miss Lulu.

Lulu

Yes. Yes. I s'pose it would take something like that….

Cornish

Oh, no, no! I didn't mean—you mustn't think I meant—What'd I say that for?

Lulu

Don't mind. They always say that to me.

[*Exit with dishes.*]

Di

Come on, Mr. Cornish. Jenny'll be waiting. Monona, let *go* of me!

Monona

I don't want you!

Dwight

Early, darling, early! Get her back here early, Mr. Cornish.

Cornish

Oh, I'll have her back here as soon as ever she'll come—well, ah—I mean….

Di

Good-by Dwight and Ina!

[*Exit **Di** and **Cornish**.*]

Dwight

Nice fellow, nice fellow. Don't know whether he'll make a go of his piano store, but he's studying law evenings.

Ina

But we don't know anything about him, Dwight. A stranger so.

Dwight

On the contrary I know a great deal about him. I know that he has a little inheritance coming to him.

Ina

An inheritance—really? I *thought* he was from a good family.

Dwight

My mercenary little pussy.

Ina

Well, if he comes here so very much you know what we may expect.

Dwight

What may we expect?

Ina

He'll fall in love with Di. And a young girl is awfully flattered when a good-looking older man pays her attention. Haven't you noticed that?

Dwight

How women generalize! My dear Ina, I have other matters to notice.

Ina

Monona. Stop listening! Run about and play.

[**Monona** *runs her circle and returns.*]

Well, look at that clock. It's almost your bedtime, anyway.

[*Enter* **Lulu**.]

Monona

No.

Ina

It certainly is.

Monona
That clock's wrong. Papa said so.

Ina
Mama says bedtime. In ten minutes.

Monona
I won't go all night.

Dwight
Daughter, daughter, daughter….

Monona
I won't go for a week.

[**Dwight** *sees on clock shelf a letter.*]

Ina
Oh, Dwight! It came this morning. I forgot.

Lulu
I forgot too. And I laid it up there.

Dwight
Isn't it understood that my mail can't wait like this?

Lulu
I know. I'm sorry. But you hardly ever get a letter.

Dwight
Of course pressing matters go to my office. Still my mail should have more careful—

[*He reads.*]

Now! What do you think I have to tell you?

Ina
Oh, Dwightie! Something nice?

Dwight

That depends. I'll like it. So'll Lulu. It's company.

Monona

I hope they bring me something decent.

Ina

Oh, Dwight, who?

Dwight

My brother, from Oregon.

Ina

Ninian coming here?

Dwight

Some day next week. He don't know what a charmer Lulu is or he'd come quicker.

Ina

Dwight, it's been years since you've seen him.

Dwight

Nineteen—twenty. Must be twenty.

Ina

And he's never seen me.

Dwight

Nor Lulu.

Ina

And think where he's been. South America—Mexico—Panama and all. We must put it in the paper.

Mrs. Bett

Who's coming? Why don't you say who's coming? You all act so dumb.

Lulu

It's Dwight's brother, mother. His brother from Oregon.

Mrs. Bett

Never heard of him.

Lulu

[*Taking photograph from shelf.*]
That one, mother. You've dusted his picture lots of times.

Mrs. Bett

That? Got to have him around long?

Dwight

I don't know. Wait till he sees Lulu. I expect when he sees Lulu you can't drive him away. He's going to take one look at Lulu and settle down here for life. He's going to think Lulu is—

Lulu

I—think the tea must be steeped now.

[*Exit.*]

Dwight

He's going to think Lulu is a stunner—a stunner....

[*The clock strikes.* **Monona** *shrieks.*]

Is the progeny hurt?

Ina

Bedtime. Now, Monona, be mama's nice little lady.... Monona, quiet, pettie, quiet....

[**Lulu** *enters with tea and toast.*]

Lulu, won't you take her to bed? You know Dwight and I are going to Study Club.

Lulu

There, mother. Yes. I'll take her to bed. Come, Monona. And stop that noise instantly.

[**Monona** *stops. As they cross* **Dwight** *spies the tulip on Lulu's gown.*]

Dwight

Lulu. One moment. You *picked* the flower on the plant?

Lulu

Yes. I—picked it.

Dwight

She buys a hothouse plant and then ruins it!

Lulu

I—I—

[*She draws* **Monona** *swiftly left; exeunt; the door slams.*]

Dwight

What a pity Lulu hasn't your manners, pettie.

Mrs. Bett

What do you care? She's got yours.

Dwight

Mother Bett! Fare thee well.

Mrs. Bett

How do you stand him? The lump!

Ina

Mama dear, now drink your tea. Good-night, sweetie.

Mrs. Bett

You needn't think I forgot about the platter, because I ain't. Of all the extravagant doin's, courtin' the poorhouse—

[*Exeunt* **Dwight** *and* **Ina.** **Mrs. Bett** *continues to look after them, her lips moving. At door appears* **Bobby.**]

Bobby

Where's Mr. Deacon?

Mrs. Bett

Gone, thank the Lord!

Bobby

I've got the grass cut.

Mrs. Bett

You act like it was a trick.

Bobby

Is—is everybody gone?

Mrs. Bett

Who's this you're talkin' to?

Bobby

Yes, well, I meant—I guess I'll go now.

[*Enter* **Di**.]

Di

Well, Bobby Larkin. Are you cutting grass in the dining room?

Bobby

No, ma'am, I was not cutting grass in the dining room.

[*Enter* **Lulu**, *collects her mother's dishes, folds cloth and watches.*]

Di

I used to think you were pretty nice, but I don't like you any more.

Bobby

Yes you used to! Is that why you made fun of me all the time?

Di

I had to. They all were teasing me about you.

Bobby

They were? Teasing you about me?

Di

I had to make them stop so I teased you. I never wanted to.

Bobby

Well, I never thought it was anything like that.

Di

Of course you didn't. I—wanted to tell you.

Bobby

You wanted—

Di

Of course I did. You must go now—they're hearing us.

Bobby

Say—

Di

Good-night. Go the back way, Bobby—you nice thing.

[*Exit* **Bobby**.]

Aunt Lulu, give me the cookies, please, and the apples. Mr. Cornish is on the front porch… mama and papa won't be home till late, will they?

Lulu

I don't think so.

Di

Well, I'll see to the hall light. Don't you bother. Good-night.

Lulu

Good-night, Di.

[*Exit* **Di**.]

Mrs. Bett

My land! How she wiggles and chitters.

Lulu

Mother, could you hear them? Di and Bobby Larkin?

Mrs. Bett

Mother hears a-plenty.

Lulu

How easy she done it... got him right over... how did she do
that?

Mrs. Bett

Di wiggles and chitters.

Lulu

It was just the other day I taught her to sew... I wonder if Ina
knows.

Mrs. Bett

What's the use of you findin' fault with Inie? Where'd you been
if she hadn't married I'd like to know?... What say?... eh?... I'm
goin' to bed.... You always was jealous of Inie.

[*Exit* **Mrs. Bett**.]

[**Lulu** *crosses to shelf, takes down photograph of Ninian Deacon,
holds it, looks at it.*]

Curtain

Scene ii

*Same set. Late afternoon. A week later. The table is cleared of
dishes, and has an oilcloth cover.* **Bobby** *is discovered outside the
window, on whose sill* **Di** *is sitting.*

Bobby

So you despise me for cutting grass?

Di

No, I don't. But if you're going to be a great man why don't you get started at it?

Bobby

I am started at it—inside. But it don't earn me a cent yet.

Di

Bobby, Bobby! I know you're great now, don't you ever think I don't, but I want everybody else to know.

Bobby

Di, when you said that it sounded just like a—a you know.

Di

Like what?

Bobby

Like a wife. Gee, what a word that is!

Di

Isn't it? It's ever so much more exciting word than husband.

[*Enter* **Lulu**, *followed by* **Monona**. **Lulu** *carries bowl, pan of apples, paring knife.* **Monona** *carries basket of apples and a towel. As* **Lulu** *rattles dishes,* **Di** *turns, sees* **Lulu**. **Bobby** *disappears from window.*]

Di

There's never any privacy in this house.

[*Exit* **Di**.]

Lulu

Hurry, Monona, I must make the pies before I get dinner. Now wipe every one.

Monona

What for?

Lulu

To make the pies.

Monona

What do you want to make pies for?

Lulu

To eat.

Monona

What do you want to eat for?

Lulu

To grow strong—and even sensible.

Monona

It's no fun asking you a string of questions. You never get mad. Mama gets good and mad. So does papa.

Lulu

Then why do you ask them questions?

Monona

Oh, I like to get them going.

Lulu

Monona!

Monona

I told mama I didn't pass, just so I could hear her.

Lulu

Why, Monona!

Monona

Then when I told her I did pass, she did it again. When she's mad she makes awful funny faces.

Lulu

You love her, don't you, Monona?

Monona

I love her best when there's company. If there was always company, I'd always love her. Isn't she sweet before Uncle Ninian though?

Lulu

I—I don't know. Monona, you mustn't talk so.

Monona

He's been here a week and mama hasn't been cross once. Want to know what he said about you?

Lulu

I—did he—did he say anything about me?

Monona

He told papa you were the best cook he'd ever ate. Said he'd et a good many.

Lulu

The cooking. It's always the cooking.

Monona

He said some more, but I can't remember.

Lulu

Monona, what else did he say?

Monona

I don't know.

Lulu

Try....

Monona

Here he is now. Ask him to his face. Hullo, Uncle Ninian! Good-by.

[*Exit* **Monona**. *Enter* **Ninian**.]

Ninian

Hello, kitten! Ask him what? What do you want to ask him?

Lulu

I—I think I was wondering what kind of pies you like best.

Ninian

That's easy. I think your kind of pies best. The best ever. Every day since I've been here I've seen you baking, Mrs. Bett.

Lulu

Yes, I—bake. What did you call me then?

Ninian

Mrs. Bett—isn't it? Every one says just Lulu, but I took it for granted…. Well, now—is it Mrs.? or Miss Lulu Bett?

Lulu

It's Miss…. From choice.

Ninian

You bet! Oh, you bet! Never doubted that.

Lulu

What kind of a Mr. are you?

Ninian

Never give myself away. Say, by George, I never thought of that before. There's no telling whether a man's married or not, by his name.

Lulu

It doesn't matter.

Ninian

Why?

Lulu

Not so many people want to know.

Ninian

Say, you're pretty good, aren't you?

Lulu

If I am it never took me very far.

Ninian

Where you been mostly?

Lulu

Here. I've always been here. Fifteen years with Ina. Before that we lived in the country.

Ninian

Never been anywhere much?

Lulu

Never been anywhere at all.

Ninian

H... m. Well, I want to tell you something about yourself.

Lulu

About me?

Ninian

Something that I'll bet you don't even know. It's this: I think you have it pretty hard around here.

Lulu

Oh, no!

Ninian

See here. Do you have to work like this all the time? I guess you won't mind my asking.

Lulu

But I ought to work. I have a home with them. Mother too.

Ninian

But glory! You ought to have some kind of a life of your own.

Lulu

How could I do that?

Ninian

A man don't even know what he's like till he's roamed around
on his own…. Roamed around on his own. Course a woman
don't understand that.

Lulu

Why don't she? Why don't she?

Ninian

Do you?

[**Lulu** *nods.*]

I've had twenty-five years of galloping about—Brazil, Mexico,
Panama.

Lulu

My!

Ninian

It's the life.

Lulu

Must be. I—

Ninian

Yes, you. Why, you've never had a thing! I guess you don't know
how it seems to me, coming along—a stranger so. I don't like it.

Lulu

They're very good to me.

Ninian

Do you know why you think that? Because you've never had
anybody really good to you. That's why.

Lulu

But they treat me good.

Ninian

They make a slavey of you. Regular slavey. Damned shame *I* call it.

Lulu

But we have our whole living—

Ninian

And you earn it. I been watching you ever since I've been here. Don't you ever go anywhere?

Lulu

Oh, no, I don't go anywhere. I—

Ninian

Lord! Don't you want to? Of course you do.

Lulu

Of course I'd like to get clear away—or I used to want to.

Ninian

Say—you've been a blamed fine-looking woman.

Lulu

You must have been a good-looking man once yourself.

Ninian

You're pretty good. I don't see how you do it—darned if I do.

Lulu

How I do what?

Ninian

Why come back, quick like that, with what you say. You don't look it.

Lulu

It must be my grand education.

Ninian

Education: I ain't never had it and I ain't never missed it.

Lulu

Most folks are happy without an education.

Ninian

You're not very happy, though.

Lulu

Oh, no.

Ninian

Well you ought to get up and get out of here—find—find some work you *like* to do.

Lulu

But, you see, I can't do any other work—that's the trouble— women like me can't do any other work.

Ninian

But you make this whole house go round.

Lulu

If I do, nobody knows it.

Ninian

I know it. I hadn't been in the house twenty-four hours till I knew it.

Lulu

You did? You thought that.... Yes, well if I do I hate making it go round.

Ninian

See here—couldn't you tell me a little bit about—what you'd *like* to do? If you had your own way?

Lulu

I don't know—now.

Ninian

What did you ever think you'd like to do?

Lulu

Take care of folks that needed me. I—I mean sick folks or old folks or—like that. Take *care* of them. Have them—have them want me.

Ninian

By George! You're a wonder.

Lulu

Am I? Ask Dwight.

Ninian

Dwight. I could knock the top of his head off the way he speaks to you. I'd like to see you get out of this, I certainly would.

Lulu

I can't get out. I'll never get out—now.

Ninian

Don't keep saying "now" like that. You—you put me out of business, darned if you don't.

Lulu

Oh, I don't mean to feel sorry for myself—you stop making me feel sorry for myself!

Ninian

I know one thing—I'm going to give Dwight Deacon a chunk of my mind.

Lulu

Oh, no! no! no! I wouldn't want you to do that. Thank you.

Ninian

Well, somebody ought to do something. See here—while I'm staying around you know you've got a friend in me, don't you?

Lulu

Do I?

Ninian

You bet you do.

Lulu

Not just my cooking?

Ninian

Oh, come now—why, I think'd you the first moment I saw you.

Lulu

Honest?

Ninian

Go on—go on. Did you like me?

Lulu

Now you're just being polite.

Ninian

Say, I wish there was some way—

Lulu

Don't you bother about me.

Ninian

I wish there was some way—

[**Monona**'s *voice chants.*]

[*Enter* **Monona**.]

Monona

You've had him long enough, Aunt Lulu—Can't you pay me some 'tention?

Ninian

Come here. Give us a kiss. My stars, what a great big tall girl! Have to put a board on her head to stop this growing.

Monona

[*Seeing diamond.*]
What's that?

Ninian

That diamond came from Santa Claus. He has a jewelry shop in
heaven. I have twenty others like this one. I keep the others to
wear on the Sundays when the sun comes up in the west.

Monona

Does the sun ever come up in the west?

Ninian

Sure—on my honor. Some day I'm going to melt a diamond
and eat it. Then you sparkle all over in the dark, ever after.
I'm going to plant one too, some day. Then you can grow a
diamond vine. Yes, on my honor.

Lulu

Don't do that—don't do that.

Ninian

What?

Lulu

To her. That's lying.

Ninian

Oh, no. That's not lying. That's just drama. Drama. Do you like
going to a good show?

Lulu

I've never been to any—only those that come here.

Ninian

Think of that now. Don't you ever go to the city?

Lulu

I haven't been in six years and over.

Ninian

Well, sir, I'll tell you what I'm going to do with you. While I'm
here I'm going to take you and Ina and Dwight up to the city,
to see a show.

Lulu

Oh, you don't want me to go.

Ninian

Yes, sir, I'll give you one good time. Dinner and a show.

Lulu

Ina and Dwight do that sometimes. I can't imagine me.

Ninian

Well, you're coming with me. I'll look up something good. And
you tell me just what you like to eat and we'll order it—

Lulu

It's been years since I've eaten anything that I haven't cooked
myself.

Ninian

It has. Say, by George! why shouldn't we go to the city *to-night*.

Lulu

To-night?

Ninian

Yes. If Dwight and Ina will. It's early yet. What do you say?

Lulu

You sure you want me to go? Why—I don't know whether I've
got anything I could wear.

Ninian

Sure you have.

Lulu

I—yes, I have. I could wear the waist I always thought they'd
use—if I died.

Ninian

Sure you could wear that. Just the thing. And throw some
things in a bag—it'll be too late to come back to-night. Now
don't you back out....

Lulu

Oh, the pies—

Ninian

Forget the pies—well, no, I wouldn't say that. But hustle them
up.

Lulu

Oh, maybe Ina won't go....

Ninian

Leave Ina to me.

[*Exit* **Ninian**.]

Lulu

Mother, mother! Monona, put the rest of those apples back in
the basket and carry them out.

Monona

Yes, Aunt Lulu.

Lulu

I can't get ready. They'll leave me behind. Mother! Hurry,
Monona. We mustn't leave such a looking house. Mother!
Monona, don't you drop those apples.

[**Monona** *drops them all.*]

My heavens, my pies aren't in the oven yet.

[*Enter* **Mrs. Bett**.]

Mrs. Bett

Who wants their mother?

Lulu

Mother, please pick up these things for me—quick.

Mrs. Bett

[*Leisurely*]

What is the rush, Lulie?

Lulu

Mother, Mr. Deacon—Ninian, you know—wants Ina and Dwight and me to go to the theater to-night in the city.

Mrs. Bett

Does, does he? Well, you mind me, Lulie, and go on. It'll do you good.

Lulu

Yes, mother. I will.

[*Exit with pies.*]

Mrs. Bett

No need breaking everybody's neck off, though, as I know of. Monona, get out from under my feet.

Monona

Grandma, compared between what I am, you are nothing.

Mrs. Bett

What do you mean—little ape?

Monona

It's no fun to get you going. You're too easy, grandma dear!

[*Exit. Enter **Ninian**.*]

Ninian

All right—Dwight and Ina are game. Oh, Mrs. Bett! Won't you come to the theater with us to-night?

Mrs. Bett

No. I'm fooled enough without fooling myself on purpose. But Lulie can go.

Ninian

You don't let her go too much, do you, Mrs. Bett?

Mrs. Bett

Well, I ain't never let her go to the altar if that's what you mean.

Ninian

Don't you think she'd be better off?

Mrs. Bett

Wouldn't make much difference. Why look at me. A husband, six children, four of 'em under the sod with him. And sometimes I feel as though nothin' more had happened to me than has happened to Lulie. It's all gone. For me just the same as for her. Only she ain't had the pain.

[*Yawns.*]

What was I talkin' about just then?

Ninian

Why—why—er, we were talking about going to the theater.

Mrs. Bett

Going to the theater, are you?

[*Enter* **Lulu**.]

Ninian

It's all right, Miss Lulu. They'll go—both of them. Dwight is telephoning for the seats.

Lulu

I was wondering why you should be so kind to me.

Ninian

Kind? Why, this is for my own pleasure, Miss Lulu. That's what
I think of mostly.

Lulu

But just see. It's so wonderful. Half an hour ago I never thought
I'd be going to the city now—with you all....

Ninian

I'm an impulsive cuss you'll find, Miss Lulu.

Lulu

But this is so wonderful....

[*Enter* **Ina**.]

Ina, isn't it beautiful that we're going?

Ina

Oh, are you going?

Ninian

Of course she's going. Great snakes, why not?

Ina

Only that Lulu never goes anywhere.

Ninian

Whose fault is that?

Lulu

Just habit. Pure habit.

Ninian

Pure cussedness somewhere. Miss Lulu, now you go and get
ready and Ina and I'll finish straightening up here.

Lulu

Oh, I'll finish.

Ninian

Go and get ready. I want to see that waist.

Lulu

Oh, but I don't need to go yet—

Ninian

Ina, you tell her to go—

Ina

Well, but Lulu, you aren't going to bother to change your dress, are you? You can slip something on over.

Lulu

If you think this would do—

Ninian

It will not do. Not for my party!

[*Shuts the door upon her.*]

Ina

How in the world did you ever get Lulu to go, Ninian? *We* never did.

Ninian

It was very simple. I invited her.

Ina

Oh, you mean—

Ninian

I invited her.

[*Doorbell rings.*]

Shall I answer it?

Ina

Will you, please?

[*Exit* **Ninian.**]

Mother, have you seen Di anywhere?

Mrs. Bett

I ain't done nothing but see her.

[*Motions to window.*]

Ina

[At window.]
Forevermore. That Larkin boy again. Di! Diana Deacon! Come here at once.

Di's Voice

Yes, mama.

[*At window.*]

Want me?

Ina

I want you to stop making a spectacle of *me* before the neighborhood.

Di

Of *you!*

Ina

Certainly. What will people think of me if they see you talking with Robert Larkin the whole afternoon?

Di

We weren't thinking about you, mummy.

Ina

No. You never do think about me. Nobody thinks about me. And mama does try so hard—

Di

Oh, mama, I've heard you say that fifty hundred times.

Ina

And what impression does it make? None.... Nobody listens to me. Nobody.

[*Enter* **Ninian** *and* **Cornish**.]

Ninian

All right to bring him in here?

Ina

Oh, Mr. Cornish! how very nice to see you.

Cornish

Good afternoon, Mrs. Deacon. How are you, Miss Di?

Ninian

I've just been asking Mr. Cornish if he won't join us to-night for dinner and the show.

Ina

Oh, Mr. Cornish, do—we'd be so glad.

Cornish

Why, why, if that wouldn't be—

Ninian

You're invited, Di, you know.

Di

Me? Oh, how heavenly! Oh, but I've an engagement with Bobby—

Ina

But I'm sure you'd break that to go with Uncle Ninian and Mr. Cornish.

Di

Well, I'd break it to go to the theater—

Ina

Why, Di Deacon!

Di

Oh, of course to go with Uncle Ninian and Mr. Cornish.

Cornish

This is awfully good of you. I dropped in because I got so lonesome I didn't know what else to do—that is, I mean….

Ninian

We get it. We get it.

Ina

We'd love to see you any time, Mr. Cornish. Now if you'll excuse Di and me one minute.

Di

Uncle Ninian, you're a lamb.

[*Exeunt* **Di** *and* **Ina**.]

Mrs. Bett

I'm just about the same as I was.

Cornish

What—er—oh, Mrs. Bett, I didn't see you.

Mrs. Bett

I don't complain. But it wouldn't turn my head if some of you spoke to me once in a while. Say—can you tell me what these folks are up to?

Cornish

Up to… up to?

Mrs. Bett

Yes. They're all stepping round here, up to something. I don't know what.

Ninian

Why, Mrs. Bett, we're going to the city to the theater, you know.

Mrs. Bett

Well, why didn't you say so?

[*Enter* **Dwight**.]

Dwight

Ha! Everybody ready? Well, well, well, well. How are you, Cornish? You going too, Ina says.

Cornish

Yes, I thought I might as well. I mean—

Dwight

That's right, that's right. Mama Bett. Look here!

Mrs. Bett

What's that?

Dwight

Ice cream—it's *ice* cream. Who is it sits home and has *ice* cream put in her lap like a ku-ween?

Mrs. Bett

Vanilly or chocolate?

Dwight

Chocolate, Mama Bett.

Mrs. Bett

Vanilly sets better…. I'll put it in the ice chest—I may eat it.

[*Takes spoon from sideboard. Exit.* **Cornish** *goes with her.*]

Dwight

Where's the lovely Lulu?

Ninian

She'll be here directly.

Dwight

Now what I want to know, Nin, is how you've hypnotized the
lovely Lulu into this thing.

Ninian

Into going? Dwight, I'll tell you about that. I asked her to go
with us. Do you get it? I invited the woman.

Dwight

Ah, but with a way—with a way. She's never been anywhere like
this with us…. Well, Nin, how does it seem to see me settled
down into a respectable married citizen in my own town—eh?

Ninian

Oh—you seem just like yourself.

Dwight

Yes, yes. I don't change much. Don't feel a day older than I ever
did.

Ninian

And you don't act it.

Dwight

Eh, you wouldn't think it to look at us, but our aunt had her
hands pretty full bringing us up. Nin, we must certainly run up
state and see Aunt Mollie while you're here. She isn't very well.

Ninian

I don't know whether I'll have time or not.

Dwight

Nin, I love that woman. She's an angel. When I think of her I
feel—I give you my word—I feel like somebody else.

[*Enter* **Mrs. Bett** *and* **Cornish**.]

Ninian

Nice old lady.

Mrs. Bett

Who's a nice old lady?

Dwight

You, Mama Bett! Who else but you—eh? Well, now, Nin, what about you. You've been saying mighty little about yourself. What's been happening to you, anyway?—

Ninian

That's the question.

Dwight

Traveling mostly—eh?

Ninian

Yes, traveling mostly.

Dwight

I thought Ina and I might get over to the other side this year, but I guess not—I guess not.

Mrs. Bett

Pity not to have went while the going was good.

Dwight

What's that, Mama Bett?

[*Enter* **Lulu**.]

Ah, the lovely Lulu. She comes, she comes! My word what a costoom. And a coif*fure*.

Lulu

Thank you. How do you do, Mr. Cornish?

Cornish

How do you do, Miss Lulu? You see they're taking me along too.

Lulu

That's nice. But, Mr. Deacon, I'm afraid I can't go after all. I haven't any gloves.

Ninian

No backing out now.

Dwight

Can't you wear some old gloves of Ina's?

Lulu

No, no. Ina's gloves are too fat for me—I mean too—mother, how does this hat look?

Mrs. Bett

You'd ought to know how it looks, Lulie. You've had it on your head for ten years, hand-running.

Lulu

And I haven't any theater cape. I couldn't go with my jacket and no gloves, could I?

Dwight

Now why need a charmer like you care about clothes!

Lulu

I wouldn't want you gentlemen to be ashamed of me.

Cornish

Why, Miss Lulu, you look real neat.

Mrs. Bett

Act as good as you look, Lulie. You mind me and go on.

[*Enter* **Ina**.]

Dwight

Ha! All ready with our hat on! For a wonder, all ready with our hat on.

Ina

That isn't really necessary, Dwight.

Lulu

Ina, I wondered—I thought about your linen duster. Would it hurt if I wore that?

Dwight

The new one?

Lulu

Oh no, no. The old one.

Ina

Why take it, Lulu, yes, certainly. Get it, Dwightie, there in the hall.

[**Dwight** *goes.*]

Cornish

Miss Lulu, with all the solid virtues you've got, you don't need to think for a moment of how you look.

Lulu

Now you're remembering the meat pie again, aren't you?

[*Enter* **Dwight**.]

Dwight

Now! The festive opera cloak. Allow me! My word, what a picture! Lulu the charmer dressed for her deboo into society, eh?

Ninian

Dwight, shut your head. I want you to understand this is Miss Lulu Bett's party—and if she says to leave you home, we'll do it.

Dwight

Ah, ha! An understanding between these two.

Cornish

Well, Miss Lulu, *I* think you're just fine anyway.

Lulu

Oh, thank you. Thank you....

[*Enter* **Di**.]

Ina

All ready, darling?

Di

All ready—and so excited! Isn't it exciting, Mr. Cornish?

Dwight

Bless me if the whole family isn't assembled. Now isn't this pleasant! Ten—let me see—twelve minutes before we need set out. Then the city and dinner—not just Lulu's cooking, but dinner! By a chef.

Ina

That's sheff, Dwightie. Not cheff.

Dwight

[*Indicating* **Ina**.]

Little crusty to-night. Pettie, your hat's just a little mite—no, over the other way.

Ina

Was there anything to prevent your speaking of that before?

Lulu

Ina, that hat's ever so much prettier than the old one.

Ina

I never saw anything the matter with the old one.

Dwight

She'll be all right when we get started—out among the bright lights. Adventure—adventure is what the woman wants. I'm too tame for her.

Ina

Idiot.

[*Back at window,* **Bobby Larkin** *appears.* **Di** *slips across to him.*]

Mrs. Bett

I s'pose you all think I like being left sitting here stark alone?

Ninian

Why, Mrs. Bett—

Ina

Why, mama—

Lulu

Oh, mother, I'll stay with you.

Dwight

Oh, look here, if she really minds staying alone I'll stay with her.

Mrs. Bett

Where you going anyway?

Lulu

The theater, mama.

Mrs. Bett

First I've heard of it.

[**Monona** *is heard chanting.*]

Ina

You'll have Monona with you, mama.

[**Mrs. Bett** *utters one note of laughter, thin and high.*]

[*Enter* **Monona**.]

Monona

Where you going?

Ina

The city, dear.

[**Monona** *cries.*]

Now quiet, pettie, quiet—

Monona

You've all got to bring me something. And I'm going to sit up and eat it, too.

Mrs. Bett

Come here, you poor, neglected child.

[*Throughout the following scene* **Mrs. Bett** *is absorbed with* **Monona**, *and* **Di** *with* **Bobby**.]

Dwight

What's Lulu the charmer so still for, eh?

Lulu

I was thinking how nice it is to be going off with you all like this.

Dwight

Such a moment advertises to the single the joys of family life as Ina and I live it.

Ina

It's curious that you've never married, Ninian.

Ninian

Don't say it like that. Maybe I have. Or maybe I will.

Dwight

She wants everybody to marry but she wishes she hadn't.

Ina

Do you *have* to be so foolish?

Dwight

Hi—better get started before she makes a scene. It's too early yet, though. Well—Lulu, you dance on the table.

Ina

Why, Dwight?

Dwight

Got to amuse ourselves somehow. They'll begin to read the funeral service over us.

Ninian

Why not the wedding service?

Dwight

Ha, ha, ha!

Ninian

I shouldn't object. Should you, Miss Lulu?

Lulu

I—I don't know it so I can't say it.

Ninian

I can say it.

Dwight

Where'd you learn it?

Ninian

Goes like this: I, Ninian, take thee, Lulu, to be my wedded wife.

Dwight

Lulu don't dare say that.

Ninian

Show him, Miss Lulu.

Dwight

I, Lulu, take thee, Ninian, to be my wedded husband.

Ninian

You will?

Lulu

I will. There—I guess I can join in like the rest of you.

Ninian

And I will. There, by Jove! have we entered the company, or haven't we?

Ina

Oh, honestly—I don't think you ought to—holy things so— what's the matter, Dwightie?

Dwight

Say, by George, you know, a civil wedding is binding in this state.

Ninian

A civil wedding—oh, well—

Dwight

But I happen to be a magistrate.

Ina

Why, Dwightie—why, Dwightie....

Cornish

Mr. Deacon, this can't be possible.

Dwight

I tell you, what these two have said is all that they have to say according to law. And there don't have to be witnesses—say!

Lulu

Don't… don't… don't let Dwight scare you.

Ninian

Scare me! why, I think it's a good job done if you ask me.

[*Their eyes meet in silence.*]

Ina

Mercy, sister!

Dwight

Oh, well—I should say we can have it set aside up in the city and no one will be the wiser.

Ninian

Set aside nothing. I'd like to see it stand.

Ina

Ninian, are you serious?

Ninian

Of course I'm serious.

Ina

Lulu. You hear him? What are you going to say to that?

Lulu

He isn't in earnest.

Ninian

I am in earnest—hope to die.

Lulu

Oh, no, no!

Ninian

You come with me. We'll have it done over again somewhere if you say so.

                    Lulu
Why—why—that couldn't be....

                    Ninian
Why couldn't it be—why couldn't it?

                    Lulu
How could you want me?

                    Ninian
Didn't I tell you I liked you from the first minute I saw you?

                    Lulu
Yes. Yes, you did. But—no, no. I couldn't let you—

                    Ninian
Never mind that. Would *you* be willing to go with me? Would
you?

                    Lulu
But you—you said you wanted—oh, maybe you're just doing
this because—

                    Ninian
Lulu. Never mind any of that. Would *you* be willing to go with
me?

                    Lulu
Oh, if I thought—

                    Ninian
Good girl—

                    Ina
Why, Lulu. Why, Dwight. It can't be legal.

                    Dwight
Why? Because it's your sister? I've married dozens of couples this
way. Dozens.

Ninian

Good enough—eh, Lulu?

Lulu

It's—it's all right, I guess.

Dwight

Well, I'll be dished.

Cornish

Well, by Jerusalem....

Ina

Sister!

Ninian

I was going to make a trip south this month on my way home from here. Suppose we make sure of this thing and start right off. You'd like that, wouldn't you? Going to Savannah?

Lulu

Yes, I'd like that.

Ninian

Then that's checked off.

Dwight

I suppose we call off our trip to the city to-night then.

Ninian

Call off nothing. Come along. Give us a send-off. You can shoot our trunks after us, can't you? All right, Miss Lulu—er—er, Mrs. Lulu?

Lulu

If you won't be ashamed of me.

Ninian

I can buy you some things in the city to-morrow.

Lulu

Oh....

Ina

Oh, mama, mama! Did you hear? Di! Aunt Lulu's married.

Di

Married? Aunt Lulu?

Ina

Just now. Right here. By papa.

Di

Oh, to Mr. Cornish?

Cornish

No, Miss Di. Don't you worry.

Ina

To Ninian, mama. They've just been married—Lulu and Ninian.

Mrs. Bett

Who's going to do your work?

Lulu

Oh, mother dearest—I don't know who will. I ought not to have done this. Well, of course, I didn't do it—

Mrs. Bett

I knew well enough you were all keeping something from me.

Ina

But, mama! It was so sudden—

Lulu

I never planned to do it, mother—not like this—

Mrs. Bett

Well, Inie, I should think Lulie might have had a little more consideration to her than this.

[*At the window, behind the curtain,* **Di** *has just kissed* **Bobby** *good-by.*]

Lulu

Mother dearest, tell me it's all right.

Mrs. Bett

This is what comes of going to the theater.

Lulu

Mother—

Dwight

Come on, everybody, if we're going to make that train.

Ninian

Yes. Let's get out of this.

Cornish

Come, Miss Di.

Ina

Oh, I'm so *flustrated!*

Dwight

Come, come, come all! On to the festive city!

Monona

[*Dancing stiffly up and down.*]
I was to a wedding! I was to a wedding!

Ninian

Good-by, Mama Bett!

Lulu

Mother, mother! Don't forget the two pies!

Curtain

Act II

Scene i

Side porch, wicker furnished. At the back are two windows, attractively curtained and revealing shaded lamps; between the windows a door, of good lines, set in white clapboards. The porch is raised but a step or two. Low greenery, and a path leading off sharply left. It is evening, a month after **Lulu**'s *marriage.*

[*Discover* **Ina, Dwight, Mrs. Bett** *and* **Monona.**]

Ina

Dwight dear, the screen has never been put on that back window.

Dwight

Now, why can't my puss remind me of that in the morning instead of the only time I have to take my ease with my family.

Ina

But, Dwight, in the mornings you are so busy——

Dwight

What an argumentative puss you are. By Jove! look at that rambler rosebush. It's got to be sprayed.

Ina

You've said that every night for a week, Dwight....

Dwight

Don't exaggerate like that, Ina. It's bad for Monona.

Ina

Dwight, look, quick. There go our new neighbors. They have a limousine—Perhaps I have been a little slow about calling. Look at them, Dwight!

Dwight

My dear Ina, I see them. Do you want me to pat them on the back?

Ina

Well, I think you might be interested.

[**Monona** *chants softly.*]

Dwight, I wonder if Monona really has a musical gift.

Dwight

She's a most unusual child. Do you know it?

[*Enter* **Di**, *from house.*]

Ina

Oh, they both are. Where are *you* going, I'd like to know?

Di

Mama, I have to go down to the liberry.

Ina

It seems to me you have to go to the library every evening. Dwight, do you think she ought to go?

Dwight

Diana, is it necessary that you go?

Di

Well, everybody else goes, and—

Ina

I will not have you downtown in the evenings.

Di

But you let me go last night.

Ina

All the better reason why you should *not* go to-night.

Monona

Mama, let me go with her.

Ina

Very well, Di, you may go and take your sister.

Monona

Goody, goody! last time you wouldn't let me go.

Ina

That's why mama's going to let you go to-night.

Dwight

I thought you said the child must go to bed half an hour earlier because she wouldn't eat her egg.

Ina

Yes, that's so, I did. Monona, you can't go.

Monona

But I didn't want my egg—honest I didn't.

Ina

Makes no difference. You must eat or you'll get sick. Mama's going to teach you to eat. Go on, Di, to the library if it's necessary.

Dwight

I suppose Bobby Larkin has to go to the library to-night, eh?

Ina

Dwight, I wouldn't joke her about him. Scold her about him, the way you did this morning.

Di

But papa was cross about something else this morning. And to-night he isn't. Good-by, Dwight and Ina!

[*Exit* **Di.**]

Monona

I hate the whole family.

Mrs. Bett

Well, I should think she would.

Ina

Why, mama! Why, Pettie Deacon!

[**Monona** *weeps silently.*]

Dwight

[*To* **Ina.**]

Say no more, my dear. It's best to overlook. Show a sweet spirit….

Mrs. Bett

About as much like a father and mother as a cat and dog.

Dwight

We've got to learn—

Mrs. Bett

Performin' like a pair of weathercocks.

[*Both talking at once.*]

Dwight

Mother Bett! Are you talking, or am I?

Mrs. Bett

I am. But you don't seem to know it.

Dwight

Let us talk, pussy, and she'll simmer down. Ah—nothing new from the bride and groom?

Ina

No, Dwight. And it's been a week since Lulu wrote. She said he'd bought her a new red dress—and a hat. Isn't it too funny—to think of Lulu—

Dwight

I don't understand why they plan to go straight to Oregon without coming here first.

Ina

It isn't a bit fair to mama, going off that way. Leaving her own mother—why, she may never see mama again.

Mrs. Bett

Oh I'm going to last on quite a while yet.

Dwight

Of course you are, Mama Bett. You're my best girl. That reminds me, Ina, we must run up to visit Aunt Mollie. We ought to run up there next week. She isn't well.

Ina

Let's do that. Dear me, I wish Lulu was here to leave in charge. I certainly do miss Lulu—lots of ways.

Mrs. Bett

'Specially when it comes mealtime.

Ina

Is that somebody coming here?

Dwight

Looks like it—yes, so it is. Some caller, as usual.

[*Enter* **Lulu**.]

Well, if it isn't Miss Lulu Bett.

Ina

Why, sister!

Mrs. Bett

Lulie. Lulie. Lulie.

Lulu

How did you know?

Ina

Know what?

Lulu

That it isn't Lulu Deacon.

Dwight

What's this?

Ina

Isn't Lulu Deacon. What are you talking?

Lulu

Didn't he write to you?

Dwight

Not a word. All we've had we had from you—the last from Savannah, Georgia.

Lulu

Savannah, Georgia....

Dwight

Well, but he's here with you, isn't he?

Ina

Where is he? Isn't he here?

Lulu

Must be most to Oregon by this time.

Dwight

Oregon?

Lulu

You see, he had another wife.

Ina

Another wife!

Dwight

Why, he had not.

Lulu

Yes, another wife. He hasn't seen her for fifteen years and he thinks she's dead. But he isn't sure.

Dwight

Nonsense. Why of course she's dead if he thinks so.

Lulu

I had to be sure.

Ina

Monona! Go upstairs to bed at once.

Monona

It's only quarter of.

Ina

Do as mama tells you.

Monona

But—

Ina

Monona!

[*She goes, kissing them all good-night and taking her time about it. Everything is suspended while she kisses them and departs, walking slowly backward.*]

Mrs. Bett

Married? Lulie, was your husband married?

Lulu

Yes, my husband was married, mother.

Ina

Mercy, think of anything like that in our family.

Dwight

Well, go on—go on. Tell us about it.

Lulu

We were going to Oregon. First down to New Orleans and then out to California and up the coast…. Well, then at Savannah, Georgia, he said he thought I better know first. So then he told me.

Dwight

Yes—well, what did he say?

Lulu

Cora Waters. Cora Waters. She married him down in San Diego eighteen years ago. She went to South America with him.

Dwight

Well, he never let us know of it, if she did.

Lulu

No. She married him just before he went. Then in South America, after two years, she ran away. That's all he knows.

Dwight

That's a pretty story.

Lulu

He says if she was alive she'd be after him for a divorce. And she never has been so he thinks she must be dead. The trouble is he wasn't sure. And I had to be sure.

Ina

Well, but mercy! Couldn't he find out now?

Lulu

It might take a long time and I didn't want to stay and not know.

Ina

Well then why didn't he say so here?

Lulu

He would have. But you know how sudden everything was. He said he thought about telling us right here that afternoon when—when it happened but of course that'd been hard, wouldn't it? And then he felt so sure she was dead.

Ina

Why did he tell you at all then?

Dwight

Yes. Why indeed?

Lulu

I thought that just at first but only just at first. Of course that wouldn't have been right. And then you see he gave me my choice.

Dwight

Gave you your choice?

Lulu

Yes. About going on and taking the chances. He gave me my choice when he told me, there in Savannah, Georgia.

Dwight

What made him conclude by then that you ought to be told?

Lulu

Why, he'd got to thinking about it.

[*A silence.*]

The only thing as long as it happened I kind of wish he hadn't told me till we got to Oregon.

Ina

Lulu! Oh, you poor poor thing....

[**Mrs. Bett** *suddenly joins* **Ina** *in tears, rocking her body.*]

Lulu

Don't, mother. Oh, Ina, don't.... He felt bad too.

Dwight

He! He must have.

Ina

It's you. It's you. *My* sister!

Lulu

I never thought of it making you both feel bad. I knew it would make Dwight feel bad. I mean, it was his brother—

Ina

Thank goodness! nobody need know about it.

Lulu

Oh, yes. People will have to know.

Dwight

I do not see the necessity.

Lulu

Why, what would they think?

Dwight

What difference does it make what they think?

Lulu

Why, I shouldn't like—you see they might—why, Dwight, I think we'll have to tell them.

Dwight

You do. You think the disgrace of bigamy in this family is
something the whole town will have to know about.

Lulu

Say. I never thought about it being that

Dwight

What did you think it was? And whose disgrace is it, pray?

Lulu

Mine. And Ninian's.

Dwight

Ninian's. Well, he's gone. But you're here. And I'm here—and
my family. Folks'll feel sorry for you. But the disgrace, that
would reflect on me.

Lulu

But if we don't tell what'll they think?

Dwight

They'll think what they always think when a wife leaves her
husband. They'll think you couldn't get along. That's all.

Lulu

I should hate that. I wouldn't want them to think I hadn' been a
good wife to Ninian.

Dwight

Wife? You never were his wife. That's just the point.

Lulu

Oh!

Dwight

Don't you realize the position he's in?... See here—do you
intend—Are you going to sue Ninian?

Lulu

Oh! no! no! no!

Ina

Why, Lulu, any one would think you loved him.

Lulu

I do love him. And he loved me. Don't you think I know? He loved me.

Ina

Lulu.

Lulu

I love him—I do, and I'm not ashamed to tell you.

Mrs. Bett

Lulie, Lulie, was his other wife—was she *there?*

Lulu

No, no, mother. She wasn't there.

Mrs. Bett

Then it ain't so bad. I was afraid maybe she turned you out.

Lulu

No, no. It wasn't that bad, mother.

Dwight

In fact I simply will not have it, Lulu. You expect, I take it, to make your home with us in the future on the old terms.

Lulu

Well—

Dwight

I mean did Ninian give you any money?

Lulu

No. He didn't give me any money—only enough to get home on. And I kept my suit and the other dress—why! I wouldn't have taken any money.

Dwight

That means that you will have to continue to live here on the old terms and of course I'm quite willing that you should. Let me tell you, however, that this is on condition—on condition that this disgraceful business is kept to ourselves.

Ina

Truly, Lulu, wouldn't that be best? They'll talk anyway. But this way they'll only talk about you and the other way it'll be about all of us.

Lulu

But the other way would be the truth.

Dwight

My dear Lulu, are you sure of that?

Lulu

Sure?

Dwight

Yes. Did he give you any proofs?

Lulu

Proofs?

Dwight

Letters—documents of any sort? Any sort of assurance that he was speaking the truth?

Lulu

Why—no. Proofs—no. He told me.

Dwight

He told you!

Lulu

That was hard enough to have to do. It was terrible for him to have to do. What proofs—

Dwight

I may as well tell you that I myself have no idea that Ninian told you the truth. He was always imagining things, inventing things—you must have seen that. I know him pretty well—have been in touch with him more or less the whole time. In short I haven't the least idea he was ever married before.

Lulu

I never thought of that.

Dwight

Look here—hadn't you and he had some little tiff when he told you?

Lulu

No—no! Not once. He was very good to me. This dress—and my shoes—and my hat. And another dress, too.

[*She takes off her hat.*]

He liked the red wing—I wanted black—oh, Dwight! He did tell me the truth!

Dwight

As long as there's any doubt about it—and I feel the gravest doubts—I desire that you should keep silent and protect my family from this scandal. I have taken you into my confidence about these doubts for your own profit.

Lulu

My own profit!

[*Moves toward the door.*]

Ina

Lulu—you see! We just couldn't have this known about Dwight's own brother, could we now?

Dwight

You have it in your own hands to repay me, Lulu, for anything that you feel I may have done for you in the past. You also have it in your hands to decide whether your home here continues. This is not a pleasant position for me to find myself in. In fact it is distinctly unpleasant I may say. But you see for yourself.

[**Lulu** *goes into the house.*]

Mrs. Bett

Wasn't she married when she thought she was?

Ina

Mama, do please remember Monona. Yes—Dwight thinks now she's married all right and that it was all right, all the time.

Mrs. Bett

Well, I hope so, for pity sakes.

Monona's Voice

[*From upstairs.*]

Mama! Come on and hear me say my prayers, why don't you?

Darkness

S c e n e i i

Ina *seated.* **Monona** *jumping on and off the porch, chanting.*

[*Enter* **Dwight**.]

Dwight

Ah, this is great… no place like home after all, is there?

Ina

Now, Monona, sit down and be quiet. You've played enough for one day.

[*Enter* **Mrs. Bett**.]

Monona

How do you know I have?

Dwight

Ah, Mama Bett. Coming out to enjoy the evening air?

Mrs. Bett

No, I thank you.

Dwight

Well, well, well, let's see what's new in the great press of our country....

[*They are now seated in the approximate positions assumed at the opening of* **Scene i**.]

Ina

Dwight dear, nothing has been done about that screen for the back window.

Dwight

Now why couldn't my puss have reminded me of that this morning instead of waiting for the only time I have to take my ease with my family.

Ina

But Dwightie, in the mornings you're so busy—

Dwight

You are argumentative, pussy—you certainly are. And you ought to curb it. For that matter I haven't sprayed that rambler rosebush.

Ina

Every single night for a month you've spoken of spraying that rosebush.

Dwight

Ina, will you cease your exaggerations on Monona's account
if not on mine. Exaggeration, my pet, is one of the worst of
female faults. Exaggeration—

Ina

Look, Dwight! our new neighbors have got a dog. Great big
brute of a thing. He's going to tear up every towel I spread on
our grass.

[*Enter* **Di**, *from the house.*]

Now, Di, where are you going?

Di

Mama, I have to go down to the liberry.

Ina

Now, Di—

Di

You let me go last night.

Monona

Mama, I can go, can't I? Because you wouldn't let me go last
night.

Ina

No, Monona, you may *not* go.

Monona

Oh, why not?

Ina

Because mama says so. Isn't that enough?

Mrs. Bett

Anybody'd think you was the king—layin' down the law an'
layin' down the law an' layin' down—Where's Lulie?

Di

Mama, isn't Uncle Ninian coming back?

Ina

Hush…. No. Now don't ask mama any more questions.

Di

But supposing people ask me. What'll I say?

Ina

Don't say anything at all about Aunt Lulu.

Di

But, mama, what has she done?

Ina

Di! Don't you think mama knows best?

Di

[*Softly.*]

No, I don't…. Well anyway Aunt Lulu's got on a perfectly beautiful dress to-night….

Ina

And you know, Dwight, Lulu's clothes give me the funniest feeling. As if Lulu was wearing things bought for her by some one that wasn't—that was—

Dwight

By her husband who has left her.

Di

Is that what it is, papa?

Dwight

That's what it is, my little girl.

Di

Well, I think it's a shame. And I think Uncle Ninian is a slunge.

Ina

Di Deacon!

Di

I do! And I'd be ashamed to think anything else. I'd like to tell everybody.

Dwight

There's no need for secrecy now.

Ina

Dwight, really—do you think we ought—

Dwight

No need whatever for secrecy. The truth is Lulu's husband has tired of her and sent her home. We may as well face it.

Ina

But Dwight—how awful for Lulu….

Dwight

Lulu has us to stand by her.

[*Enter* **Lulu**.]

Lulu

That sounds good. That I have you to stand by me.

Dwight

My dear Lulu, the family bond is the strongest bond in the world. Family. Tribe. The—er—pack. Standing up for the family honor, the family reputation is the highest nobility.

[*Exit* **Di** *by degrees. Left.*]

I tell you of all history the most beautiful product is the family tie. Of it are born family consideration—

Ina

Why, you don't look like yourself… is it your hair, Lulu? You look so strange….

Lulu

Don't you like it? Ninian liked it.

Dwight

In that case I think you'd show more modesty if you arranged your hair in the old way.

Lulu

Yes, you would think so. Dwight, I want you to give me Ninian's Oregon address.

Dwight

You want what?

Lulu

Ninian's Oregon address. It's a funny thing but I haven't it.

Dwight

It would seem that you have no particular need for that particular address.

Lulu

Yes I have. I want it. You have it haven't you, Dwight?

Dwight

Certainly I have it.

Lulu

Won't you please write it down for me?

[*She offers him tablet.*]

Dwight

My dear Lulu, now why revive anything? No good can come by—

Lulu

But why shouldn't I have his address?

Dwight

If everything is over between you why should you?

Lulu

But you say he's still my husband.

Dwight

If my brother has shown his inclination as plainly as I judge that
he has it is certainly not my place to put you in touch with him
again.

Lulu

I don't know whose place it is. But I've got to know more—I've
got to know more, Dwight. This afternoon I went to the post
office to ask for his address—it seemed so strange to be doing
that, after all that's been—They didn't know his address—I
could see how they wondered at my asking. And I knew how
the others wondered—Mis' Martin, Mis' Curtis, Mis' Grove.
"Where you hiding that handsome husband of yours?" they
said. All I could say was that he isn't here. Dwight! I won't
live like that. I want to know the truth. You give me Ninian's
address.

Dwight

My dear Lulu! My *dear* Lulu! You are not the one to write to
him. Have you no delicacy?

Lulu

So much delicacy that I want to be sure whether I'm married or
not.

Dwight

Then I myself will take this up with my brother. I will write to
him about it.

Lulu

Here's everything—if you're going to write him, do it now.

Dwight

My dear Lulu! don't be absurd.

Lulu

Ina! Help me! If this was Dwight—and they didn't know whether he had another wife or not and you wanted to ask him and you didn't know where he was—oh, don't you see? Help me.

Ina

Well of course. I see it all, Lulu. And yet—why not let Dwight do it in his own way? Wouldn't that be better?

Lulu

Mother!

Mrs. Bett

Lulie. Set down. Set down, why don't you?

Lulu

Dwight, you write that letter to Ninian. And you make him tell you so that you'll understand. I know he spoke the truth. But I want you to know.

Dwight

M—m. And then I suppose as soon as you have the proofs you're going to tell it all over town.

Lulu

I'm going to tell it all over town just as it is—unless you write to him.

Ina

Lulu! Oh, you wouldn't!

Lulu

I would. I will.

Dwight

And get turned out of the house as you would be?

Ina

Dwight. Oh, you wouldn't!

Dwight

I would. I will. Lulu knows it.

Lulu

I shall tell what I know and then leave your house anyway
unless you get Ninian's word. And you're going to write to him
now.

Dwight

You would leave your mother? And leave Ina?

Lulu

Leave everything.

Ina

Oh, Dwight! We can't get along without Lulu.

Dwight

Isn't this like a couple of women?… Rather than let you in for a
show of temper, Lulu, I'd do anything.

[*Writes.*]

Monona

[*Behind* **Ina**.]
Mama, can I write Uncle Ninian a little letter, too?

Ina

For pity sakes, aren't you in bed yet?

Monona

It's only quarter of.

Ina

Well you may go to bed *now* because you have sat there
listening. How often must mama tell you not to listen to grown
people.

Monona
Do they always say something bad?

Ina
Monona, you are to go up to bed at once.

[*She makes her leisurely rounds for kisses.*]

Monona
Papa, it's your turn to hear me say my prayers tonight.

Dwight
Very well, pettie. When you're ready call me.

[*Exit* **Monona**.]

There, Lulu. The deed is done. Now I hope you're satisfied.

[*Places the letter in his pocket.*]

Lulu
I want you to give me the letter to mail, please.

Dwight
Why this haste, sister mine? I'll mail it in the morning.

Lulu
I'll mail it now. Now.

Dwight
I may take a little stroll before bedtime—I'll mail it then.
There's nothing like a brisk walk to induce sound restful sleep.

Lulu
I'll mail the letter now.

Dwight
I suppose I'll have to humor your sister, Ina. Purely on your
account you understand.

[*Hands the letter.*]

Ina

Oh, Dwight, how good you are!

Lulu

There's—there's one thing more I want to speak about. If—if you and Ina go to your Aunt Mollie's then Ninian's letter might come while you're away.

Dwight

Conceivably. Letters do come while a man's away.

Lulu

Yes. And I thought if you wouldn't mind if I opened it—

Dwight

Opened it? Opened *my* letter?

Lulu

Yes, you see it'll be about me mostly. You wouldn't mind if I did open it?

Dwight

But you say you know what will be in it, *Miss* Bett?

Lulu

I did know till you—I've got to see that letter, Dwight.

Dwight

And so you shall. But not until I show it to you. My dear Lulu, you know how I hate having my mail interfered with. You shall see the letter all in good time when Ina and I return.

Lulu

You wouldn't want to let me—just see what he says?

Dwight

I prefer always to open my own letters.

Lulu

Very well, Dwight.

[*She moves away. Right*]

Ina

And Lulu, I meant to ask you: Don't you think it might be better if you—if you kept out of sight for a few days?

Lulu

Why?

Ina

Why set people wondering till we have to?

Lulu

They don't have to wonder as far as I'm concerned.

[*Exit*]

Mrs. Bett

I'm going through the kitchen to set with Grandma Gates. She always says my visits are like a dose of medicine.

[*Exit* **Mrs. Bett**.]

Ina

It certainly has changed Lulu—a man coming into her life. She never spoke to me like that before.

Dwight

I saw she wasn't herself. I'd do anything to avoid having a scene—you know that…. You do know that, don't you?

Ina

But I really think you ought to have written to Ninian. It's—it's not a nice position for Lulu.

Dwight

Nice! But whom has she got to blame for it?

Ina

Why, Ninian.

Dwight

Herself! To tell you the truth, I was perfectly amazed at the way she snapped him up here that afternoon.

Ina

Why but Dwight—

Dwight

Brazen. Oh, it was brazen.

Ina

It was just fun in the first place.

Dwight

But no really nice woman—

Ina

Dwightie—what did you say in the letter?

Dwight

What did I say? I said, I said: "Dear Brother, I take it that the first wife story was devised to relieve you of a distasteful situation. Kindly confirm. Family well as usual. Business fair." Covers it, don't it?

Ina

Oh, Dwightie—how complete that is.

Dwight

I'm pretty good at writing brief concise letters—that say the whole thing, eh?

Ina

I've often noticed that....

Dwight

My precious pussy.... Oh, how unlike Lulu you are!

[*Right.* **Di** *and* **Bobby** *appear, walking very slowly and very near.*]

[**Dwight** *rises, holds out his arms.*]

Ina

Poor dear foolish Lulu! oh, Dwight—what if it was Di in Lulu's place?

Dwight

Such a thing couldn't happen to Di. Di was born with ladylike feelings.

[*They enter the house.* **Ina** *extinguishes a lamp.* **Dwight** *turns down the hall gas. Pause.* **Di** *and* **Bobby** *come to the veranda.*]

Di

Bobby dear! You don't kiss me as if you really wanted to kiss me to-night....

Darkness

Scene iii

The same. Evening, a week later. Stage Hooded with moonlight, house lighted. At the piano, just inside the window, **Lulu** *and* **Cornish** *are finishing a song together,* **Lulu** *accompanying.*

> How sweet the happy evening's close,
> 'Tis the hour of sweet repose—
>   Good-night.
>
> The summer wind has sunk to rest,
> The moon serenely bright
> Unfolds her calm and gentle ray,
> Softly now she seems to say,
>   Good-night.

[*As they sing,* **Di** *slips into the house, unseen.*]

Cornish
Why, Miss Lulu, you're quite a musician.

Lulu
Oh, no. I've never played in front of anybody—

[*They come to the porch.*]

I don't know what Ina and Dwight would say if they heard me.

Cornish
What a pretty dress that is, Miss Lulu!

Lulu
I made this from one of Ina's old ones since she's been gone. I don't know what Ina and Dwight are going to say about this dress, made like this, when they get home.

Cornish
When are they coming back?

Lulu
Any time now. They've been gone most a week. Do you know I never had but one compliment before that wasn't for my cooking.

Cornish
You haven't!

Lulu
He told me I done up my hair nice. That was after I took notice how the ladies in Savannah, Georgia, done up theirs.

Cornish
I guess you can do most anything you set your hand to, Miss Lulu: Look after Miss Di and sing and play and cook—

Lulu
Yes, cook. But I can't earn anything. I'd like to earn something.

Cornish

You would! Why, you have it fine here, I thought.

Lulu

Oh, fine, yes. Dwight gives me what I have. And I do their work.

Cornish

I see. I never thought of that....

[*Pause.*]

Lulu

You're wondering why I didn't stay with *him!*

Cornish

Oh, no.

Lulu

Yes you are! The whole town's wondering. They're all talking about me.

Cornish

Well, Miss Lulu, you know it don't make any difference to your friends what people say.

Lulu

But they don't know the truth. You see, he had another wife.

Cornish

Lord sakes!

Lulu

Dwight thinks it isn't true. He thinks—he didn't have another wife.... You see, Dwight thinks he didn't want me.

Cornish

But—your husband—I mean, why doesn't he write to Mr. Deacon and tell him the truth—

Lulu

He has written. The letter's in there on the piano.

Cornish

What'd he say?

Lulu

Dwight doesn't like me to touch his mail. I'll have to wait till he comes back.

Cornish

Lord sakes!… You—you—you're too nice a girl to get a deal like this. Darned if you aren't.

Lulu

Oh, no.

Cornish

Yes you are, too! And there ain't a thing I can do.

Lulu

It's a good deal to have somebody to talk to….

Cornish

Sure it is.

Lulu

… Cora Waters. Cora Waters, of San Diego, California. And she never heard of me.

Cornish

No. She never did, did she? Ain't life the darn—

[*Enter* **Mrs. Bett.**]

Mrs. Bett

I got Monona into bed. And it's no fool of a job neither.

Lulu

Did you, mother? Come and sit down.

Mrs. Bett

Yes. She went to bed with a full set of doll dishes…. Ain't it nice with the folks all gone?… I don't hear any more playin' and singin'. It sounded real good.

Lulu

We sung all I knew how to play, mama.

Mrs. Bett

I use' to play on the melodeon.

Cornish

Well, well, well.

Mrs. Bett

That was when I was first married. We had a little log house in a clearing in York State. I was seventeen—and he was nineteen. While he was chopping I use' to sit on a log with my sewing. Jenny was born in that house. I was alone at the time. I was alone with her when she died, too. She was sixteen—little bits of hands she had—

[*Yawns. Rises, wanders toward door.*]

Can't we have some more playin' and singin'?

Lulu

After a little while, mama—dear.

Mrs. Bett

It went kind of nice—that last tune you sung.

[*Hums the air. Enters house.*]

Cornish

I must be going along too, Miss Lulu.

Lulu

I can't think why Di doesn't come. She ought not to be out like this without telling me—

[**Mrs. Bett** *appears beside the piano, lifts and examines the letters lying there.*]

Cornish

Well, don't you mind on my account. I've enjoyed every minute I've been here.

Lulu

Mother! Those are Dwight's letters—don't you touch them.

Mrs. Bett

I ain't hurting them or him neither.

[*Disappears, the letters in her hand.*]

Cornish

Good-night, Miss Lulu. If there was anything I could do at any time you'd let me know, wouldn't you?

Lulu

Oh, thank you.

Cornish

I've had an awful nice time, singing, and listening to you talk—well of course—I mean the supper was just fine! And so was the music.

Lulu

Oh, no.

[**Mrs. Bett** *appears at the door with a letter.*]

Mrs. Bett

Lulie. I guess you didn't notice. This one's from Ninian.

Lulu

Mother—

Mrs. Bett

I opened it—why of course I did. It's from Ninian.

[*Holds out unfolded letter and an old newspaper clipping.*]

The paper's awful old—years back, looks like. See. Says "Corie Waters, music hall singer—married last night to Ninian Deacon"—Say, Lulie, that must be her.

Lulu

Yes, that's her. That's her—Cora Waters…. Oh, then he *was* married to her just like he said!

Cornish

Oh, Miss Lulu! I'm so sorry!

Lulu

No, no. Because he wanted me! He didn't say that just to get rid of me!

Cornish

Oh, that way….I see….

Lulu

I'm so thankful it wasn't that.

Mrs. Bett

Then everything's all right once more. Ain't that nice!

Lulu

I'm so thankful it wasn't that.

Cornish

Yes, I can understand that. Well, I—I guess I ought to be going now, Miss Lulu…. Why, it *is* Miss Lulu Bett, isn't it?

Lulu

[*Abstractedly, with the paper.*]
Yes—yes—good-night, Mr. Cornish. Good-night

Cornish

Good-night, Miss Lulu…. I wonder if you would let me tell you something.

Lulu

Why—

Cornish

I guess I don't amount to much. I'll never be a lawyer. I'm no good at business and everything I say sounds wrong to me. And yet I do believe I do know enough not to bully a woman—not to make her unhappy, maybe even—I could make her a little happy. Miss Lulu, I hate to see you looking and talking so sad. Do you think we could possibly arrange—

Lulu

Oh!

Cornish

I guess maybe you've heard something about a little something I'm supposed to inherit. Well, I got it. Of course, it's only five hundred dollars. We could get that little Warden house and furnish up the parlor with pianos—that is, if you could ever think of marrying me.

Lulu

Don't say that—don't say that!

Mrs. Bett

Better take him, Lulie. A girl ought to take any young man that will propose in front of her mother!

Cornish

Of course if you loved him very much then I'd ought not to be talking this way to you.

Lulu

You see Ninian was the first person who was ever kind to me. Nobody ever wanted me, nobody ever even thought of me. Then he came. It might have been somebody else. It might have been you. But it happened to be Ninian and I do love him.

Cornish

I see. I guess you'll forgive me for what I said.

Lulu

Of course.

Cornish

Miss Lulu, if that five hundred could be of any use to you, I wish you'd take it.

Lulu

Oh, thank you, thank you, I couldn't.

Cornish

Well, I guess I'll be stepping along. If you should want me, I'm always there. I guess you know that.

[*Exit*]

Mrs. Bett

Better burn that up. I wouldn't have it round.

Lulu

But mother! Mother dear, try to understand. This means that Ninian told the truth. He wasn't just trying to get rid of me.

Mrs. Bett

Did he want you to stay with him?

Lulu

I don't know. But I think he did. Anyway, now I know the truth about him.

Mrs. Bett

Well, I wouldn't want anybody else to know. Here, let me have it and burn it up.

Lulu

Mama, mama! Aren't you glad for me that now I can prove Ninian wasn't just making up a story so I'd go away?

Mrs. Bett

[*Clearly and beautifully.*]
Oh, Lulu! My little girl! Is that what they said about you? Mother knows it wasn't like that. Mother knows he loved you…. How still it is here! Where's Inie?

Lulu

They've gone away, you know….

Mrs. Bett

Well, I guess I'll step over to Grandma Gates's a spell. See how her rheumatism is. I'll be back before long—I'll be back….

[*Exit. For a moment* **Lulu** *breaks down and sobs. Rises to lay* **Dwight**'s *letter through the window on piano. Slight sound. She listens. Enter* **Di** *from house. She is carrying a traveling bag.*]

Lulu

Di! Why Di! What does this mean? Where were you going? Why, mama won't like your carrying her nice new satchel….

Di

Aunt Lulu—the idea. What right have you to interfere with me like this?

Lulu

Di, you must explain to me what this means…. Di, where can you be going with a satchel this time of the night? Di Deacon, are you running away with somebody?

Di

You have no right to ask me questions, Aunt Lulu.

Lulu

Di, you're going off with Bobby Larkin. Aren't you? Aren't you?

Di

If I am it's entirely our own affair.

Lulu

Why, Di. If you and Bobby want to be married why not let us get you up a nice wedding here at home—

Di

Aunt Lulu, you're a funny person to be telling *me* what to do.

Lulu

I love you just as much as if I was married happy, in a home.

Di

Well, you aren't. And I'm going to do just as I think best. Bobby and I are the ones most concerned in this, Aunt Lulu.

Lulu

But—but getting married is for your whole life!

Di

Yours wasn't.

Lulu

Di, my dear little girl, you must wait at least till mama and papa get home.

Di

That's likely. They say I'm not to be married till I'm twenty-one.

Lulu

Well, but how young that is.

Di

It is to you. It isn't young to me, remember, Aunt Lulu.

Lulu

But this is wrong—it is wrong!

Di

There's nothing wrong about getting married if you stay married.

Lulu

Well, then it can't be wrong to let your mother and father know.

Di

It isn't. But they'd treat me wrong. Mama'd cry and say I was disgracing *her*. And papa—first he'd scold me and then he'd joke me about it. He'd joke me about it every day for weeks, every morning at breakfast, every night here on the porch—he'd joke me.

Lulu

Why, Di! Do you feel that way, too?

Di

You don't know what it is to be laughed at or paid no attention to, everything you say.

Lulu

Don't I? Don't I? Is that why you're going?

Di

Well, it's one reason.

Lulu

But Di, do you love Bobby Larkin?

Di

Well…. I could love almost anybody real nice that was nice to me.

Lulu

Di… Di….

Di

It's true.

[**Bobby** *enters.*]

You ought to know that…. You did it. Mama said so.

Lulu

Don't you think that I don't know....

Di

Oh, Bobby, she's trying to stop us! But she can't do it—I've told her so—

Bobby

She don't have to stop us. We're stopped.

Di

What do you mean?

Bobby

We're minors.

Di

Well, gracious—you didn't have to tell them that.

Bobby

No. They knew *I* was.

Di

But, silly. Why didn't you tell them you're not.

Bobby

But I am.

Di

For pity sakes—don't you know how to do anything?

Bobby

What would you have me do, I'd like to know?

Di

Why tell them we're both—whatever it is they want us to be. We look it. We know we're responsible—that's all they care for. Well, you are a funny....

Bobby

You wanted me to lie?

Di

Oh! don't make out you never told a fib.

Bobby

Well, but this—why, Di—about a thing like this….

Di

I never heard of a lover flatting out like that!

Bobby

Anyhow, there's nothing to do now. The cat's out. I've told our ages. We've got to have our folks in on it.

Di

Is that all you can think of?

Bobby

What else is there to think of?

Di

Why, let's go to Bainbridge or Holt and tell them we're of age and be married there.

Lulu

Di, wherever you go I'll go with you. I won't let you out of my sight.

Di

Bobby, why don't you answer her?

Bobby

But I'm not going to Bainbridge or Holt or any town and lie, to get you or any other girl.

Di

You're about as much like a man in a story as—as papa is.

[*Enter* **Dwight** *and* **Ina**.]

Dwight

What's this? What's this about papa?

Ina

Well, what's all this going on here?

Lulu

Why, Ina!

Di

Oh, mama! I—I didn't know you were coming so soon. Hello, dear! Hello, papa! Here's—here's Bobby....

Dwight

What an unexpected pleasure, *Master* Bobby.

Bobby

Good-evening, Mrs. Deacon. Good-evening, Mr. Deacon.

Dwight

And Lulu. Is it Lulu? Is this lovely houri our Lulu? Is this Miss Lulu Bett? Or is this Lulu something else by now? You can't tell what Lulu'll do when you leave her alone at home. Ina—our festive ball gown!

Lulu

Ina, I made it out of that old muslin of yours, you know. I thought you wouldn't care—

Ina

Oh, that! I was going to use it for Di but it doesn't matter. You are welcome to it, Lulu. Little youthful for anything but home wear, isn't it?

Dwight

It looks like a wedding gown. Why are you wearing a wedding gown—eh, Lulu?

Ina

Di Deacon, what have you got mama's new bag for?

Di

I haven't done anything to the bag, mama.

Ina

Well, but what are you doing with it here?

Di

Oh, nothing! Did you—did you have a good time?

Ina

Yes, we did—but I can't see…. Dwight, look at Di with my new black satchel.

Dwight

What is this, Diana?

Di

Well, I'm—I'm not going to use it for anything.

Ina

I wish somebody would explain what is going on here. Lulu, can't you explain?

Dwight

Aha! Now, if Lulu is going to explain that's something like it. When Lulu begins to explain we get imagination going.

Lulu

Di and I have a little secret. Can't we have a little secret if we want one?

Dwight

Upon my word, she has a beautiful secret. I don't know about your secrets, Lulu.

[*Enter* **Mrs. Bett**.]

Mrs. Bett

Hello, Inie.

Ina

Oh, mother dear….

Dwight

Well, Mother Bett….

Mrs. Bett

That you, Dwight?

[*To* **Bobby**.]

… Don't you help me. I guess I can help myself yet awhile.

[*Climbs the two steps.*]

[*To* **Di**.]

Made up your mind to come home, did you?

[*Seats herself.*]

I got a joke. Grandma Gates says it's all over town they wouldn't give Di and Bobby Larkin a license to get married.

[*Single note of laughter, thin and high.*]

Dwight

What nonsense!

Ina

Is it nonsense? Haven't I been trying to find out where the new black bag went? Di! Look at mama….

Di

Listen to that, Bobby. Listen!

Ina

That won't do, Di. You can't deceive mama, and don't you try.

Bobby

Mrs. Deacon, I—

Dwight

Diana!

Di

Yes, papa.

Dwight

Answer your mother. Answer *me*. Is there anything in this absurd tale?

Di

No, papa.

Dwight

Nothing whatever?

Di

No, papa.

Dwight

Can you imagine how such a ridiculous story started?

Di

No, papa.

Dwight

Very well. Now we know where we are. If anybody hears this report repeated, send them to *me*.

Ina

Well, but that satchel—

Dwight

One moment. Lulu will of course verify what the child has said.

Lulu

If you cannot settle this with Di, you cannot settle it with me.

Dwight

A shifty answer. You're a bird at misrepresenting facts....

Lulu

Oh!…

Dwight

Lulu, the bird!

Lulu

Lulu, the dove to put up with you.

[*Exit.*]

Ina

Bobby wanted to say something.…

Bobby

No, Mrs. Deacon. I have nothing—more to say. I'll—I'll go now.

Dwight

Good-night, Robert.

[**Ina** *and* **Dwight** *transfer bags and wraps to the House.*]

Bobby

Good-night, Mr. Deacon. Good-by, Di.

[**Di** *follows* **Bobby**. *Right.*]

Di

Bobby, come back, you hate a lie—but what else could I do?

Bobby

What else could you do? I'd rather they never let us see each other again than to lose you in the way I've lost you now.

Di

Bobby!

Bobby

It's true. We mustn't talk about it.

Di

Bobby! I'll go back and tell them all.

Bobby

You can't go back. Not out of a thing like that. Good-by, Di.

[*Exit.*]

[*Enter* **Dwight** *and* **Ina.**]

Di

If you have any fear that I may elope with Bobby Larkin, let it rest. I shall never marry him if he asks me fifty times a day.

Ina

Really, darling?

Di

Really and truly, and he knows it, too.

Dwight

A-ha! The lovelorn maiden all forlorn makes up her mind not to be so lorn as she thought she was. How does it seem not to be in love with him, Di—eh?

Di

Papa, if you make fun of me any more I'll—I'll let the first train of cars I can find run over me....

[*Sobs as she runs to house.*]

Mrs. Bett

Wait, darling! Tell grandma! Did Bobby have another wife too?

[*Exeunt* **Mrs. Bett** *and* **Di.**]

Ina

Di, I'd be ashamed, when papa's so good to you. Oh, my! what parents have to put up with....

Dwight

Bear and forbear, pettie—bear and forbear…. By the way, Lulu, haven't I some mail somewhere about?

Lulu

Yes, there's a letter there. I'll get it for you.

[*She reaches through the window.*]

Dwight

A-ha! An epistle from my dear brother Ninian.

Ina

Oh, from Ninian, Dwight?

Dwight

From Ninian—the husband of Miss Lulu Bett…. You opened the letter?… Your sister has been opening my mail.

Ina

But, Dwight, if it's from Ninian—

Dwight

It is my mail.

Ina

Well, what does he say?

Dwight

I shall read the letter in my own time. My present concern is this disregard for my wishes. What excuse have you to offer?

Lulu

None.

Ina

Dwight, she knows what's in it and we don't. Hurry up.

Dwight

She is an ungrateful woman.

[*Opens the letter, with the clipping.*]

Ina

[*Over his shoulder.*]
Ah!… Dwight, then he was…

Dwight

M—m—m—m. So after having been absent with my brother for a month you find that you were not married to him.

Lulu

You see, Dwight, he told the truth. He did have another wife. He didn't just leave me.

Dwight

But this seems to me to make you considerably worse off than if he had.

Lulu

Oh, no! No! If he hadn't—hadn't liked me, he wouldn't have told me about her. You see that, don't you?

Dwight

That your apology?… Look here, Lulu! This is a bad business. The less you say about it the better for all our sakes. You see that, don't you?

Lulu

See that? Why, no. I wanted you to write to him so I could tell the truth. You said I mustn't tell the truth till I had the proofs.

Dwight

Tell whom?

Lulu

Tell everybody. I want them to know.

Dwight

Then you care nothing for our feelings in this matter?

Lulu

Your feelings?

Dwight

How this will reflect on us—it's nothing to you that we have a brother who's a bigamist?

Lulu

But it's me—it's me.

Dwight

You! You're completely out of it. You've nothing more to say about it whatever. Just let it be as it is… drop it. That's all I suggest.

Lulu

I want people to know the truth.

Dwight

But it's nobody's business but our business… for all our sakes let us drop this matter Now I tell you, Lulu—here are three of us. Our interests are the same in this thing—only Ninian is our relative and he's nothing to you now. Is he?

Lulu

Why—

Dwight

Let's have a vote. Your snap judgment is to tell this disgraceful fact broadcast. Mine is, least said soonest mended. What do you say, Ina?

Ina

Oh, goodness—if we get mixed up in a scandal like this we'll never get away from it. Why, I wouldn't have people know of it for worlds.

Dwight

Exactly. Ina has stated it exactly. Lulu, I think you should be reconciled.

Ina

My poor poor sister! Oh, Dwight! when I think of it—what
have I done, what have *we* done—that I should have a good
kind loving husband—be so protected, so loved, when other
women… Darling! You *know* how sorry I am—we all are —

Lulu

Then give me the only thing I've got—that's my pride. My pride
that he didn't want to get rid of me.

Dwight

What about my pride? Do you think I want everybody to know
that my brother did a thing like that?

Lulu

You can't help that.

Dwight

But I want you to help it. I want you to promise me that you
won't shame us like this before all our friends.

Lulu

You want me to promise what?

Dwight

I want you—I ask you to promise me that you will keep this
with us—a family secret.

Lulu

No! No! I won't do it! I won't do it! I won't do it!

Dwight

You refuse to do this small thing for us?

Lulu

Can't you understand anything? I've lived here all my life—on
your money. I've not been strong enough to work they say—
well, but I've been strong enough to be a hired girl in your
house—and I've been glad to pay for my keep…. But there
wasn't a thing about it that I liked. Nothing about being here

that I liked…. Well, then I got a little something, same as other folks. I thought I was married and I went off on the train and he bought me things and I saw different towns. And then it was all a mistake. I didn't have any of it. I came back here and went into your kitchen again—I don't know why I came back. I suppose it's because I'm most thirty-four and new things ain't so easy any more—but what have I got or what'll I ever have? And now you want to put on to me having folks look at me and think he run off and left me and having them all wonder. I can't stand it. I can't stand it. I can't….

Dwight

You'd rather they'd know he fooled you when he had another wife?

Lulu

Yes. Because he wanted me. How do I know—maybe he wanted me only just because he was lonesome, the way I was. I don't care why. And I won't have folks think he went and left me.

Dwight

That is wicked vanity.

Lulu

That's the truth. Well, why can't they know the truth?

Dwight

And bring disgrace on us all?

Lulu

It's me—It's me—

Dwight

You—you—you—you're always thinking of yourself.

Lulu

Who else thinks of me. And who do you think of—who do you think of, Dwight? I'll tell you that, because I know you better than any one else in the world knows you—better even than Ina. And I know that you'd sacrifice Ina, Di, mother, Monona,

Ninian—everybody, just to your own idea of who you are.
You're one of the men who can smother a whole family and not
even know you're doing it.

Dwight

You listen to me. It's Ninian I'm thinking about

Lulu

Ninian….

Dwight

Yes, yes… Ninian!… Of course if you don't care what happens
to him, it doesn't matter.

Lulu

What do you mean?

Dwight

If you don't love him any more….

Lulu

You know I love him. I'll always love him.

Dwight

That's likely. A woman doesn't send the man she loves to prison.

Lulu

I send him to prison! Why, he's brought me the only happiness
I've ever had….

Dwight

But prison is just where he'll go and you'll be the one to send
him there.

Lulu

Oh! That couldn't be…. That couldn't be….

Dwight

Don't you realize that bigamy is a crime? If you tell this thing
he'll go to prison… nothing can save him.

Lulu

I never thought of that....

Dwight

It's time you did think. Now will you promise to keep this with us, a family secret?

Lulu

Yes. I promise.

Dwight

You will?...

Lulu

Yes... I will.

Dwight

A... h. You'll be happy some day to think you've done this for us, Lulu.

Lulu

I s'pose so....

Ina

This makes up for everything. My sweet self-sacrificing sister!

Lulu

Oh, stop that!

Ina

Oh, the pity of it... the pity of it!...

Lulu

Don't you go around pitying me! I'll have you know I'm glad the whole thing happened.

Curtain

Act III (2nd Version)

*The same. Discover **Mrs. Bett**, tidying the porch and singing. It is the following morning.*

[*Enter **Lulu** with bag.*]

Mrs. Bett

Where you going now, for pity sakes?

Lulu

Mother. Now, mother darling, listen and try to understand.

Mrs. Bett

Well, I am listening, Lulie.

Lulu

Mother, I can't stay here. I can't stay here any longer. I've got to get clear away from Dwight and Ina.

Mrs. Bett

You want to live somewhere else, Lulie?

Lulu

I can't live here and have people think Ninian left me. I can't tell the truth and bring disgrace on Ninian. And I can't stay here in Dwight's kitchen a day longer. Oh, mother! I wish you could see—

Mrs. Bett

Why, Lulie, I do see that.

Lulu

You do, mother?

Mrs. Bett

I've often wondered why you didn't go before.

Lulu

Oh, mother, you dear—

Mrs. Bett

You needn't think because I'm old I don't know a thing or two.

Lulu

You want me to go?

Mrs. Bett

It's all I can do for you now, Lulie. Just to want you to go. I'm old and I'm weak and I can't keep care of you like when you was little.

Lulu

Oh, mother, I'm so glad!

Mrs. Bett

I ain't exactly glad—

Lulu

Dearest, I mean I was so afraid you wouldn't understand—

Mrs. Bett

Why wouldn't I understand, I'd like to know? You speak like I didn't have a brain in my skull.

Lulu

No, dear, but—

Mrs. Bett

You mind me, Lulie, and go on. Go on…. Say, scat's sake, you can't go. You ain't got any money.

Lulu

Yes, mother, I have. I've got twelve dollars.

Mrs. Bett

And I ain't got much. Only enough to bury me nice.

Lulu

Don't you worry, mother. I'll be all right. I'll get work.

Mrs. Bett

Mother wants to help you. Here, Lulie, you take my funeral fifty. Joke on Dwight to make him bury me.

Lulu

Oh, no, mother, I couldn't.

Mrs. Bett

You mind me, Lulie. Do as mother tells you.

Lulu

Mother, dearest! Oh, I wish I could take you with me!

Mrs. Bett

You needn't to worry about me. If I get lonesome I can give Dwight the dickens.

Lulu

Good-by—dear—good-by. I'll go the back way, they won't see me.

[**Lulu** *kisses her and turns away. Left.*]

Mrs. Bett

Lulie. Mother loves you. You know that, don't you?

Lulu

Dearest, yes—yes, I do know.

[*She goes.* **Mrs. Bett** *trembles, turns, sees her dust cloth, goes on working and begins to hum.*]

[*Enter* **Dwight**.]

Dwight

Ready for breakfast, Mama Bett?

> ### Mrs. Bett
>
> No, I ain't ready.

> ### Dwight
>
> Neither is the breakfast. Lulu must be having the tantrim.

> ### Mrs. Bett
>
> I s'pose you think that's funny.

> ### Dwight
>
> Lulu ought to think of you—old folks ought to have regular meals—

> ### Mrs. Bett
>
> Old? Old? Me, old?

> ### Dwight
>
> Well, you're hungry. That's what makes you so cross, Mama Bett.

> ### Mrs. Bett
>
> All you think of is food, anyhow.

> ### Dwight
>
> Who has a better right? Who provides the food we eat?

> ### Mrs. Bett
>
> That's all you're good for.

> ### Dwight
>
> Well, I may not amount to much in this old world of ours but I flatter myself I'm a good provider.

> ### Mrs. Bett
>
> If I was going to brag I'd brag original.

> ### Dwight
>
> You mustn't talk like that. You know you're my best girl.

> ### Mrs. Bett
>
> Don't you best-girl me.

Dwight

There, there, there....

Mrs. Bett

Now look at you. Walking all over me like I wasn't here—like I wasn't nowhere.

Dwight

Now, Mama Bett, you're havin' the tantrim.

Mrs. Bett

Am I? All right then I am. What you going to do about it? How you going to stop me?

Dwight

Now, now, now, now....

[*Enter* **Ina**.]

Ina

Dwight, I can't think what's happened to Lulu. Breakfast isn't even started.

Dwight

Lulu must be having a rendezvous.

[*Grandma snorts.*]

Ina

That's randevoo, Dwightie. Not rendezvous.

Dwight

You two are pretty particular, seems to me.

Mrs. Bett

Oh, no! We ain't used to the best.

[**Di** *is at the door.*]

Di

Hello, family! What's the matter with breakfast?

Mrs. Bett

There ain't any.

Ina

Di, let's you and I get breakfast just to show Aunt Lulu that we can.

Mrs. Bett

Say if you two are going to get breakfast, I'll go over to Grandma Gates for a snack.

[*Enter* **Monona**.]

Monona

What do you s'pose? Aunt Lulu's trunk is locked and strapped in her room.

Ina

Monona, stop imagining things.

Monona

Well, it is. And I saw her going down the walk with her satchel when I was washing me.

Dwight

Lulu must be completely out of her mind.

Mrs. Bett

First time I've known her to show good sense in years.

Ina

Why, mama!

Dwight

Mother Bett, do you know where Lulu is?

Mrs. Bett

Mother knows a-plenty.

Ina

Mama, what do you mean?

Mrs. Bett

I know all about Lulie being gone. She went this morning. I told her to go.

Ina

Why, mama! How can you talk so! When Dwight has been so good to you and Lulu....

Mrs. Bett

Good, yes, he's give us a pillow and a baked potato—

Dwight

So! You and Lulu presume to upset the arrangement of my household without one word to me.

Mrs. Bett

Upset, upset—You cockroach!...

Ina

Monona! Stop listening. Now run away and play. Di, you go and begin breakfast.

Di

Yes, mummy.

Monona

Aw, let me stay.

Ina

[*Exeunt* **Di** *and* **Monona**.]

Go at once, children. Mother, you ought not to use such language before young people.

Mrs. Bett

Don't you think they're fooled. What do you suppose Di was going to run away with Bobby Larkin for, only to get away from you.

Dwight

Mother Bett!

Mrs. Bett

What do you suppose Lulu married Ninian for—only to get shed of both of you.

Ina

Oh please, please, somebody think a little bit of me. Dwight, do go after Lulu—go to the depot—she couldn't get away before the 8:37.

Dwight

My dear Ina, my dignity—

Ina

Oh, please do go!

Dwight

Oh, my heavens! what a house full of women—

Ina

Dwight, we can't get along without Lulu.

Dwight

Upsetting things about my ears....

[*Exit.*]

Ina

Mama, I do think it's too bad of you—oh! now I'll try to get some breakfast.

[*Exit.*]

Mrs. Bett

Going to try to, he-e!

[*Enter* **Monona**.]

Monona

Oh, grandma isn't it fun with so much going on!

Mrs. Bett

What's that, you little ape?

Monona

Oh, I just love it! Everybody makes such funny faces.

Mrs. Bett

Some people are born with funny faces. Monona, ain't you ever going to grow up?

Monona

Grandma, I am grown up.

Mrs. Bett

You don't act like it.

Monona

Well, grown folks don't neither.

Mrs. Bett

Sh-hh-hhh, stop talking back to me.

Monona

Everybody shushes me. If I don't talk, how'll they know I'm there?

Mrs. Bett

I guess they could bear up if they didn't know you was there.

Monona

I'd better get in, or I'll catch it.

[**Monona** *sings a silly song.*]

Mrs. Bett

[*Rocking in rhythm with the song.*]
Scot's sake, what am I doing! Them wicked words.

[*Enter* **Di**.]

Di

Monona, mama wants you.

Monona

I'd better go or I'll catch it. I'll catch it anyway

[*Exit*]

[*Enter* **Ninian**.]

Di

Uncle Ninian! Well it's just about time you showed up.

Ninian

You're right, Di. But I came as soon as I could.

Di

You might as well know. I think you're a perfect slunge.

Mrs. Bett

Land sakes!

Ninian

Mrs. Bett.

Mrs. Bett

Don't you come near me! Don't you speak to me! You whited centipede!

Ninian

That's what I expected and that's what I deserve.

Mrs. Bett

Move on! Move on!

Ninian

Let me tell you something first, Mother Bett.

Mrs. Bett

Don't you "mother" me.

Ninian

Yes, that's just what I mean, *Mother* Bett. I've found that the woman I married died in Rio years ago. Here's a letter from the consul.

Mrs. Bett

Dead? Ain't that nice! But what ailed you all the time? A man with any get-up-and-get would have known that all along.

Ninian

I'm not excusing myself any, Mother Bett.

Mrs. Bett

Well, perhaps you're as good as you know how to be. Anyway, your mother's responsible for a good deal without counting you.

Ninian

Mother Bett, where is Lulu?

Mrs. Bett

Who, Lulie? Oh, she's run away.

Ninian

What do you say?

Mrs. Bett

She's gone off on the train this morning. I told her to go.

Ninian

Mother Bett, Mother Bett—where has she gone?

Mrs. Bett

Gone to call her soul her own, I guess.

Ninian

But Mother Bett, where did Lulu go?

Mrs. Bett

She might be at the depot.

Ninian

Can I catch her?

Mrs. Bett

You can catch her if ye can run in them white—mittens.

Ninian

Run? Watch me.

[*Exit running.*]

Di

Oh! Grandma, isn't it just too romantic?

Mrs. Bett

What do you mean—rheumatic?

[*Enter* **Monona**.]

Monona

Breakfast's ready, grandma.

Mrs. Bett

Breakfast! I wouldn't know coffee from flapjacks.

Monona

I've been catching it all morning and I didn't do a thing.

Mrs. Bett

What's that, little ape?

Monona

Grandma, honestly, do you see why because Aunt Lulu ran
away the whole family should pick on me?

Mrs. Bett

Come here, you poor neglected child!

Monona

Mama's getting breakfast and she's burned all over and she's so cross—m-m-m. Why here she comes now!

Mrs. Bett

Who?

Di

Aunt Lulu!

[*Enter* **Lulu**.]

Lulu

Mother—

Monona

Oh, goody—now they'll pick on you instead of me.

Mrs. Bett

[*Softly.*]

Monona! You run down the road as tight as you can and catch your Uncle Ninian quick—Sh-sh-sh—

Monona

Uncle Ninian! Oh—oh!

[*Exit*]

Lulu

Mother—what do you think I've heard?

Mrs. Bett

Land knows! my head's whirlin'. Who found you?

Lulu

Found me?

Mrs. Bett

I can count up to 'leven in this house that's went after you or went after them that went after them—Oh land!…

Lulu

Mother, the station agent said to me just now when I went to buy my ticket, he said, "You just missed your husband. He went hurrying up the street." I couldn't go till I knew.

Di

Why, Aunt Lulu, haven't you heard—

Mrs. Bett

Sh-h-h-h—Leave it burst.

[*Enter* **Dwight**.]

Dwight

So… after making me traipse all over town for you and before breakfast…. What is the meaning of this, Lulu? Answer me.

Mrs. Bett

Sit down, Dwight. Take off your hat why don't you?

[*Enter* **Ina**.]

Ina

Forevermore.

Lulu

Were you looking for me, Dwight?

Dwight

What about our breakfast, may I ask?

Lulu

Haven't you had your breakfast, Dwight? I had mine in the bakery.

Mrs. Bett

In the bakery! On expense!

Ina

Lulu, where have you been?

Lulu

How good of you to miss me!

Ina

Lulu, you don't act like yourself

Lulu

That's the way I heard the women talk in Savannah, Georgia.
"So good of you to miss me."

Dwight

Lulu, let's have no more of this nonsense....

Lulu

Whose nonsense, Dwight? I've left your home for good and all.
I'm going somewhere else to work.

Ina

Why, Lulu, what will people think of Dwight and me if we let
you do that?

Dwight

So you thought better of the promise you made to us last
evening not to tell our affairs broadcast.

Lulu

Your affairs? No, Dwight, you can tell them anything you like
when I'm gone.

Ina

How am I ever going to keep house without you? Dwight,
you've simply got to make her stay. When I think of what I
went through while she was away... everything boils over, and

what I don't expect to b-b-boil b-b-burns. Sister, how can you be so cruel when Dwight and I—

Dwight
Patience, patience, pettie… Lulu, I ask you to stay here where you belong.

Lulu
No, Dwight, I'm through.

Dwight
So, sister mine, have you found some other man willing to run away with you?

Lulu
That will do, Dwight. You've pretended so long you can't be honest with yourself, any of the time. Your whole life is a lie.

Mrs. Bett
Save your breath, Lulie.

[*Enter* **Monona** *with* **Ninian**.]

Dwight
At least, Miss Lulu Bett, neither Ina nor I ever had to lie about our marriage.

Monona
Here he is, grandma.

Lulu
Oh….

Ninian
What's that your saying, Dwight?

Ina
Forevermore!

Lulu
Ninian….

Ninian

Lulu…. So I didn't miss you.

Dwight

Ha! ha!… The happy bridegroom comes at last. What's the meaning of this, Ninian?

Ninian

I'll bet he's made life beautiful for you since you got back. Anything more to say, Dwight?

Dwight

Yes, Lulu was planning to run away…. I was telling her she'd better stay here at home where she'd have us to stand by her.

Ninian

Yes, I've heard how you stood by her. You're a magnificent protector, you are!

Dwight

Look here, Nin, don't you feel that you have to sacrifice yourself. Lulu is well enough off here.

Ina

She was quite happy until you came, Ninian.

Ninian

You hypocrites!

Mrs. Bett

Hypocrites! He-e!

Ina

Children, stop listening to older people.

Di

Oh, mama!…

Monona

[*Crying.*]
Oh… Let me stay!

Ina

Children!…

[*Exeunt* **Di** *and* **Monona**.]

Ninian, how can you say such things to us!

Ninian

Lulu has suffered as much from you as she has from me.

Mrs. Bett

That's right, Ninian. Plain talk won't hurt nobody around here.

Ninian

Lulu, can you forgive me?

Lulu

But Cora Waters… what of her?

Dwight

Yes, what about your other wife?

Ninian

I haven't any other wife—just Lulu.

Mrs. Bett

Cora Waters is dead. I knew it all along.

Lulu

Ninian, is it true?

Ninian

Yes, it's true.

Mrs. Bett

He's confided in his mother. He told me all about it.

Ninian

Will you come back to me, Lulu?

Mrs. Bett

Better take him, Lulie. You can have that fifty to furnish up the parlor.

Lulu

Oh, mother! I wish we could have you with us.

Ninian

Do you forgive me?

Lulu

I forgave you in Savannah, Georgia.

Curtain

Act III (1st Version)

[As originally produced December 21, 1920.]

The piano store: Empty, bare, three or four up-right pianos with bright plush spreads and plush-covered stools. Back, a dark green sateen curtain. It is the following morning.

*[Discover **Cornish** at a little table, on which is opened a large black book.]*

*[Enter **Monona**, carrying basket of parcels.]*

Monona

Oh, Mr. Cornish....

Cornish

Hello, there, Monona! How's everything?

Monona

Everything's perfectly awful up to our house.

Cornish

Miss Lulu's all right, I hope?

Monona

Aunt Lulu is—

Cornish

There! I knew it. I know this thing was going to wind up in a fit of sickness—

Monona

Sick.... No. She's gone.

Cornish

Gone! Miss Lulu gone?

> Monona

Run away.

> Cornish

Oh, with who?

> Monona

Nobody, I guess. She skipped out of the house early this morning. It was me saw her going down the walk with her bag. It was me told everybody. It was me found her trunk packed and locked in her room. That's all.

> Cornish

This is terrible, terrible—and your people not home yet?

> Monona

I should say they are. Came last night.

> Cornish

But what are they doing to find her?

> Monona

Papa said he wouldn't do a thing. Mamma's been getting breakfast and she's burned all over, and she's so cross—m-m!

> Cornish

Yes, but aren't they trying to find Lulu—your Aunt Lulu—

> Monona

Grandma says she knows she's dead. Probably she's drowned in the river and they'll get her out with her hair all stringy—

> Cornish

See here. I think I'll come up to your house. I'll put a little notice on my door—

> Monona

I better go now. I'll catch it anyhow. I've been catching it all the morning and I didn't do a thing. Mr. Cornish, honestly, do you see why, because Aunt Lulu ran away, the whole family should pick on me?

                    Cornish
Well, we must all help as much as we can, Monona—

                    Monona
Up to our house, honestly, you'd think I was the one that had done it. And I may!

[*Exit, running.*]

                    Cornish
I'll be right there, as soon as I can lock up.

[*He disappears behind the green curtain. Pause.*]

[*Enter **Lulu**.*]

                    Lulu
Mr. Cornish. Mr. Cornish.

[**Cornish** *appears.*]

                    Cornish
Well!

                    Lulu
Well!

                    Cornish
You're out early.

                    Lulu
Oh, no!

                    Cornish
My, but I'm glad to see you. Won't you sit down?

Lulu

I can only stay a minute. Wasn't that Monona just went out of here?

Cornish

Yes, that was Monona.

Lulu

Did she say anything about me?

Cornish

She—she said you'd run away. She—she must have been mistaken.

Lulu

No, she wasn't. I have.

Cornish

Why, Miss Lulu!

Lulu

Or I'm going on the 10:10. My bag's in the bakery. I had my breakfast in the bakery…. I've left them for good.

Cornish

Then I suppose he cut up like a hyena over that letter being opened.

Lulu

Oh, he forgave me that.

Cornish

Forgave you!

Lulu

Overlooked it, rather.

Cornish

Anyway he's convinced now about that other Mrs. Ninian Deacon?

Lulu

Yes, but you mustn't say anything about that, please, ever.

Cornish

Even now? Well, I'll be jumped up. Even now? Then—I guess I see why you're going.

Lulu

It isn't only that. I'm going… I'm *going!*

Cornish

I see. Would—would you tell me where?

Lulu

Maybe. After a while.

Cornish

I do want you to. Because I—I think you're a brick.

Lulu

Oh, no!

Cornish

Yes, you are. By George! you don't find very many *married* women with as good sense as you've got. That is, I mean—

Lulu

All right. I know. Thank you.

Cornish

You've been a jewel in their home—I know that. They're going to miss you no end.

Lulu

They'll miss my cooking.

Cornish

They'll miss more than that. I've watched you there…

Lulu

You have?

Cornish

You made the whole place go.

Lulu

You don't mean just the cooking?

Cornish

No.

Lulu

I never had but one compliment before that wasn't for my cooking. He told me I done up my hair nice…. That was after I took notice how the ladies in Savannah, Georgia, done up theirs.

Cornish

Well, well, well!…

Lulu

I must go now. I wanted to say good-by to you….

Cornish

I hate to have you go. I—I hate to have you go.

Lulu

Oh, well!

Cornish

Look here, I wish—I wish you weren't going.

Lulu

Do you? Good-by.

Cornish

Can't I come to the depot with you?

Lulu

You can't leave the store alone.

Cornish

Yes. I'll put a little notice on the door…

Lulu

No. That would be bad for the business. Good-by.

Cornish

Good-by, Miss Lulu! Good-by, good-by, good-by!…

Lulu

There's something else. I'm going to tell you—I don't care what
Dwight says.

[*Takes letter from her handbag.*]

As long as I told you the other part, I'm going to tell you this.

Cornish

I want to know everything you'll let me know.

Lulu

See—at the office this morning was this. It's from Ninian.

Cornish

Well, I should think he'd better write.

Lulu

Nobody must know. It was bad enough for the family before,
but now… here it is:

> "… just want you to know you're actually rid of me.
> I've heard from her, in Brazil. She ran out of money
> and thought of me, and her lawyer wrote to me.…"

… he incloses the lawyer's letter.

> "I've never been any good—Dwight would tell you
> that if his pride would let him tell the truth once in
> a while. But there isn't anything in my life makes me
> feel as bad as this… "

… well, that part doesn't matter. But you see.

He didn't lie to get rid of me—and she was alive just as he
thought she might be!

Cornish

And you're free now.

Lulu

That's so—I am. I hadn't thought of that…. It's late. Now I'm really going. Good-by.

Cornish

Don't say good-by.

Lulu

It's nearly train time.

Cornish

Don't you go…. Do you think you could possibly stay here with me?

Lulu

Oh!…

Cornish

I haven't got anything. I guess maybe you've heard something about a little something I'm supposed to inherit. Well, it's only five hundred dollars…. That little Warden house—it don't cost much—you'd be surprised. Rent, I mean. I can get it now. I went and looked at it the other day but then I didn't think… well, I mean, it don't cost near as much as this store. We could furnish up the parlor with pianos… that is, if you could ever think of such a thing as marrying me.

Lulu

But—you know! Why, don't the disgrace—

Cornish

What disgrace?

Lulu

Oh, you—you—

Cornish

There's only this about that. Of course, if you loved him very much then I ought not to be talking this way to you. But I didn't think—

Lulu

You didn't think what?

Cornish

That you did care so very much about him. I don't know why.

Lulu

I wanted somebody of my own. That's the reason I done what I done. I know that now.

Cornish

I figured that way…. Look here, I ought to tell you. I'm—I'm awful lonesome myself. This is no place to live. Look—look here.

[*He draws the green curtain, revealing the mean little cot and washstand.*]

I guess living so is one reason why I want to get married. I want some kind of a home.

Lulu

Of course.

Cornish

I ain't never lived what you might say private.

Lulu

I've lived too private.

[*Pause.*]

Cornish

Then there's another thing. I—I don't believe I'm ever going to be able to do anything with the law.

Lulu

I don't see how anybody does.

Cornish

And I'm not much good in a business way. Sometimes I think that I may never be able to make any money.

Lulu

Lots of men don't.

Cornish

Well, there it is. I'm no good at business. I'll never be a lawyer. And—and everything I say sounds wrong to me. And yet I do believe that I'd know enough not to bully a woman. Not to make her unhappy. Maybe—even, I could make her a little happy.

Lulu

Lots of men do.

[*Voices.*]

[*Enter* **Ina, Dwight** *and* **Mrs. Bett.**]

Ina

Oh, Dwight! she's still here.

Dwight

So this is where we find our Lulu!

Lulu

Did you want me, Dwight?

Ina

Want you? Why, Lulu! are you crazy? Of course we want you. Why aren't you home?

[*Nursing her wrist, which is bandaged, with the other hand, which is bandaged, too.*]

Mrs. Bett

Lulie, Lulie, we thought you'd gone off again.

Lulu

Mother, darling....

Dwight

Here am I kept home from the office, trying my best to take your place. You're a most important personage, Miss Lulu Bett.

Lulu

What did you want of me?

Ina

Want of you? Why, my goodness....

Dwight

If you had tasted bacon fried as the bacon was fried which I have tasted this day—

Ina

Oh, Dwight, that's not funny!

Dwight

No. And the muffins were not funny either. Yes they were!

Lulu

How good of you to miss me!

Ina

Lulu, you don't act like yourself.

Lulu

That was the way I heard the women talk in Savannah, Georgia. "So good of you to miss me."

Dwight

Lulu, what does this mean? No more of this nonsense.

Lulu

Whose nonsense, Dwight?

Dwight

We know that your trunk is locked and strapped in your room
and you were seen going down the street with a bag. You
have flown here, presumably to discuss your situation with an
outsider. Is this fair to us?

Lulu

What do you want me to do, Dwight?

Ina

Do? Why, we want you to come home.

Lulu

Home!

Dwight

Also to explain your amazing behavior.

Cornish

May I do that, Miss Lulu?

Lulu

No—no thank you. I think I'd like to speak for myself. Dwight,
I've left your home for good and all.

Ina

Sister....

Mrs. Bett

Lulie... Lulie!...

Dwight

Ah-ha! You have thought better of the promise you made to Ina
and me last evening not to tell our affairs broadcast.

Lulu

I've thought no better of it—and no worse. I couldn't. But I've
been thinking of something else. Of you, Dwight.

Dwight

Ah—I'm flattered.

Lulu

… Let it go at that…. In any case, I've left your home.

Ina

But where are you going?

Lulu

I meant to go somewhere else and work.

Ina

Go somewhere else and work. Cook? Lulu, have you no consideration for Dwight and me at all? What would people think if we let you do that….

Dwight

Patience, patience, pettie. Let's have no more of this, Lulu. I imagine you're not quite well. Come home with us, now, there's a good girl.

Lulu

No, Dwight.

Ina

Lulu, I simply can't keep house without you. When I think of going through with what I went through this summer while you were away…. Everything b-boils over and what I don't expect to b-boil b-burns….

[*Sobs.*]

Dwightie, you've got to make her stay.

Dwight

Pettie—control yourself…. Lulu, I ask you, I implore you, to come back home with us.

Cornish

Miss Lulu….

Lulu

Yes?

Cornish

May I tell them?

Lulu

What is there to tell them?

Cornish

I think Miss Lulu and I are going to—arrange.

Lulu

O but not yet—not yet.

Dwight

What—you? You and Cornish? I should think not. How can you?

Lulu

Cora Waters is alive. Ninian's heard from her. There's her lawyer's letter.

Ina

Forevermore!

Mrs. Bett

What you talking—what you talking. I want to know but I ain't got something in my head…. Lulie, you ain't going to get married again, are you—after waiting so long?

Dwight

Don't be disturbed, Mother Bett. She wasn't married that first time. No marriage about it.

Ina

Dwight! If Lulu marries Mr. Cornish, then every- body'll have to know about Ninian and his other wife.

Lulu

That's so. You would have to tell, wouldn't you? I never thought of that. Well—you can get used to the idea while I'm gone.

Dwight

Gone?

Ina

Gone where?

Mrs. Bett

Where you goin' now, for pity sakes?

Lulu

Away. I thought I wanted somebody of my own. Well, maybe it was just myself.

Dwight

What ridiculous talk is this?

Cornish

Lulu—couldn't you stay with me—

Lulu

Sometime, maybe. I don't know. But first I want to see out of my own eyes. For the first time in my life. Good-by, mother.

Mrs. Bett

Lulie, Lulie....

Lulu

[*At the door.*]

Good-by. Good-by, all of you. I'm going I don't know where— to work at I don't know what. But I'm going from choice!

[*Exit*]

[**Cornish** *follows her.*]

Mrs. Bett

Who's going to do your work now, I'd like to know?

Curtain

About the Author

Zona Gale was born August 26, 1874 in Portage, Wisconsin. After graduating from the University of Wisconsin, she worked as a journalist in Milwaukee and New York City. In 1904, Gale returned to Portage and concentrated on her literary career. Her early novels and stories presented an idyllic view of village life (often set in the aptly named Friendship Village, which had many parallels to her hometown). Her activism in progressive politics riled some of her Portage neighbors, and Gale's rosy view of small-town life soured by the end of the First World War. Her fifth novel, *Birth* (1918), was such a radical thematic departure that the *New York Times'* review bemoaned, "Where, oh where, is the Zona Gale of 'Friendship Village'?" (18 Nov. 1918). Her next novel, *Miss Lulu Bett* (1920), was a critical and commercial success, and she won the 1921 Pulitzer Prize for Drama for the stage adaptation. Though she continued to produce novels, plays, and short stories for the rest of her life, she never again achieved the success of *Birth* and *Miss Lulu Bett.* In 1928, Gale married Portage banker (and childhood friend) William L. Breese. She died of pneumonia on December 27, 1938.